one little wish

BOOK ONE OF THE LITTLE THINGS SERIES

GINA LAMANNA

For updates on new releases, please sign up for my newsletter at www.ginalamanna.com.

Feel free to get in touch anytime via email at gina.m.lamanna@gmail.com!

SYNOPSIS

Dear Diary,

I know three things:
1. I didn't kill anyone.
2. Mack Montgomery is a troublemaker.
3. I am running out of time.

You've got to believe me, Diary. I didn't have anything to do with those murders, I promise you. For crying out loud, I'm the only person in this tiny Texas town who *doesn't* own a gun! But I can't help feeling like someone is out to get me. The only question is *who*... and why.

While we're at it, let's get one other thing straight. None of this would have happened if it weren't for the shadow called Mack Montgomery. That man may be hot-as-sin and the talk of the high school reunion, but let me tell you one thing. He is up to something, Diary. He is so full of questions, yet somehow, I can't seem to find one single answer. One second he's breaking into my house and accusing me of murder, and the next, he's turned those soft baby blues on me, making my stomach do all sorts of somersaults.

I'm running low on time, Diary. If I can't find the murderer, and if Mack Montgomery doesn't go back to where he belongs... I'm afraid that my one little wish may never come true.

xoxo,
Scarlett

Acknowledgements

To you, my readers! Thank you for your friendship and support.

I appreciate each and every one of you!

A huge hug & thank you to all who helped "whip this book into shape" in time for publication:

- Stacia - for controlling my runaway commas.

- Connie – for your encouraging words!

- Gillian – for reading anything I send your way, pretty or not.

- Neila – you're wonderful!

- Dianne – please show me your ways in fashion.

- Barb – your kind words always mean more than you know.

- Kim – for your friendship & making me smile.

- Joy – for your advice, inspiration, and enthusiasm!

To Mom & Dad — For being there even when my "wishes" didn't make sense.

To Alex. For making all my wishes come true, and for believing in my craziest ones. я тебя люблю!

To Meg & Kristi— For being the best sisters I could wish for - sometimes.

To my Oceans Apart ladies— For each of you, I wish a "Happily Ever After."

To Sprinkles On Top Studios, my awesome cover designer. Photo Courtesy of Deposit Photos

And last but not least, to all my family and friends, thanks for making me laugh.

~Evelina~

If you are a dreamer, come in.
If you are a dreamer, a wisher, a liar,
A hope-er, a pray-er, a magic bean buyer,
If you're a pretender, come, sit by my fire.
For we have many a flax golden tale to spin.
Come in, come in.

~Shel Silverstein~

CHAPTER 1

Dear Diary,

I S THAT WHAT I SHOULD call you? To be honest, this is my first ever journal, and I'm not quite sure what to write in here. Do you even *like* the name Diary? Anyway, you're probably wondering who on earth I am, blabbin' on and on during our first date. Well, hello, Diary. My name is Scarlett Powers, and I'm pleased to make your acquaintance.

If there's one thing you should know about me, it's this: I'm a simple girl, from a simple town, with a simple wish. Except, my one simple wish is too complicated to get into right now, especially with all the trouble I'm in at the moment.

I don't understand it, Diary. There ain't no good reason for me to stumble over one dead body, let alone two of them. I didn't have anything to do with those murders, I promise you, Diary. I promise, okay?

Don't listen to what all the townsfolk say because they don't know anything about me. This whole high school reunion fiasco is just ruining my life, when all I want is for everything to go back to normal. I want my nanny job back, and I want the whispers to stop. I want everyone to mind their own business, and for cryin' out loud, I want Mack Montgomery to go back to where he belongs, which is far away from my tiny town.

Now, let me tell you one more thing, Diary. These people have messed with the wrong woman. At the end of the day, I may be just a simple girl with a simple life and a simple wish, but here's the kicker: I plan on fightin' like hell to make that one little wish come true.

Anyway, thanks for listening, Diary. If I didn't have you, I have no clue who I could talk to about this mess. You'll be hearin' a lot from me; that's for certain. Good night, Diary.

Love,
Scarlett

Chapter 2

O F ALL THE DAYS TO run late, I'd picked the worst one. Hiking up my skirt, I jogged down Main Street, the dust swirling around my ankles. At this rate, I would be muddy before I even stepped foot inside the church.

I nodded hello to Mrs. Maples as she drove past in her fancy new truck. Her husband waved from the passenger seat, a doughnut in hand. That wouldn't be good for the poor guy's cholesterol.

Quickening my pace to a sprint, I thought it was a little bit sad I knew the status of Mr. Maples's cholesterol. But in a town of this size, a pinprick on the map of America, too much information had a way of leaking out for all the public to hear. Which was ironic, since people liked to think that secrets were gold, when really, they were more like pennies.

That didn't stop the townsfolk from trying to stow their secrets under lock and key, doling them out to the deserving few. I wasn't one of the deserving few by a long shot, however I *was* invisible most of the time, which meant people let secrets slip around me that they probably shouldn't. It didn't much matter since I didn't have anyone to tell.

My feet carried me down the dusty road. Trees lined either side of the street, and the sun beat down hard on my bare shoulders. I had worn a shawl earlier, but it was already too hot to wear while sprinting my tail across town.

Finally, the small auto repair shop came into view. The dilapidated building had a crooked roof just barely hanging on.

Mud-caked tires held up spattered trucks, each in a state of disrepair. One new, shiny, dark car sat in the lot, and I wondered who would be in a town of this size, driving a car with a price tag of *that* size.

"Hey, Frank!" I hollered, banging open the screen door of the tiny shack Frank called a storefront. "Is my baby done?"

Frank Benton, one of two local mechanics, took his sweet time stepping out of the garage, wiping his hands on a towel that hung from his waist. "Sweetheart, I thought you were coming yesterday."

"I called you like six times, Frank." My breath came in gulps. "I was nannying, and Gray's mom was running late. I couldn't get here before you closed, and I knew it was poker night for you and the boys, so I didn't want to keep you late."

"Good thing, too, seein' how I cleaned those boys out." Frank leaned in with a wink. "But don't tell my wife that since I'm saving the cash to take her to a surprise dinner. A real nice restaurant outside of the city. Maybe with steak. I think I'll even get one of them fancy beers they're always bragging about in the commercials."

"Good for you, Frank." I grinned. "Lou Anne will love it. That's real sweet of you."

"She's a good woman. I don't show her enough of life's luxuries."

"Speaking of fancy…" I leaned on the counter. "Whose beauty of a vehicle is that out there?" I nodded toward the sleek, midnight-black car with a logo so upscale I didn't even know the name that went along with it.

Frank turned to me, his eyes bright. "You didn't hear?"

"Hear what?"

"That's the car I'm holding for Mack." Frank smiled so broadly, the space where he was missing a front tooth showed. "Mack called and said he'd be back for Reunion Day after all. He's supposed to pick it up tomorrow. I can't believe you, of all people, didn't know."

Me, of all people. I had no reason to know. I hadn't seen Mack for ten years, and the last time I'd seen him, well… it hadn't ended on pleasant terms.

"He's..." I cleared my throat. "I thought he wasn't coming. That's what The Ladies said." The Ladies were a group of feisty, eighty-year-old women who ran the town through gossip, book club, and pecan pie.

"Well, The Ladies didn't get a call late last night saying that Mack changed his mind." Frank gave a whistle, eyeing the car. "You won't believe what it took to get this puppy here. Beautiful."

I swallowed. My heart was doing a dance to its own beat despite the flush of dismay creeping up my face. "That's great, Frank. I'm sure it'll be good for business." I forced my face into a smile. "Look, I'm sorry to rush you, but is my car ready? I'm gonna be late to church, otherwise."

Frank blinked. "It's mostly ready."

"Mostly? I thought you said she was done yesterday."

"She *was,* but there's one thing I can't do here at my shop." He shrugged, his expression sheepish. "You're gonna have to take her over to Joe's Body Shop to get the scrape waxed out."

"There wasn't a scrape on my car when I brought her in here." I frowned. "Frank, what'd you do?"

"It's a tiny little scrape. I already called Joe and told him about my mistake." Frank's eyes softened in apology. "I really am sorry, Scarlett. You just have to drive your vehicle over there, and Joe will fix her right up. He said he can do it in one day, and you'll have it back tomorrow."

"Can't you fix it here?" I pointed at the sign just behind Frank: Frank's Auto Body Service and Repair Shop.

"It's not my specialty."

"Then your sign is misleading," I grumbled. "You are misleading your customers."

"Darlin', I said I'm *sorry.*"

"You know I can't afford another fix!" I threw my arms up in the air. "I don't *got* extra money just lyin' around, Frank. I'm a nanny. I'm not rolling in dough over here."

Frank raised his hands in a *Whoa, Nelly* sort of gesture. "Joe's just gonna put it on my tab. Sometimes I send him business; sometimes he sends me some. It'll all even out, not a penny of cost for you."

"And now I'm gonna be late to church." I huffed a bit but relented at Frank's apologetic expression. "Fine, fine, I'll bring her to Joe's. If I hurry, maybe I can drop it off and make it in time for the opening hymn."

"I'm headed up to the church if you need a ride." Frank gestured behind him to the lot full of dusty pickups. "What do you say?"

I shook my head. "That's all right. I'm just gonna pay and get out of here. I don't wanna put you out, but I appreciate the offer."

I handed over some bills that I'd carefully stacked, one on top of the other. I'd counted the money at least three times and saved for six weeks to get enough. At the last second, I thrust the stack into Frank's hands, not wanting to think about how much the new transmission had cost.

I grabbed the proffered keys and hustled out back to where my lavender VW Beetle sat, looking shiny and new amid the blue, red, and black trucks the size of monsters. The diamond frame around my license plate shone brightly under the Sunday morning rays. Of course, the diamonds were fake, but even if they were chintzy, I liked the sparkle.

"Come on, girl." I patted my baby on the roof. She was my first ever purchase—big purchase, at least—and I probably talked to her as much as some people talked to their cats. "Let's go get that scratch looked at."

I narrowed my eyes at the small black mark on the driver's door, but I pushed away the mean words I wanted to say to Frank. He'd apologized, and it wouldn't do me any good to say another word. When there were only two mechanics in town, my options for repairs were limited. Getting on Frank's bad side would be *no bueno* for future services.

I drove to the other end of the block, my car cruising like a brand-new machine. I gave her a few affectionate pats on the dashboard, turned the radio up, rolled the windows down, and enjoyed the five-minute drive the best I could.

I was only halfway through the first song by the time I pulled into Joe's Body Shop, and I had one foot out the door before my car even stopped rolling.

I waltzed up to the shop. "Joe?" I called out as I walked through the door. "Hey, Joe, did you get a message from Frank? He said you were gonna fix a scratch on my baby for him."

There was no response.

The shop was plain, a little bit dingy, with some clutter on the desk and a few sad-looking chairs forgotten in the corner. I walked around to the other side of the front counter, taking a peek at the calendar laid out in plain view. "Joe?"

Normally, I'd do no such thing since I didn't snoop by nature. But Pastor Kent wasn't going to halt the service and wait for me, and the town talked about me enough as it was. I didn't need another tally in my naughty column.

"Huh. Should be open, according to this here," I murmured. I read through the shop's hours list and tried one more time. "Joe?"

"What are you hollerin' about?" A short, fat man with a black mustache appeared in the doorway. "Joe's not here right now. He went down the street to grab a Hot Pocket. What can I help you with?"

"A Hot Pocket? It's eight in the morning," I said. "Why's he need a Hot Pocket?"

"You here to question his diet, or can I help you with something?"

The man's nametag said Ralph, yet I knew his name was Ryan. He'd been a few years ahead of me in school. "Why's your nametag say Ralph?"

"Why you asking so many questions?" Ryan asked.

I sighed. "Never mind. Did Joe say anything about doing a

job on my vehicle for Frank? I just had my transmission fixed at Frank's, and he scratched the car. Said Joe would do a better job fixing it, and that I'd be able to get her back by tomorrow."

"Yeah, whatever."

"Yeah, whatever *yes* or whatever *no*?"

"Yeah, whatever. Leave your car here."

"But I want her back," I said. "And the cost should be put on Frank's tab. The scratch wasn't my fault."

"Fine."

"Fine?" I waved a hand in question. "Are you always so agreeable?"

"I can be." Ryan shrugged, looking down at his fingernails, his disinterest obvious. "Joe and Frank always swap business. Just write a note here, and I'll leave it for Joe."

"You're not gonna give it to him?" I could feel my eyes turning stormy. "You're not even listenin' to me. This is my precious car, and I want you to promise me you'll look after her."

"I'm gonna pin your note right up here." Ryan smacked the board behind him. "Got it?"

I relented and murmured my agreement, then jotted down a note and handed it over. I watched until Ryan tacked it up on the board.

"This all right, lady?"

"Don't call me lady, Ralph Ryan," I said. "My name's Scarlett."

"Fine."

"I want my car back, and I want it tomorrow, please." I pointed at Ryan. "And I expect *not* to receive a bill. Are we on the same page here, buddy?"

Ryan shrugged again. "Sure. Fine. Now, do you have someone coming to pick you up, or you need a ride somewhere? Joe'd be upset if I didn't offer to drop you off at church."

"I wouldn't wanna put you out." I tossed the car keys to Ryan. "I got transportation. They're called legs, and I've gotta *fly*."

I turned, leaving Ryan standing there with his arms crossed

above a stomach as round as an inner tube. The scrap-metal door clanked shut behind me as I slipped off my sandals, grabbed them, and ran toward church. My hair went wild, and my dress blew up past my knees, but I refused to be late.

CHAPTER 3

B<small>Y THE TIME</small> I <small>REACHED</small> the front steps of the Southern Baptist Church, my lungs had just about collapsed from the humidity of the late August day. The air was so heavy it felt as though I were breathing from underneath a wet blanket. My armpits were a little sweaty, and even though I did my best to air them out discreetly, I could see Miss Bennington's frown from across the room at my display of unladylike behavior.

Normally, I'd go apologize to her. After all, in order to remain invisible one mustn't cause waves. But today, I had more important things to worry about. Noelle was coming to town. Glittery, sparkly, chic Noelle. Back in high school, we'd been inseparable. Then, she'd gone off to fashion school in New York and was making a name for herself there. I stayed here in Luck, getting bitten by mosquitos and hosing the dust from my shoes twice a week.

Noelle came to town about once every three years. She didn't come more often because, as she put it, nothing much was left here except for me and her parents. Plus, she made more money than God, so she could afford to fly her parents up north, instead of sitting in Luck and sweating in the summer sun.

It quickly became clear that I wasn't the only one feeling anxious for the day. The air buzzed with excitement, whispers flitted through the lobby, and people's eyeballs scanned the crowd faster than ever before. We were *all* waiting for those who'd escaped, those who'd gotten away, and gone on to bigger and better things.

Tomorrow was Reunion Day, and that meant that all the little birdies who'd spread their wings and flown away to greener pastures would return home, flocking back to dusty old Luck.

The week would be full of watching, whispering, and one-upping everyone else—comparing who had more kids, who made more money, and who had traveled the farthest. Well, that was easy for me, seeing how I wouldn't be winning any awards. I hadn't even graduated high school, but that didn't mean I wouldn't be waiting, watching, and whispering with the rest of them.

CHAPTER 4

Dear Diary,

I CAN'T GET THIS DAMN MASCARA to stay on my eyelashes! What is *with* these brushes? Anyway, it's me again, Scarlett. My last name isn't really important. Not because I'm famous like Oprah, but because nobody in this town cares enough to remember my last name for anything good. Which is probably for the best, seeing how nothin' good ever came of a Powers girl, anyhow.

Hang on a minute, Diary. I'm sorry. You probably don't even know which town I'm talkin' about. I live in a place called Luck, Texas. It's not on the map, so don't even bother looking. We've got a population of nine hundred forty-two, but most people round that number up to a grand, even though the mathematics are all sorts of wrong.

Here in Luck, we have great manners. We put on makeup to go to the weekly book club, bake a mean pecan pie, and spend half the summer swatting the mosquitos from our skin. It's probably the same in the rest of Texas, but I wouldn't know. I never left Luck. When in Luck, stay in Luck. At least, that's what the sign says on Main Street. Our motto here is to keep your friends close, your enemies closer, and a gun under your pillow. That's just how things go in this town.

Look what you made me do, Diary— I'm already ramblin' on and on, never shuttin' up. Also, I'd like to apologize in advance that you got stuck with me and not someone glamorous like Noelle

Summers, whose life is full of glitter and fancy clothes. You'd probably like to read about her instead of me, I bet. But that's okay. I like my life.

The thing is, I live the most ordinary life you could ever imagine. I don't have a bunch of friends. I'm a chameleon here on the dusty streets of small-town Texas. People talk at me all the time, but they don't want to hear what I have to say. That's where you come in, Diary, because I've got things to say. If I don't write them down, the words just might pop out of my mouth at the city council meeting, and that wouldn't be polite.

But I'm off to church now. My best friend Noelle's coming to town. I hope she hasn't forgotten about me. I'm nervous, Diary. Will it be the same as always? Well, I guess we'll have to see.

xo,
Scarlett

CHAPTER 5

E VERY SINGLE HEAD IN CHURCH turned. Even the pastor. When she walked in, Pastor Kent stopped yammering right in the middle of a speech about us coughing up money into the collection basket.

She was none other than Noelle Summers.

My face heated up as I saw my best friend, but I wasn't sure if I could still call her that. After I thought about it, I wasn't quite sure what constituted a best friend. We talked on the phone once per month, but that was it. She probably had a lot more glamorous friends up in the Big Apple—friends who didn't have mud streaking their faces and slightly sweaty armpits.

But all my nerves flew right out the window when Noelle looked my way and a smile lit up her face. The smile was just for me, and I knew it. She waved, pushed past Mrs. Maples and her doughnut-addicted husband, and joined me in the pew.

"Well, go on, y'all. Stop starin', now," she said in a perfect drawl. "Sorry I'm late. My plane was delayed."

Pastor Kent spluttered as he began lecturing once more, reminding everyone to donate as much as possible because we needed a new roof on the building.

I tuned out the pastor and blinked back tears as I laid eyes on my friend for the first time in three years. "Noelle, you made it!"

"Don't you get all teared up, girlie," she said. Her long, dark hair was slicked into a chic ponytail, and her eyes were perfectly decorated with eyeliner. Her lashes were silky, luxurious, and clump-free. "I brought you something."

"You did?" My own somewhat blondish hair frizzed out, dancing to the beat of its own drum. I couldn't get it to cooperate, no matter how hard I tried, so I didn't try any longer.

"I did, you wanna see?"

"How 'bout after church?"

"This can't wait." Noelle glanced up and down the pews, then sneaked something from her bag. She shoved a package into my hands. "Open it."

I looked down, stifling a gasp at the pretty, pink-and-white-striped, little bag. "This isn't what I think it is… is it?"

Noelle raised her eyebrows, a gleeful expression covering her face at my reaction. "Better look and see."

I tried to remove the bright tissue paper without making a racket, but at least four heads turned my way. Miss Bennington, who sat three rows ahead of us, put a finger to her lips. Her eyebrows were so furrowed, she'd have to get all-new Botox to get rid of those wrinkles.

Noelle clapped a hand over her mouth, hiding a giggle. "Go on," she hissed in my ear. "These people don't understand."

My face burned as I pulled the tissue paper out square by square. Normally, I'd do no such thing and disrupt the sermon, but today was a special day. Noelle and I had always broken the rules. Although somehow, everyone loved her, and I'd always ended up with punishments coming out the wazoo. I'd give just about anything to be as lovable, beautiful, and gorgeous as Noelle. Then again, I was lucky just to be her friend.

"Noelle!" I tried to whisper her name, but it came out as a high-pitched squeak. "You didn't! Oh my, goodness gracious."

Every head in the church turned toward me, which was unfortunate because at that very moment I'd unearthed the gold nugget at the bottom of that pink-and-white package. Except the gift wasn't gold; it was red—bright, sparkling, lacy red.

The entire congregation, I'm ashamed to admit, turned their heads as I held up the skimpiest pair of devil panties in the entire universe. I wasn't even sure how they were supposed to cover my rear end because they were so teensy-tiny.

Gasps skittered through the room like a wave, causing my face to absolutely flame with embarrassment, shame, and all sorts of emotions that made my cheeks look like overripe tomatoes forgotten on the vine.

Pastor Kent let out a low whistle.

Miss Bennington made the sign of the cross. "Child, what are you thinking bringing those sinful things to church?" she hissed. "Lord Almighty."

"Shall we say a prayer for her?" Mrs. Maples asked. She elbowed her doughnut-addicted husband. "Larry, shut your eyes and apologize to the good Lord."

Noelle looked around. "Y'all need to calm down. This is real, honest-to-goodness Victoria's Secret. She'll put them away now, so relax. Just hush and listen to Pastor Kent."

As usual, people listened when Noelle spoke. All grace and charm, she could get the entire town to jump off a bridge if she asked nicely.

Thankfully, one by one, everyone turned their attention back to Pastor Kent, who buried his nose in the readings. We all pretended he hadn't looked when the panties came out, but there was no denying that his eyes had wandered.

"Those are real, true Victoria's Secret underwear," Noelle whispered a few minutes later. "And there's a matching bra in that bag to boot. I hope I got you the right size."

I looked down at my chest. "I haven't grown a whole bunch since you last saw me, so I'm sure it's perfect."

Noelle laughed. "You've got just the right amount of chest, girlie. I can't wait to have you try them on."

"After church, Noelle. My goodness! I'm in enough trouble as it is, holdin' up my underwear for the whole town to see." But I was certain my eyes shone bright, and my heart was lighter than it had been in years. Noelle was back. And not only was she back, we'd picked up as if she'd never left.

CHAPTER 6

Dear Diary,

S HE'S BACK! CAN YOU BELIEVE it? I don't know what I've done right in life to get a gift from Noelle Summers. She even remembered my sizes from back when we used to circle our dream purchases in the Victoria's Secret catalog. We don't have a Victoria's Secret within a few hours of this town, so I've never had anything so fancy. It's Walmart for me, or else the local Dollar General.

Diary, let me tell you, Noelle brought me back this lingerie set so sinful that I can't even imagine wearin' it in front of anyone except myself. And even then, I'd probably blush if I saw my reflection in the mirror. As a general rule, I'm not a blushin' type of girl.

I wish I had someone to see me wearin' it. But let's be honest, there ain't nobody in this town that wants to see me in that thing. I haven't had a date in over three years. But who knows? Noelle tells me to dress to make myself feel good. Maybe I'll wear them on Reunion Day, and then *I'll* be the one with a secret. But the difference between me and everyone else? When it comes to secrets, I know how to keep 'em to myself.

xo,
Scarlett

CHAPTER 7

"GO ON IN, JUST REAL quick." Noelle gave me a shove in the direction of the closet. "Why haven't they fixed the bathroom yet?" She'd led me down to the church basement after Pastor Kent had finished speaking, before anyone else had a chance to grab her attention and chat her ears right off her head.

"They tried, but I heard it sprung another leak early this morning."

"Nobody's around. Just slip into it real quick."

"Can't I wait 'til I get home?"

Noelle shook her head, pointing once more to the closet door. The air was cooler down there, and the floor was deserted. Only mamas with crying babies and people using the restrooms went down there. Since the restrooms were out of order, the place was abandoned.

"That's just wicked, Noelle."

"What's so wicked about a pair of undies? Up in New York, models walk around the streets wearin' them. They parade on television in skimpier clothes than that there."

I hesitated. I liked getting into trouble with Noelle, but I wasn't sure I'd be comfortable in the lingerie set she'd given me. I'd rather wait until I got home and could analyze the fit in the comfort of my own bedroom.

Noelle rolled her eyes and put her hand on the closet door. "Real quick, 'cause I have lunch plans with my parents. I wanna see if they fit before you get the chance to run away. I *know* you won't put them on if I don't make you."

I groaned. "It's no use saying no, is it?"

She grinned and shook her head. "Get in there."

"It's good to have you back." I smiled. "Honest to goodness, Noelle. I've missed you."

"And I've missed you." She gave my booty a nice, firm smack as she yanked open the door. "Now, don't make me tell you again."

I took a step into the closet, helped by a gentle push on the lower back from Noelle. But as I stepped into the dark abyss, I couldn't believe my eyes. I screamed and screamed and backed way up. The Victoria's Secret bag tipped upside down and spilled its goods all over the place.

Noelle tried to catch me, but I flailed around wildly out of control. Nobody could tame me, not a soul.

"What is it?" she asked. "Lord almighty, stop screamin'. You're gonna wake the dead."

I shook my head. Raising a trembling finger, I pointed. "I don't think so, Noelle. He's already dead."

Noelle looked into the closet. "Damn."

I didn't even comment on her swearing in the church basement.

"He *is* dead," she said. "And I don't think he's wakin' up."

CHAPTER 8

Dear Diary,

Y OU'LL NEVER GUESS WHAT HAPPENED today!?
I found a dead body. That sinful underwear Noelle
got for me, well, I went to try it on. But the bathroom
at church was closed, so I stumbled into a closet at her insistence.
Then, I stumbled right onto Frank's body.

I don't know how it got there, Diary, but this town already
talks enough about my troublemakin' tendencies. Since I was the
last person to see Frank alive, everyone's tongues are really gonna
be waggin' now.

Except, I didn't kill him, Diary. You *know* I didn't. I just picked
up my car, my little baby, and went on my way! I didn't kill anyone.
I don't even think I have it in me to kill someone, but especially
not someone like Frank. What really makes me sad is that his wife
is never gonna get that fancy dinner now.

Hang on a second... let me back up. Since I know for a fact
that I didn't kill Frank, then there *has* to be someone else who saw
him alive after me. If I can find the last person who saw him alive,
well, I'm willing to bet that's the same person who made him dead.

Love,
A very troubled Scarlett

CHAPTER 9

"AND THEN SHE KISSED THAT frog, and he turned into a prince," I said in a soft and soothing voice. I turned the page. "But then the princess told that man she wouldn't marry him unless he got a job."

"I like that lady." Grayson's sweet, pink cheek rested against my leg. His sandy-brown hair flopped loosely over his forehead and spread out like an angel's halo over the pillow resting on my thighs. The little man's chest rose and fell, his words just a whisper before his dreams claimed him for the evening.

I ran my fingers over his hair, down the soft skin of his forehead, and the perfect scent of baby powder and shampoo filtered up to me. "I like her too," I whispered. "She's a tough cookie."

"I'm a tough cookie," Gray breathed, his eyelashes fluttering over his round, cherubic face. "Tough… cookie…" The last words were mere afterthoughts as his breathing steadied, the rhythmic motion of his chest calming me.

My fingers stroked his hair, and my heart swelled as I looked at the sweet boy sleeping on my lap. "Goodnight, Gray."

I leaned down, kissed him on the forehead, and sat there for a long time. My eyes glazed over, my hand ran through his locks, which were as fine as angel hair, and I let my body relax for the first time that day.

It was still Sunday, but it had been a long Sunday. After phoning the police that morning, I'd had to sit around and explain to them how I'd found Frank's body. My face burned as I thought of how

22

I'd had to show them my devil panties just to *prove* I wasn't making up my story. They were suspicious of me and said it was mighty coincidental that I'd stumbled into the very same closet as Frank. I thought it had been bad luck.

Then again, I've got just about the worst luck out there, so I shouldn't have been surprised. My luck got even worse when the cops discovered that I'd been the last person to visit Frank's shop. At least, I was the last person they *knew* about. I couldn't explain that bit away because it was the truth, and I had no reason to lie about it. But after I stepped back and considered it, I realized the truth sounded a bit odd.

Why had Frank sent me away to Joe's shop for a tiny scratch? I shuddered. *And who'd gotten to him after me, but before the church service?* Had the murderer been at the shop when I'd been there? Had he been sitting right there in the pew at the sermon, looking around, just biding his time? Had the man, or woman, I suppose, donated to the collection basket? Had the killer shaken my hand during "grip and grin" fellowship time?

Grayson coughed, his small body shuddering. I pulled him closer as I pushed away the dark thoughts. I was innocent. Shouldn't that be enough?

The screen door opened downstairs. Annie's footsteps pattered across the kitchen floor, and the crinkle of a grocery bag echoed as she plopped it on the counter.

Gently, I lifted the pillow from my lap and set it back on the bed while guiding Gray's head to an easy resting place. He yawned, rolled over, and smiled in his sleep before settling into a cozy little cocoon of blankets.

I kissed that gorgeous head of his one last time, thinking that he was the reason for so much of my happiness. Nannying was hard work, but it was worth it. Especially when Gray's little hands gripped mine, and his slobbery little kisses landed on my cheeks.

I smiled and slipped the book I'd been reading out from

underneath Gray. Some of the pages were already bent in half, the spine of the book nearly crushed. I set it on the nightstand, thinking I'd just have to make another. Gray already had a stack of books I'd written just for him. They were nothing special, just some stories I'd jotted down. I liked to draw on them, and Gray liked to help. At his insistence, I'd bound all the pages, and he already had a shelf full of them.

I wrote other stories too, ones for ears much older than Grayson's, but those were locked in a closet in my little home. I didn't write because I thought I was good at it. I wrote because we didn't have a darn library in town.

A few of us locals have been fighting for one for ages, but the city council members didn't think it would be a good use of our limited funds. So, until the council got some sense knocked into their heads, I'd just keep on writing the stories I wanted to read. They could keep out the books, but they couldn't take away the words.

I jogged down the steps and found Annie with her back to me, loading groceries into the fridge. She had ten years on me, easy, but I'd never asked her real age. Gray was almost four. Since I was twenty-eight, that would put Annie pretty close to forty. Which meant she'd better get crackin' if she wanted Gray to have siblings.

But Annie's husband spent more time traveling on business than he did at home with his family. I wasn't the queen of relationships, but from what I understood, a husband and a wife needed to spend some time together before they had a baby. That just wasn't happening in the Harper household. I hadn't seen Mr. Harper for weeks.

"What are you watching me for?" Annie asked, tossing her blond hair over her shoulder without looking up from the fridge. "Hand me that can of tomatoes."

I leapt into action, handing over one canned good after the next until the bag was empty. "Gray was good tonight," I said. "He'll be reading books alone before we know it."

Annie shook her head. "That nonsense you leave by his bed? I suppose I'll have to have Chris bring back some real books next time he comes home."

I swallowed. "There's nothing offensive in those books. And some of them, Gray even helps color the pictures. I think he likes the stories."

"They're garbage," Annie said, cracking open a bottle of bubbly water. There were ten more on the counter, but she must not have felt the need to ask me if I wanted one. Or maybe I just didn't look thirsty.

"They might not win the Nobel prize for cleverness," I said carefully. "But they're fun. They teach Gray to read and encourage him to be creative. If he doesn't like the stories, we rework them together."

She shook her head. "We need to get him some *real* literature."

"Well, you know, The Ladies and I have book club once a week," I said. "You're invited if you'd like to come and read grown-up books. In fact, we're working hard to get a library for this town. Maybe you'd like to help our cause, seeing as how you find literature so important for the next generation."

She smacked her lips, the fizziness of the bubbles hissing in the background sounded mighty refreshing. My throat was dry. I coughed. Annie scooped up the rest of the bottles and shoved them into the fridge. I swear, if I didn't love Gray so much, I'd have more than a few words to say to that woman about her manners alone, but I swallowed them for the moment and kept quiet.

"I'll just have Chris send us a few books from the airport." Annie looked at the calendar pinned to the outside of her refrigerator. "Looks like he's headed to NYC to fly to London tomorrow. They ought to have some books there."

"The library project could really use some support from more local Luck citizens," I said. "Especially ones as esteemed as yourself." What I didn't add was that she had a lot of money that might help our cause. But she didn't seem too keen on sharing her family's money, even though the only reason she'd gotten rich in the first place was a fat inheritance.

I didn't see the point of her bein' rich if she couldn't even spare a bottle of water for her nanny. Did she sit and stare at her dollar bills all day? What was she savin' them all for anyway?

Annie crossed her arms. "Do you really think you have time to be concentrating on a *library*?" Her eyes flashed in my direction. "I had half a mind to tell you not to show up today, but I really needed my massage, and my backup babysitter was busy."

My jaw dropped open. "But I tuck Gray in every Sunday night! Why would today be any different?"

"I don't want a *murderer* caring for my child," Annie said, her voice turning cold and harsh. "The town is talking, Scarlett. Can you tell me why every time something strange happens here your name comes up?"

"I didn't kill Frank!" Her accusations upset me so much, I could barely breathe. "What are you talkin' about? Who is sayin' that?"

"Everyone!" She shook her head. "First, you go raising those panties up in church like the American flag. The next thing we know, you're peeking into dark closets in the basement and unearthing dead bodies. Dead bodies that you'd talked to when they were alive, just this very morning."

"I picked up my car from Frank's," I sputtered. "He was plenty alive when I left him too. As for the other thing, well, that was a completely unrelated incident. It was a gift from Noelle."

"Yes, but Noelle didn't talk to Frank this morning." Annie leaned on the counter. "Noelle's name never comes up every time strange things happen around here. She's not off causing trouble left and right."

I swallowed my hot words once more, trying to convince myself to keep those polite manners I'd been raised with, but it was mighty difficult. What Annie wasn't saying came across as loudly as if she'd shouted it: Noelle wasn't a Powers girl, and Powers girls were no good. Everyone knew that. They'd known it ever since my mother had stumbled into town, according to the rumors. But they were just that—rumors.

"Miss Annie, you know me." My voice had taken on a bit of a pleading tone. "I can't even kill the mice in this house. I certainly couldn't... I couldn't... I didn't kill Frank!"

Annie rolled her eyes toward the ceiling. "I sure hope so, Scarlett. I'd hate to see you end up like your mother."

"You didn't even *know* her." I couldn't help the venom that came out in my words. I'd had enough of Annie's barbed comments. They'd lashed out at me like a scorpion's tail and stung, the poison seeping into my bloodstream so deeply that at times, I almost believed the rumors. "And if you think I could kill Frank, then it turns out you don't know me, either."

"I'm just repeatin' what everyone else is thinkin'." Annie crossed her arms. "You know it just as well as I do."

I grabbed my purse from the counter. "Goodnight, Miss Annie. I'll be back tomorrow night like you asked, but only for Gray." I paused, halfway out the door. "Unless you think I'm a danger to your son, who I love more than anyone in this world."

Miss Annie bit her lip, and her eyes slid over to the calendar on her fridge once again. I knew exactly what she was thinking. She was thinking that her dye-job at the salon was non-refundable without twenty-four hours' notice.

I blew out a short breath from between my lips. "You can go to your hair appointment, Miss Annie. I know you want to. You can't be walking around during Reunion Day with your roots showing."

Miss Annie's eyes flashed, caught in her own dilemma, as she walked over to the door. "Goodnight, Scarlett." I'd hardly gotten my other foot onto the porch before she slammed that door shut.

She hadn't even paid me for the night, but there was no way I was going back inside and facing that woman. No amount of money would make it alright for me to cry in front of her. She'd see it as a sign of weakness and eat me alive.

I stepped off the front step, my eyes stinging. No matter how many times I heard one biting phrase after the next, it never felt nice being accused of things I didn't do. Whether it was breaking one of her china teacups or killing a man, it didn't matter. If I'd done any of those things, I'd 'fess up. Hot tears threatened to slide down my face. I swiped my cheeks as I took one step into the darkness, wondering how, after all the years I'd known her, Annie could think I was capable of killing a man.

CHAPTER 10

WITH ONE FOOT IN FRONT of the other, I made my way down the deserted road to the old barn I lived in at the moment. It was on Hal Newton's property, and he was so old that he didn't care about all the rumors swirling around town about my troublemaking. He was just happy to have an extra couple of hundred bucks a month to fund his beer habit. He didn't ask much, and I didn't talk. It really was a great partnership.

Plus, he was good with Gray. The old man hated people, but he loved children. I didn't blame him much. Every once in a while, the three of us would have a picnic on the lawn between our houses. Those were the only times I'd seen the man smile.

The property was located about a mile outside of town. By town, I meant Main Street. Luck was so small I found it hard to call it a town, but we townsfolk liked to be optimistic about its size. One road led into town, and the same one led out of it past old Hal Newton's farm—simple, just like everything else here.

My little home, a semi-restored thing on the border of Hal's property and the Lannister's farm, sat about a half mile away from Hal's house. My home was accessible by a little foot path and some beaten-down grass, which signified the new road I'd made for my vehicle.

On foot, it took about twenty minutes to get from Gray's home to mine, and that night was a nice night for a walk. I needed a minute to calm down. The mosquitos were few and far between, making for a rare summer's eve. The stars twinkled brightly and

29

open fields stretched as far as I could see under the moon's sparkling glow. Luck could be a serene, beautiful place when nobody else was awake. It wasn't the town I didn't like. The town was perfect. The people were what made things complicated.

About halfway through the walk, I picked up on another sound in addition to my feet crunching on the gravel shoulder. I stopped to listen for a moment and realized I heard the sound of a car approaching. And the car was coming fast.

I barely had time to step off the side of the road before it raced by. The dark, shiny car just whipped right past and showered me with a cloud of dust. Only one person in Luck drove like that.

Mack was back.

And that knowledge did strange things to my stomach.

Thanking my lucky stars he hadn't noticed me, I kept right on walking. I didn't have the nerve to face him right now. I was dressed in a dusty old sundress, dirt streaked my face, and my hair was wild from the gust of wind he'd stirred up. One or two salty tears might have slid their way down my cheeks after the words I'd had with Annie. The last thing I needed was for Mack to see me cry. A long time ago, I'd cried over him, and I'd vowed then and there that it would be the last time. I hadn't cried over a boy since.

Unfortunately, in the distance I spotted the headlights from that fancy dark car turn around and point themselves right back at me. I stepped off the side of the road, trying to tell myself it was so he wouldn't run me over. In reality, I didn't want him to see me like that.

Sure, I'd known he would be back for Reunion Day, but he wasn't supposed to arrive until the next day. Planning to hunker down and avoid the public places while he was around, I'd stocked up on groceries the day before. I hadn't planned for him to catch me off guard.

Then… oh my goodness gracious. He was stopping. Right there next to me.

"Scarlett Powers, how are you doing, sweetheart?" None other than Mack Montgomery rolled down the passenger window and leaned over, that Hollywood smile of his competing with the moonlight for brightness. He didn't stop smiling, not even at the sight of my dirty dress or my mud-splattered face.

"Mack." I shifted slightly under his penetrating gaze. "How are you doing?"

His smile quirked in an endearing, perfectly lopsided grin, full of the same boyish chaos that had left town in a whirlwind ten years ago. "I hoped I'd be seeing you around here."

I forced my face to imitate his smile. "I'm gonna be honest, Mack. I was sorta hoping I wasn't gonna be seeing you."

Mack gave a shake of his head. "Well, that's no way to greet a visitor. Let me buy you a drink one night this week, Scarlett."

"I don't think that's a great idea."

"Why not?"

I gave a half-hearted shrug. "You said it yourself, Mack. You're 'just' a visitor. Why hash all that old stuff up when you'll be gone again in a few days? Easier to just leave everything under the rug, don't you think?"

Mack's forehead crinkled, and the look on his face was one of surprise. "You don't mean that."

"Of course I do!" I threw my arms up, taking one step toward the car. "I don't even know you anymore, Mack. It's been ten years. We were able to let things rest for a decade. Why dredge up old business now?"

Mack tilted his head sideways. "I just asked you to grab a drink, Scarlett. We don't gotta talk about old times."

When I didn't respond, he threw his car in park, opened the door, and stepped out of the vehicle. He took his sweet time hooking his thumbs in his pockets and strolling around the shiny car. He stopped close enough for me to reach out and touch him, if I wanted.

His blue eyes burned brightly, and I could feel his vibrant energy buzzing without even resting a hand on his skin. Those golden locks of his flopped over his forehead and made for just the right amount of cute and sexy. He had just the right amount of hair to run my hands through and hold on tight.

And by God, that man could fill out a pair of jeans and a gray V-neck T-shirt like nobody I'd ever seen before. It wasn't the first time I'd wondered why Hollywood wanted him behind the scenes as a stunt driver instead of front and center. Ladies around the world would have swooned if Mack Montgomery's body had shown up on the silver screen without a shirt.

"Why do you want to get a drink with me?" I asked.

Mack crossed his arms. "Because it's been a long time, and that's the point of Reunion Day. Catching up with old friends. It ain't a date, Scarlett. I was just gonna buy you a beer. A martini, if that's still your thing. If you don't want to, just say no."

I swallowed. "No."

Mack blinked. "No?"

"You gave me the option." I took one step away from Mack. "And I took it. No, Mack. I don't think it's a good idea."

Mack stepped closer, closing the gap I'd just created. "Why not?"

"I don't have to answer to you, not after all this time."

Mack gave an astounded shake of his head. "Where are you walkin' this time of night all by yourself?"

"I'm goin' home."

"You don't have a car?"

"It's in the shop," I said. "You clearly haven't heard yet."

"About Frank?" Mack tipped his head sideways. "Yeah, I heard. I heard your car was at his place this morning, but I thought you picked it up."

I bit my lip. "Long story."

"Ignore those people whisperin' about you," Mack said. "They all know you didn't do anything to Frank."

"It's not any of your business what this town thinks, seeing how you don't live here anymore."

Mack reached up a hand and ran his fingers through those gorgeous locks, leaving a trail of disheveled hair in his wake. "Fine. I was just trying to be polite. I won't force you to get a drink with me, though I wish you'd consider it."

"I'm sorry, Mack."

"Let me give you my number in case you change your mind."

"I'm not gonna change my mind," I said. "I don't want your phone number."

"Let me give you a ride home, at the very least."

"I don't need a ride home. It's a ten-minute walk and a beautiful night," I said. "I've been doin' just fine on my own. No offense, but I don't need anyone swooping in right now to help me out."

"I'm not swooping in to help you out. I'm just trying to get my money's worth on this car rental." Mack gestured toward his pretty vehicle. "You know how expensive it was to get an Audi down here for a few days? Frank, God rest his soul, had to pull in favors from three counties over."

I gave Mack a smile. "I'm fully capable of getting home by my lonesome, without the help of an Audi." I knew I should be more considerate, more polite. After all, he was a guest of Luck at the moment. But it was a slippery slope. "In fact, I've been doing it for almost twenty-eight years now, believe it or not."

"Do you remember our pact?" Mack asked. The question smacked me upside the head, out of the blue. "Do you remember?"

I swallowed hard. "Goodnight, Mack."

I couldn't help the stubborn streak in me, the one that made my feet start walking away from Mack, even though I knew in my soul it was silly to turn down a ride for half a mile. What could happen in half a mile? That was a two-minute car ride. Surely, I could control myself around Mack for two minutes.

My eyes started to sting again the farther I got from Mack. My heart screamed at me to turn around, apologize for my rudeness, and give Mack a hug. I wanted to get a drink with him, ask about his life, and make sure he had a nice stay in Luck, Texas for the next few days.

At the same time, the stubborn streak that got me into so much trouble was a double-edged sword. As much as it got me into sticky situations, it also saved my life. That stubbornness was the reason I didn't let the whispers get to me and break me down. If I weren't such a stubborn bitch, the town would have run me into the ground years ago.

After a minute of walking, the crunch of a second set of footsteps joined me. I stared at my feet, marching onward and upward, and tried to ignore the pleasant sensation of a man by my side. I resisted the urge to look up—or worse, to reach out and grab Mack's hand. It would be too easy to fall into old patterns that had been so hard to get rid of the first time.

"Are you okay?" Mack asked. "Sweetheart, you're breakin' my heart. I can't stand to see you like this."

I sniffed, pretending I'd suddenly developed a case of serious allergies, even though I wasn't fooling anyone.

"What's wrong?" Mack reached out, his hand sliding onto my shoulder, his fingers grasping my skin as he turned me to face him. "You can't tell me my face brought on tears now, can you? Did I do this to you?"

I looked up, seeing a deep sadness in Mack's blue eyes. My own watered, but no tears slipped out.

"I knew I was a bastard, but I didn't know I'd hurt you this bad." Mack's low voice rolled over the empty plains. The moonlight glinted off of those blue irises, sending my stomach lurching into the clear depths of his eyes.

I'd never felt smaller in my life. My shoulders crumpled, my arms hugged my body, and I let myself fall into Mack's arms. Sobs came up from the deepest cavities of my chest as he hugged me as close as anyone had ever hugged me.

"I didn't kill Frank," I whispered against his chest. My tears wet his shirt, causing a pool of dampness to bloom from underneath my cheek. Although I was willing to bet his gray shirt cost more money than I made from a day's work, I couldn't pull myself away. "Why do they think I did it?"

"You're just in shock." Mack rubbed circles on my back, his breath hot against my hair. "Nobody thinks you did anything."

"Then why are they saying it?" Somewhere inside, I found the strength to break free from Mack's arms and step backward. I'd found that spark of anger, and I used it to beat out the sadness. My eyes still clouded with unshed tears, but this time, I wiped them away with frustration.

Instead of answering, Mack reached out and took my hand. My chest heaved at first, and my mind warred between shaking his hand loose or forfeiting to his comforting touch. The latter idea won out. Mack's fingers wove through mine, and he led me down the country road, with the sound of crickets accompanying us home.

The next time I looked up, we'd reached my little barn. I'd barely noticed the walk back. My mind had been deliciously blank, numb to the world around me. I hadn't had time to think about the dead body I'd discovered. It must have all come out in one tornado of angry tears.

"I'm sorry about that." I turned to Mack and dropped his hand. "I don't know what came over me. I think I just hadn't processed finding Frank's body. On top of that, with the town talkin'… it all just came out in an explosion. I'm sorry you had to see that."

Mack looked at the barn behind me. "So, this is where you live? Ol' Hal still own this property?"

I nodded, grateful he'd let my apology rest and didn't feel the need to poke and prod it to death.

"Well, I hope you have a good rest of your evening, Miss Scarlett." Mack leaned in, the scent of him filling the air all around us, a bit of fresh pine, a hint of expensive shower gel, the minty freshness of his breath. He pressed his lips against my cheek in a chaste kiss, then gave me that gorgeously lopsided smile as he stepped back. "I'd offer to call you, but I don't think you want that."

I looked at my shoes.

"And I'd offer to leave my number, but you already said no to that too." Mack gave me a salute as he took a few steps back. "It was great to see you, Scarlett. I hope I run into you again while I'm in town, but if not…" He cleared his throat. "Well, I hope you're happy."

Turning, I unlocked the door and stepped into the entryway of my tiny little home. I stood in the doorway looking back at Mack. "Now that you walked me home, you've gotta walk back to your car, and that don't seem right. Are you sure you don't want to come in for a cup of coffee? I can call Sal."

Mack smiled at the mention of Sal, who'd been driving taxis since the town was first formed. "I think you might be right, Scarlett. It's for the best if I get going."

My heart fluttered, a wisp of fear curling in my stomach, as Mack turned and strolled away. If possible, he looked just as good from the back as he did from the front, with strong legs and strong arms. I realized Hollywood hadn't stolen as much of the small-town cowboy out of Mack as I might have suspected.

As he gave me one last smile and wave, I closed the door, and my heart sank all the way down to my feet. I'd just run off the only man I'd ever loved.

Then again, if we'd been meant to be, maybe he wouldn't have left in the first place.

CHAPTER 11

Dear Diary,

WHAT A DAY. I AM tired. Bone-tired. But I just have to write to you because my brain is on the fritz wondering if what I said to Mack was right or wrong. I know what he did all them years ago was wrong, but what if... what if he did it for a reason?

More importantly, even if he did leave for a reason, well, it didn't change the fact that it hurt me real bad. So why can I not stop feeling as if I care for him, Diary? It's crazy!

I wasn't all that polite with him, either, and I'm ashamed of that. I was raised with better manners than that, and one thing I've never been called is rude. But my problem, Diary, is this: If I start being nice to Mack, what's to stop the next thing from happening? Because I can't have Mack leaving my bed in the morning and never coming back. I couldn't handle that. Remember how I told you I had that one little wish? Well, I thought he was the answer. Turns out, I was wrong.

XoXo, a very confused Scarlett

CHAPTER 12

"I S SHE READY?" I ASKED, wiping my brow as I climbed the front steps to Joe's Auto Body Shop.

As before, Ralph-or-Ryan stood behind the counter, while there was no sign of Joe anywhere. That day, Ryan's jumpsuit read Miguel.

"She's ready," Ryan-or-Miguel said, gesturing toward my beautiful lavender Beetle. The cute little car put a smile on my face. "Though I'm not sure why she was sent over here, I'll be honest."

I squinted, looking hard for the black mark. It wasn't there. "It looks like you did a great job. She's good as new. What are you talkin' about?"

Ryan shrugged. "Didn't take more than a little bit of elbow grease to get that 'scratch' out. Wasn't more'n a smudge of dirt, turns out. Nothing that couldn't've been taken care of by Frank." Ryan's shoulders stiffened, and his cheeks turned pink. "May he rest in peace."

I bowed my head for a moment. "Well, regardless, I appreciate your work. Um, I suppose I can just pay for it, seeing as how Frank... well, let me just take care of it, so we don't have to worry about the tab."

Ryan waved a hand. "Forget about it. Like I said, it didn't even take any product to clean her up. Just a bit of muscle." Ryan-or-Miguel leaned on the counter, his voice low. "Joe hasn't been around the shop since you stopped by yesterday, so he didn't even know you were here. If you take her and get out of here, I won't say nothin' if you don't."

"Really? Wow, I'd be real grateful," I said. "That's real kind of you, Ryan."

"My pleasure." Ryan gave a nod. "Don't wanna bother Joe about this, 'specially since I don't know what I'd be charging you for, anyhow. Not to mention, with what happened to Frank yesterday…" Ryan shook his head. "It's my pleasure to do a bit of good for him if I can."

I gave a small smile of agreement. "It sure does mean a lot to me."

"Say, I heard you were over there right before, well… they found him."

"I found him, Ryan." The smile froze on my face. "You didn't hear?"

From the red tinge of Ryan's ears, I guessed he *had* heard and just didn't want to say anything about it.

"Nah, I hadn't heard," he muttered, though we both knew it was a lie.

"Ryan, if you got a question, just ask me," I said. "I hope you're not 'forgetting' to charge me because you think I'll come after you, otherwise."

Ryan spluttered a nonsense phrase, and I sighed.

"I didn't kill him, Ryan. Look at me." I did a twirl in my red sundress, a pretty one I'd picked out especially for the day. It had buttons where the thick straps met the top of the soft fabric. "Do you really think I could've taken on Frank? Come on. I can hardly open a jar of pickles, let alone kidnap a man and move his body to the church basement."

While Ryan had the grace to look embarrassed, I focused on telling myself that my outfit choice had nothing to do with the fact that Mack was in town, and neither did me swiping a bit of devilish-red lipstick on. But both my diary and I knew the truth.

If I was going to run into Mack that day, I wasn't going to be dirt-streaked and crying. I was going to stand proud and bright.

"I'm gonna head out now, and I thank you for your kindness in helping me out with this situation," I said with a small finger wave at Ryan. "If I can do anything for you, you let me know, all right?"

Ryan gave a curt nod. "Yes, ma'am."

On the way out the door, I paused and turned around. Maybe it was a bit sinful of me, but I had a thought right then and there. Ryan didn't know what to think of me. He didn't know whether he should be scared, terrified, or embarrassed. There was no reason I couldn't use his confusion to get a few answers.

"Say, Ryan." I leaned against the doorframe. When he gave me a curious stare, I bit my lip, realizing too late that I had just put fresh red gloss on them babies. I ran my tongue over my teeth, and Ryan squirmed while he waited for me to finish. "Do you know anyone who might have wanted Frank dead?"

"Why would I know that?" Ryan's expression grew alarmed. "I just work here, all right? I don't care about the rivalry between Joe and Frank. As far as I can tell, they seem to work together just fine."

I frowned. "I thought they'd got over that silly old rivalry. They seemed like they were working well together. I thought it was a good sign that Frank sent me over here to fix the body of my car. Frank said him and Joe'd been trading business for a while now."

"It's nothing like it used to be." Ryan's face darkened, probably remembering the days when Joe and Frank had fought each other tooth and nail for each customer. There were only so many cars in our small town. As it turned out, there was enough going wrong with the vehicles to keep two shops in business. "But they had a fight last week. I don't know about what." Ryan raised his arms in submission before I could ask. "I walked in on the tail end of it. Then Frank stormed out."

"You didn't catch anything it was about?"

Ryan shook his head. "I asked Joe about it, but he blew me off.

Said it was nothing but a disagreement over an oil change. Like I said, I just work here. I don't get involved with politics."

"And after that?"

"What do you mean?" Ryan bounced his shoulders up and down. "Nothing. Joe stomped around here moody all week, but I just figured he was sour over the argument. The rivalry isn't good for either of them."

"But Frank wouldn't have sent my car over here if they were fightin' again, would he?" I pursed my lips. "Frank said Joe could just add the payment to his tab. Surely, they wouldn't trust each other to work on credit if they were arguing about an oil change."

"That is odd. I guess I never thought much about it."

A movement over Ryan's shoulder caught my attention. I pointed a finger. "Hey, you, get away from my car!" I turned to Ryan. "Who is that?"

"That's Miguel." Ryan thumbed at the name on his jumpsuit. "He's been with us for a few months now, just doing the basic stuff. Real talented around an engine."

I glanced at the small Latino man, watching as he wiped my windows down. "Ah, I didn't know you'd hired a new employee."

"He just showed up looking for work one day. He didn't mind doing the boring work, so we just kept him on."

"Do you think he might have a clue of what's happening?" I asked. "Maybe I could ask him a few questions."

"You can try." Ryan grinned. "But he don't speak English."

My shoulders slumped. "Huh. Well, maybe I'll just talk to Joe when he's back. Do you know when you're expecting him back?"

Ryan shook his head. "I wasn't expecting him gone, so your guess is as good as mine. Why you so interested, anyway?"

I stuck a hand on my hip. "I'm just curious. Trying to figure out what happened here. The whole town thinks I had something to do with Frank being murdered, and nothing can stop a rumor in its tracks like the truth." I hesitated. "Maybe if I can find someone else who had a reason to want Frank dead, then they'll lay off me."

Ryan's eyes softened. "Ain't that the police's job?"

"I talked to them for hours yesterday, but I didn't have anything to tell them."

"Is it true you found his body with Noelle Summers, that beautiful thing?" Ryan asked. "I heard you were trying on the devil's undies, and that's how he ended up dead."

"Will you listen to the words coming out of your mouth, Ryan Hall? That's just nonsense! It don't matter what I was trying on. It wasn't gonna kill anyone. Frank was already dead."

"I'm just telling you what I heard."

"If Joe comes back, can you tell him to give me a call?" I asked. "Don't tell him I was here. Let's keep that our little secret."

"Sure thing."

"Has he ever missed work before?" I raised an eyebrow. "Just seems weird to me, him being gone, Frank's body being found. I don't know why exactly, but my gut is giving me a bad feeling about this."

"You think Joe's dead too?" Ryan's eyes widened to the size of hay barrels. "No."

"I'm not saying that. Don't you go spreading talk, now." I lowered my voice. "I'm *not* saying Joe's dead by any means. But, what if Joe's hiding from something? Or someone?"

"You think Joe killed Frank?" Ryan shook his head. "No way."

"I don't know what I'm saying, except that this whole thing smells fishy."

Ryan's face crinkled in thought. "Isn't Monday afternoon book club day?"

"Yeah, I gotta get going, or else I'm gonna be late." I glanced at the clock on the wall. "Can you tell Miguel I don't need the rest of my windows cleaned. I gotta hit the road."

"Doesn't Joe's wife go to book club?" Ryan asked. "She might know. Joe doesn't usually skip out on work like this. Then again, I wasn't worried because Angie would've called me if she was worried about Joe."

"You're right." I exhaled a breath. "Angie should be there today. I'll let you know if I hear anything important."

"I'd appreciate that, Miss Scarlett. Now, you drive safe. And if you get the chance, try your windshield wipers. I threw on an extra pair for free since yours were getting grimy."

"Thanks, Ryan. I won't forget it." I smiled, jogged down the steps, and nodded a thank-you to Miguel before climbing in my vehicle.

Just before I pulled out of the parking lot, my phone rang. I kept my foot on the brake while I dug in my purse. I smiled once I saw Noelle's name pop up on my caller ID.

"Hey, I was just thinking," Noelle started as soon as I picked up, before I could so much as breathe onto the line. "You gals still do that nerdy book club thing on Mondays?"

"Yeah, of course! I'm just on my way there now. I thought you were spending the day with your parents?"

"I was, but my mom has been talking to me about 'settling down' for the past three hours. Do you mind if I come along?" Noelle coughed. "I ain't much of a reader, but I sure as hell will take books over listening to one more reason I'm becoming an old maid."

I grinned. "I'm on my way. And don't worry, I'm the only person who reads the books anyways, so you'll fit right in."

"Great! I'll bring wine."

"Like I said, you're a natural."

"And you're a lifesaver." Noelle's voice grew quiet. "Can't wait to see you, honey. You keeping your chin up?"

"I'm doing just fine," I said, meaning it. I pulled out of the parking lot, smiling with real gusto for the first time since I'd stumbled onto Frank's body. "At least, I am now."

CHAPTER 13

Dear Diary,

NOBODY KNOWS I WRITE BOOKS. Not even my book club. Really, you're the only person who knows. Well, you and Grayson, but seeing as how he's not even four years old, that hardly counts. Anyway, writing books isn't the point of our little club. Don't let the title fool you; our "book club" is nothing more than an excuse to drink mimosas on a Monday.

The other members of the group let me choose all the books since they don't bother to read along. But it's fun, anyway. I don't have many friends in this town, but at least these ladies don't look at me like I'm bonkers. Then again, they're just as bonkers. So, book club or mimosa club, I suppose it doesn't matter.

Especially not today, since I'm not thinking of any book at all. I'm only worried about what Angela has to tell me about her husband's absence. I don't care what Ryan says. Something is wrong with this picture. I just can't figure out what.

It's just icing on the cake that Noelle is coming along for the ride. I can't help but smile when that girl is in the same room as me. Reunion Day always brings two things, the bad and the good. Seeing as how I ran into the "bad" last night, I'm anxious to get my fill of the "good" today. I'm done cryin', Diary. I'm ready to get to the bottom of this business.

And if Mack happens to see me walking downtown in this

pretty red dress that I bought for a special occasion, then so be it. Because I didn't dress up for him.

Not really.

Okay, fine, I might have.

But there's nothing wrong with showing a man what he missed out on, right?

Tune in later, Diary. I'll keep you posted.

xoxx Scarlett xoxx

CHAPTER 14

"I S THAT WHO I THINK it is?" Noelle asked, her eyes flashing toward me, brimming with questions. "Is that *Mack*?"

I nodded. *Just my luck.* I pulled onto Main Street right as Mack's fancy Audi whipped around the corner going the other way, its taillights fading into the distance. All my dressing up had been for nothing.

"Oh, girl, I can read you like a book." Noelle shook her head. "You're right. I *do* belong in this book club. I've got you nailed, cover to cover. See what I just did there?"

"You're just full of jokes." A blush warmed my cheeks. "It's just *Mack*."

"When's the last time you wore lipstick?" Noelle raised an eyebrow. "Don't get me wrong. I was proud of you when you showed up with red lips. I know you're the *au naturel* type. A swipe of mascara is all you need, in fact. I'm jealous. You know that. Which is why I *knew* something was up the second I climbed into this car. Your lipstick. You wanted Mack to notice you!"

"No." The lie fell flat even to my ears.

"And that red dress." Noelle shook her head, and her eyes were bright with mischief. "I knew you weren't dressing up for me! You little devil, you. Speaking of, are you wearing those panties I gave you? They'd match perfectly."

My fingers gripped the steering wheel tighter. "No! Of course not. Nobody wants to see me in those. Don't be silly." The truth was I'd considered slipping into them that morning after I'd draped the soft fabric of the red dress over my body. But I couldn't do it. It had just felt wrong. Plus, nobody would be seeing them, anyhow.

"I don't know why you keep saying that. You're as gorgeous as can be." Noelle blinked. "You've got a canvas for a face, let's be honest. The makeup artists up at my fashion school would die to hold a brush to your cheeks."

"Well, I'd die before I'd let them. I'm fine just the way I am."

Noelle shrugged. "I'm not arguing. I think you're gorgeous, and I just said so. Plus, all that walking around town instead of driving keeps you so skinny. You eating enough?"

"Stop worrying! I'm fine, Noelle." I paused. The silence was heavy as Noelle stared, waiting for me to explain. I exhaled a long breath. "Okay, something happened last night."

"Mack? I knew it!" Noelle gasped. "You didn't take him right back, did you? Did you at least make him grovel before you let him into your house? Or did you go to his place?"

"Noelle, I didn't sleep with him!"

"Oh." She straightened her lips into a polite smile. "Good for you. Girl, you have willpower because time has aged that man well. *Mmm-mmm.*"

"You want him?"

"He's not my type," Noelle said. "Plus, I'm not moving back here. As much as I miss you, honey, I'm at home in the city."

I sighed. "I know that. And my place is here, in this small town. Why did God do that, Noelle? He gave me the best friend a girl could ask for, and then pulled us five million miles apart."

"I know, I know." Noelle reached over and clasped my hand. "But that's sayin' something special about us, I think. Even five thousand miles can't keep us out of trouble. Speaking of trouble, if you speed up now, I'm pretty sure I saw Mack pull off way down the road at Ernie's gas station. We can 'accidentally' waltz by him there. What do you say?"

"That's too obvious! I can't afford to be embarrassed again." I explained about what'd happened last night, everything from Gray's mother reaming me out to my collapse into Mack's arms. I hadn't meant to spill *all* of the beans, but Noelle had that effect on me. I just couldn't stop talking once I started. "So this red dress is mostly for me, but if Mack happened to see me and notice that I wasn't covered in a pile of mud with salt streaks down my face, that would've been okay. I'm not trying to get him back, just show him I'm not a mess."

"Well, let's go show him."

"We're going to be late for book club."

"You're such a nerd." Noelle grinned. "And I love you for it. Book club it is, but I'm only saying that because I intend to have a few mimosas, and maybe it'll be *more* fun to run into him once we're giggly on champagne. What do you say?"

"I have to say that champagne sounds good." Then, I quickly filled her in on what had happened at Joe's Auto Body Shop. "So let's get Angela some champagne. You remember Joe's wife? The one with the weird knuckles? She'll be more likely to be honest if she's had a few mimosas."

"Promise me one thing."

"What's that?" I glanced at her as I parked the car in front of the cafe we used for our meetings.

"After you find out information from Angela, you take a break. You don't babysit Gray until late tonight, right?"

I nodded. "And only for a short time while Mrs. Harper gets her hair done."

"Perfect." Noelle grinned. "Then promise me that you'll have a good time. You'll drink mimosas with me, and then we can go to a late lunch together. Maybe do a bit of shopping to sober you up before your date with Gray tonight. I'm only in town for a few days, and I want to have some fun with you. Okay?"

Nothing sounded better. Plus, I needed to get my mind off

things for a little bit. Thinking nonstop about Joe, Frank, Mack, Annie, and this entire town was driving me nuts.

"You've got yourself a deal."

Noelle leaned over and gave me a hug and a kiss on the cheek. "Great. Now, let's go see those old biddies. I've gotta make sure they're just as terrible as ever."

CHAPTER 15

THE COZY CAFE SERVED AS the meeting place for more town gatherings than not. PTA meetings were held on Sunday evenings, and the Crafty Knitters met on Friday nights when everyone else was busy doing things like going to the bar or watching movies. More than one "debate" had been held at the cafe for candidates running for a local town office, while "rebellious" teens were dragged out by their ears at least once a week at midnight, the unofficial curfew on school nights.

Our book club had the place reserved for Mondays at lunchtime. Mondays were the days I had off while Grayson went to a friend's house. Later, I'd pick him up and handle bed and bath time while Mrs. Harper got her hair done or her nails touched up.

"Doesn't Monday at lunch interfere with anyone else's schedule?" Noelle ran her own dainty nails through her hair, tossing the long, dark locks behind her shoulders. "I can't imagine finding time in the middle of the day. I know you don't work until night, but what about the others?"

She wore simple jeans and a form-fitting black top. The outfit was so simple yet so exquisite. I'd bet it had cost upward of a hundred dollars, at least. Even my "fancy" red dress had been a bargain at eight dollars from the thrift store.

I shrugged. "Well, seeing as how the main three members have been retired for twenty years, their schedules are wide open. The other ladies either have jobs within walking distance, or stay at home during the day. I imagine it's a different pace of life here than New York. Everyone in town knows it's book club day."

Noelle laughed. "Yes, I suppose. It's nice coming back here." She looked thoughtful. "Sometimes, I wonder if it wouldn't be nice to move back home. Everything's so much simpler here. People don't make as much money, but they don't need as much either."

"Be still my heart!" I faked a heart attack, clasping at my chest. "Do you mean it, Noelle? Are you considering moving back?"

The dreamy look on her face faded, and she grinned at me. "Not really. I like to think about it now and again, but I think I was made for the city. I *like* the hustle and bustle. I like that not everybody knows I'm going to book club, or who I'm dating, or what I ate for breakfast."

"Noelle Summers, do you have a boyfriend?" My jaw dropped as Noelle reached for the passenger door handle. I reached over and hooked my finger in the back belt loop of her jeans. "Don't you dare step one foot out of this car without telling me about it, missy."

Noelle collapsed back in her seat, the sly grin of a fresh, secret love sliding onto her face. "He's not my boyfriend."

I clasped my hand over my mouth and stifled a giggly scream. "Noelle! Why'd you wait so long to tell me?"

"I didn't! We just had our second date, but..." Noelle shook her head. "I have a good feeling about this one, Scarlett. A really good feeling."

"Spill the beans, already! I'm dying here."

Noelle tilted her nose up. "You said it yourself. We're gonna be late to book club."

"Just tell me one thing," I said. "Have you... you know... done it?"

"I just said two dates, Scarlett. New York hasn't turned me into a hoodlum!" Noelle shook her head, her eyes sparkling. "But we did a bit of the other stuff, kissin' and things. And you know what? I'm gonna shave my legs *extra* good for our next date, just in case."

"Promise you'll call me the *second* after your next date with him!" I said. "My goodness, I'm so happy for you. I know you've been sayin' each time we talk that dating up in that city is so hard."

"It is hard. Although, I think it's harder down here because you know the whole pool of guys to choose from. Up there…" Noelle sighed. "Up in the city, there's still the hope that not all the good ones are taken. Here in Luck, you know too much about all these guys. Billy Handler picked his nose all through third grade. How could I kiss him? And Angelo Wexler pooped his pants in kindergarten. I know that was a long time ago, but come on."

I didn't comment since Noelle's words were too true. But unlike her, I didn't have plans to get out of Luck, which made the dating pool for me shrink smaller and smaller by the second.

"Oh, I'm sorry," Noelle said. "I didn't mean that. I'm sure there's plenty of men here that would love you and be good to you." Her eyes scanned my crestfallen face. "And if you don't have a date by the time Christmas rolls around, how about you come up and visit me? Who knows? Maybe if this guy works out, he'll have some friends. We can double date."

"You mean it?" My palms grew sweaty just thinking about a trip to the city that never sleeps. I wasn't sure I was cut out for that lifestyle. What if I got smushed by a taxi? So many things could happen in a big city. The options were endless.

"You're already thinking of all the reasons not to," Noelle said. "I know how your brain works, and I can see your gears turning, but don't you worry. I'd take care of you." She pushed open the car door. "Now, come on. I see three sets of prying eyes peeking out from the windows, just waiting to gather some gossip. Let's go inside."

I followed Noelle to the door, unable to suppress the thought that maybe all the good guys *were* taken here in Luck. What did that mean for me? It sure wasn't helping my one little wish. That was for certain. But I belonged here in this terrible, gossip-filled town. It was where I'd grown up. I had roots. I was comfortable and happy.

However, as I stepped up to the door of The Cozy Cafe, I wondered if maybe all of those things were excuses.

Maybe I was just scared.

CHAPTER 16

"NOELLE SUMMERS!" THE DOOR TO the cafe was flung open by three sets of old, wrinkly hands, all vying for the first grip on Noelle's arm. "You're back!"

I stood behind my friend on the steps, unable to hide a smile as three old ladies hauled Noelle in through the door, touching her hair, pinching her cheeks, and prodding at her thin stomach.

"Ladies, relax," I said, following Noelle inside. "Don't maul the girl, or she'll never come back."

"Oh, hello, Scarlett," someone muttered as an afterthought before all three women went back to examining the size of Noelle's chest and commenting on the color of her lipstick.

Noelle grinned like a champ. Since she seemed to be holding her own, I slipped past the swarm of book clubbers and walked up to the counter. "Two cappuccinos today, Mary Anne. On me."

"Bet you've been waiting a long time to say that, huh?" Mary Anne, the owner of The Cozy Cafe, was just as cozy herself. She was round, cushy, and wore a mustard-yellow dress with a floral print that had probably doubled as kitchen wallpaper in the seventies. She grinned. "I haven't seen you smile that big in a while, honey."

"Yeah, well." I turned to look at the group. "Something about that girl seems to make everyone smile."

Mary Anne chuckled. "Give yourself some credit. The two of you together, that's the magic."

I crossed my arms, watching the reunion between the three old ladies and my best friend. "I'm going to have to pull them off of her, aren't I?"

"They're just excited." Mary Anne added espresso to the machine. "Noelle can handle it, if anyone can."

The three old ladies responsible for mauling Noelle were named, in no particular order, Tiny, Tootsie, and Tallulah. Together, they made up the former girl band named, very creatively, GURLZ. Or at least, that was what they said.

After listening to them talk about their girl band days, one would have thought they were the next best thing to Britney Spears, pre-meltdown. In reality, the biggest break those ladies had ever gotten was a jingle in a local commercial for Lou's Hardware Store. And the only reason they'd gotten that gig was because Lou was married to Tiny, and Tiny wore the pants in that relationship.

"Are they extra excitable today, or is it just me?" I glanced at the eighty-plus-year-old women fawning over Noelle's hair. "They seem peppier than usual."

"You're right on." Mary Anne lowered her voice, pouring milk into a steamer pot. "They just found out the Reunion Day committee is letting them sing ten seconds of their hit song during setup."

"Setup?"

"They start setting up the auditorium at five tomorrow afternoon." Mary Anne shrugged. "Guests don't arrive until seven, but GURLZ didn't seem to care. They bullied the planning committee so much, eventually they just caved in and gave them a slot to sing their hearts out during setup."

"That's a good time," I said. "Seein' as how their bedtime is eight, anyway."

Mary Anne laughed. "They won't even notice there's no audience." She looked at the three ladies fondly. "They're just happy to sing. Well, I should say scream. It's definitely more screaming than singing. Here's your cappuccinos, darlin'. You go rescue Noelle now before they tear her apart."

Carrying two steaming cappuccinos, I elbowed my way past the members of GURLZ then handed a cup to Noelle. "Ladies." I narrowed my eyes at the three women. "Give her some space to breathe."

"I know this is book club, and I don't want to interrupt, so let's sit down." Noelle nodded toward the comfy couches surrounding a well-worn coffee table. "I brought you ladies gifts, but I can't get them out of my purse until I have my hands free."

The mention of "gifts" did the trick. Noelle plopped on one of the loveseats, patting the space next to her for me to sit. After getting seated, I added a packet of sugar to my coffee and one to Noelle's.

"You remembered!" she said. "I swear, I'm the only person in New York who adds sugar to their coffee. I don't understand why. We do so much walking, the calories just burn right off."

"What about these gifts you speak of?" Tiny, true to her name, was the smallest of the bunch.

The three ladies sat crammed next to each other on the couch, different as could be. What Tiny lacked in physical size, she made up for in personality. She was like a firecracker: lots of punch packed into a small packet, and not afraid to light up the place with curse words when she got angry. Her hair curled in white locks close to her scalp, and she wore a tank top that said "Angel" across her chest... her very droopy chest. A neon-pink bra peeked out from underneath the tank top, and a smattering of tattoos decorated her left arm. She was a motorcycle mama if I'd ever seen one, minus the motorcycle.

Noelle unearthed three thin tubes from her purse and handed them across to the three ladies smushed together. "Lip gloss. It's *Chanel*. Real, live Chanel."

"I call red!" Tootsie elbowed her bandmates out of the way as she snatched the most vibrant shade of crimson of the three tubes. Tootsie, a full-figured woman, was known mostly for her hair. It was piled high in a beehive 'do, the shade somewhere between fire-truck red and the neon pink of Tiny's bra. She had so much hair, it stuck up probably a foot over her head. Even though that might be an exaggeration, you definitely didn't want to get stuck behind Tootsie in the movie theater.

Lastly, Tallulah, the most posh one of the group, carefully examined a pale shade of pink lipstick. "This'll bring out my skin tones."

"I had you in mind when I picked that one out." Noelle winked.

Tallulah grinned. She had skin tones the color of creamy milk chocolate, and her soft brown eyes were so large, I often caught myself gazing into them. She had a soothing, mesmerizing stare and a warm personality to match. With a deep voice as silky and soulful as could be, she was the real singer of the group.

"What do you say?" I chided the GURLZ.

"Thank you," three voices chorused. The women already seemed intent on unscrewing the caps and comparing the lip glosses.

"Are we waiting for anyone else?" Noelle asked.

"We usually start ten minutes late," I said. "Which means everyone shows up twenty minutes late. Let's give them a few more minutes."

Half an hour later, three more ladies had joined us, which was two more than usual. Probably, they were just curious to catch up with Noelle, which was fine by me. I was just happy to see that Angela, Joe's wife, had shown up. Not only had she shown up, she'd strolled in sporting a rock the size of Arkansas.

"Angela, what is that on your hand?" Tiny leapt to her feet and yanked Angela toward her the second the poor woman stepped through the door. "Where on earth did Joe get something this size?"

"Unless it's not from Joe?" Tootsie, red-beehive wobbling dangerously, shook her head. "Maybe you've got a lover on the side?"

"Tootsie, that's rude." Tallulah spoke, her voice calming the room down. "Let's come and sit, shall we? Let's let Scarlett talk about the book for five minutes like usual, and then we can chat."

"Oh, there's not really any story to my ring." Angela showed off her ring, swooping around the room as Mary Anne waltzed over with a tray of brightly colored mimosas. Angela picked one up, wrapping her talon-like nails around the glass, then extended those weird knuckles for all of us to see. "It's from my Joey. Isn't it a beaut?"

"Business has been good at the shop?" I asked, trying for casual.

Angela's eyes flicked toward me before turning back to the rock. "I suppose so. I think he's working on a new deal, or whatever. He had to go on a last-minute business trip yesterday." Angela giggled. "I don't ask questions. I just take the jewelry."

"That is way more boring than I expected," Tiny said, her gravelly voice a testament to years of smoking. "Thought you'd gotten yourself a lover. A real sexy one, like in these books Scarlett picks out."

I blushed. "Tiny, Angela is married. She should be gettin' jewelry from her husband." I smiled at Angela. "It's beautiful. I'm glad things are goin' so well with you and Joe."

"Why wouldn't they be?" Angela's eyebrows drew in as she frowned, her bottle-blond hair swishing as she glared at me. "Joe and I are a perfect couple."

"I just meant… sometimes business and traveling are hard," I said. "Long distance relationships. You know, I'm just happy that you guys are making it work."

The venom from Angela's gaze faded as she glanced fondly at her ring. "Yeah, I don't mind if he leaves town for a few days if he keeps bringing back presents like this."

"When's he coming back?" I asked.

The room quieted, and I realized my question sounded as though I were prying.

"Why?" Angela asked in her nasally voice. "Can't you just be happy about my ring? Why the questions, Scarlett?"

Again, my cheeks tinged with red. "I just needed some work done on my car, and I was hoping that Joe might be willing to fit me in. But I thought maybe he'd be overloaded now, what with… with Frank…"

The room quieted again, but this time everyone bowed their heads.

"God rest his soul," Tallulah said. "Such a shame."

Angela cleared her throat. "Yes, it really is a shame. Although, maybe *Scarlett* can shed some light on the situation, seeing as how she found the body and all?" Angela phrased it as a question, but her judgmental glare insinuated everything that wasn't said.

"I was there too," Noelle said, her own gaze leveling at Angela. "Do you have any specific questions? Maybe I can answer them."

"Oh, uh… no, no of course not." Angela looked at her hands. "I just meant, I didn't mean anything."

"Good. How about we get started on the book?" Noelle turned to me, giving me a subtle wink.

"Oh, really, it's okay," I said. "If people aren't in the mood, we can skip it."

"Grab a mimosa, ladies," Noelle instructed. "Because I want to hear about this whole 'reading' thing you gals do."

I removed the book we'd been reading from my bag and set it on the coffee table.

The other ladies each reached for mimosas, then stared at the book with fascination as if it were some sort of alien creature.

"So, was it good?" Tootsie looked up at me. "What's it about?"

"We really don't have to do this," I said, glancing around. "We can skip the book talk for the week."

"No! I wanna do the reading." Tiny crossed her arms. "It's my turn. I've been preparing all week with my sexy voice."

"Your sexy voice?" Noelle raised her eyebrows. "I think I've been missing out, not being in a book club over in New York."

"Oh, yes." Tootsie lowered her voice, leaning in and whispering across the table. "Nobody here reads the book except for Scarlett, so we make her pick out a passage to read each week. I asked her to pick out a sexy one for my week."

"Page fifty-two," I said. "If you're interested."

"So, how sexy are we talking?" Noelle asked, her eyes darkening with excitement. "This is fun. You guys really *do* need a library. In fact, you need something *better* than a library."

"Better than a library?" I asked. "Such as?"

"A bookstore!" Noelle's eyes glittered. "I can see it now. A nice, new and used bookstore. This town is so small, you could even run parts of it like a library and allow people to loan out books if they want."

"The money is the problem," I said. "We don't have money to build a library *or* a bookstore."

"That's where my savvy marketing skills come in," Noelle said. "I have an idea."

"An idea, you say?" Tootsie leaned in, her beehive nearly smacking Noelle in the face. "Do tell."

"Well, you know the old saying…" Noelle waited, but when nobody chimed in, she continued. "Sex sells."

"I like it!" Tiny raised her small fist in the air. "I'm for sale. I just gotta run it by Lou first, but he's pretty open to me putting my body on display."

I wrinkled my nose at the eighty-year-old woman. "No, Tiny. You ain't sellin' your body. I told you that like a hundred times! Noelle, I love you, but we are *not* sellin' sex to raise money for a bookstore."

"Relax, you crazy ladies." Noelle shot Tiny a curious glance. "First off, I didn't know that about Lou… very, very interesting.

Second of all, I'm not talking about selling sex. I'm talking about advertising it."

"You mean like billboards with a picture of us three naked?" Tiny gestured toward her bandmates. "We've discussed things like that in the past and always tried to keep most of our clothes on, but I suppose if it's for the good of the bookstore. What I'm trying to say is I'm available for nudity as long as it's for a good cause."

Tootsie nodded. "Just as long as I can keep my makeup on and my hair done, I don't care about clothes."

"No!" I said. "Nobody's removing their clothes."

The room fell silent as everyone's eyes looked behind me at something, or someone, I couldn't see. When the door smacked shut, I closed my eyes and wondered who in the world had heard me instructing everyone to keep their clothes on.

"Well, that doesn't sound like much fun." Mack's low, manly voice filled the entire room. "Clothes are so damn restrictive."

I closed my eyes tighter, taking long, deep breaths.

"I agree!" Tiny said, waving a hand. "Usually, the fun don't start 'til the clothes come off."

"Well, I think you can have plenty of fun with your clothes on… or off." Mack's footsteps thunked across the floor, coming closer and closer. "Just takes the right person."

Sensing his presence behind me, I opened my eyes and caught a glimpse of Tootsie fanning herself. Angela's mouth was hanging open so wide, I could see that little dangly-thingamajig at the back of her throat.

I turned around, positive my cheeks were as red as a tomato. "Mack," I said, looking up. He wore a different pair of jeans today. They were washed out and worn, less fancy than the ones he'd had on the day before. A black T-shirt stretched against his chest and tightened across his biceps as he crossed his arms. "What brings you here?"

"I just stopped by your place, and you weren't home," Mack

said. "I happened to run into Mrs. Harper at the store, and she kindly informed me you'd be here for book club. I just had no idea it was *this* sort of a book club. The sexy kind."

I swallowed. "This is the respectable kind of book club."

"Yeah, in fact we're just getting started on the 'read out loud' portion of the meeting. Want to join?" Tiny gestured toward an open chair at the opposite end of the table from me.

I breathed a sigh of relief. If Mack would just take a few steps away from me, I might be able to think a bit better. With him standing next to me, my neurons were on the fritz, and I couldn't form coherent sentences.

"He doesn't want to join," I said quickly. "Did you need something, Mack?"

"I just wanted to say hi," he said. "Isn't that what Reunion Day is about? Catching up with old pals?"

I exhaled loudly. "Well, *hello*! There. Are you happy?"

"Don't be *rude*," Tallulah chided, her voice deep and rolling. "Take a seat, Mack. You'll enjoy this. I can already tell."

Instead of taking the empty seat across the room, Mack situated himself on the armrest of the loveseat with his rear end just inches away from my elbow.

I gave it a little nudge. "Excuse me, you're in my space bubble." I gave his butt one more poke with my elbow. "Do you mind?"

Mack ignored my prods and leaned over, scooping up the book that Tiny had placed face down on the table, its pages still open to the disastrous section at the end of chapter four.

I lunged for the book, but he held it just out of reach. "Is this where we left off?"

My cheeks, if they weren't red before, were sunburnt as all heck right now. "No!"

"We've never read it," Tiny said. "Scarlett's the only one who reads these things. Then she picks out her favorite passage to read to us."

"This was not my favorite!" I reached again for the book, but Mack's playful eyes met mine, and he tucked the book on the opposite side of his body. "Tiny, you're the one who asked me to pick out a sexy scene. It wasn't my choice."

"That's what she always says." Tiny winked at Mack. "She always blames it on us."

I started to retort again, but Noelle laid a hand on my leg.

"There's nothing wrong with bein' sexy," Noelle said, first scanning my face then glancing at Mack. "In fact, I was just talking about the power of sex. It sells. I called Scarlett a nerd on the way over here today, but I think I might have been wrong about this whole 'reading' business. If I'd known we were gonna gossip about good-looking guys and read sexy stuff, well then she's not a nerd—she's a goddess. Count me in from here on out."

"I agree." Mack ran a hand through his chaotic hair. "If you can't have fun with it, what's the point? Right?"

The ladies all nodded, even Angela. The only person not nodding was me, but that's because I was too busy trying to set that book on fire with my eyes. Unfortunately, seeing as how I hadn't attended Hogwarts, it didn't work.

"In fact, did you know this town is having trouble raising money for a bookstore?" Noelle asked, her voice airy and innocent. "And I just think that's silly. Books are important."

"Yes," I said, gritting my teeth. "I happen to think so too. Children's books, educational books, historical books—"

"Romance books," Noelle cut in, with a wink in my direction. "Picture this proposal: We buy the open lot right there next to The Cozy Cafe." Noelle gestured outside. "We build a small, cute, little shop with books all over the place. That part of the job can be left to Scarlett, since she actually reads. My contribution could be the backroom."

"The backroom?" Tiny raised an eyebrow. "I like the sound of that."

Noelle nodded. "A place for book club to meet. Y'all could host events, signings, wine and cheese night, and you'd never have to compete for space with the rest of The Cozy Cafe guests."

"I like that wine and cheese night talk," Tiny said, "but I think we gotta take things a step further."

"I was *just* getting there." Noelle grinned. "What if that backroom has a little bar? Perfect to serve mimosas. People can buy a drink, we'll fill up the place with cushy chairs, and they can relax and read a book."

"I like it," Tootsie said. "But where does the sexy stuff come in?"

"I propose we make *three* rooms. The backroom," Noelle said, "and then the back *back* room."

This time, even Tallulah leaned in. "What are you talking about?"

"You know what I'm talking about." Noelle moved nose to nose with Tallulah, her voice soft. "A sexy store. Nothing too crazy, just the basics. Some lingerie, lip gloss."

"Fuzzy pink handcuffs?" Tiny asked. "Lou likes them puppies."

"Fuzzy pink handcuffs," Noelle agreed. "Games. Whipped cream. You name it."

"Blindfolds?" Tootsie asked.

"You got it," Noelle said. "Blindfolds and even those little nighties that barely cover your tush."

Tallulah sucked in a breath. "I always wanted one of them."

"This town ain't got nothing like that," Angela said, her ring shining under the sunlight streaming through the windows. "I think that might be nice. Could really bring us ladies together."

Noelle glanced at Mack. "The men could come too, but I doubt they'd want to."

Mack was doing a good job looking very busy with his fingernails.

"What does that have to do with books?" I asked. "I'm not drawing the connection."

"It's an all-purpose shop!" Noelle said. "Think about it like those

Tupperware parties or whatnot, except this is way more fun. Come for the books, stay for the drinks, go home with a sexy surprise!"

"Might infuse some young blood into this book club," Mary Anne called from across the room. "I like the idea, myself. I might've tried to read stuff too if I'd known it was *fun*. I just remembered reading all them sad books in school, and I don't like being sad."

"See?" Noelle turned to me. "I think this could really work. People will read more, which is what you want, right? They'll have a safe place to go and chat about stuff that nobody talks about. There ain't anything to be ashamed about."

I shook my head. "We ain't getting funding for a sexy store," I said, looking down. "Not if we can't even convince them about a library."

"Maybe I can talk to a few people while I'm in town," Noelle said. "The worst they can say is no."

I shrugged. "I suppose. But what about kids' books? I wanted a library to get books for Gray."

"The back rooms will be closed off," Noelle said. "Eighteen and over, only. The front of the bookstore you could decorate any way you want. Make a kids' corner or something. Just think, you wouldn't have to squeeze book club in at lunchtime. You could have it on Thursday nights or something. Girls' night out."

"I'm in," Tootsie said, echoed quickly by Tiny, followed by Tallulah. Angela nodded in agreement, along with the other two ladies who'd quietly been following the conversation.

"Mack?" I turned to him. "What are your thoughts?"

"I think Noelle's right," Mack deadpanned. "And you ain't got anything to be ashamed about."

"If that's the case, Mr. Montgomery," I said, gathering up all my courage, "then turn to page fifty-two and give that reading a go. Let's see how good *you* are at this reading business."

For the first time, Mack looked a bit uneasy. "I don't normally read this stuff."

"But you seemed *so* keen to try it out." I reached over and opened the book for him. "And like you said, sex ain't anything to be ashamed about."

Mack cleared his throat, looking down at the page. First, his ears turned red. Then, a small sheen of sweat lined his forehead as his eyes scanned the contents of the chapter. His hand shook as he flipped the page, then his eyes nearly bugged out of his head.

He leaned over, whispering in my ear. "Is that even *possible*?" He pointed to the text. "That sounds physically impossible."

I grinned, looking around the room at the other ladies, who looked positively gleeful at Mack's discomfort.

"Go on, read it aloud," Tiny said. "I can read with you, if you'd like."

"I'm just…" Mack trailed off. "Do those things really *heave*?"

"Read it out loud!" Tootsie called out. "I want to hear what's heavin' and where."

"You girls call our, ahem… our, uh… you call it *that*?" Mack looked up, snapping the book shut. "You know what? I forgot I have to go pick something up."

"What do you have to pick up?" I asked sweetly.

"Um, my… uh." Mack glanced around. "Belt. I need a belt."

"The one you have on ain't good enough?" Tiny asked. "You're just scared to read."

Mack glanced down, as if surprised to find he was already wearing a belt. "Well, look at that. No, I'm not scared, just… um…"

"We release you from the GURLZ club." Tootsie waved a hand. "We knew you'd be too faint-hearted to join book club."

"You may leave," Tiny said. "And let us continue discussing our fake boyfriends in peace."

Mumbling something about *impossible,* Mack turned, heading out the door. Judging by the zig-zag pattern he took, I would've guessed he'd been the one drinking mimosas, not the rest of us.

As soon as the door slammed behind him, all the ladies burst out laughing.

"So, my turn?" Tiny reached out and grabbed the book. "I'm really curious what's heaving in here."

"And I'm curious what can make a sex-on-a-stick man like that blush." Tallulah looked over at me. "Say, before he disappeared, didn't you and Mack—"

"Just read," I interrupted, thrusting the book into Tiny's hands.

Tiny took the book, read a paragraph, then grinned. "Wait 'til you ladies hear this. I didn't even know that could bend this way…"

CHAPTER 17

"WELL, THAT WAS... ENLIGHTENING," NOELLE said after we'd bid everyone goodbye. The two of us had grabbed lunch next door, staving off the last of the mimosas bubbling in our systems. "I had no idea a book club could be so fun."

I smiled, unlocking the car before we climbed inside. "I'm glad you liked it! You're a nerd now too."

"About that bookstore idea." Noelle looked across the center console. "What do you say? Should we pursue it? I'd love to help on the backroom stuff. You know, I do have a fashion degree, and I'd love to design a few things. With the town being so small, we wouldn't need to do bulk orders. I could just hand make a few nice garments to start with and go from there."

"Let me think about it," I said. "Maybe Reunion Day isn't the time to be asking around for money. We've already put a lot of the city's funds into the event, and plus, everyone thinks the idea of a bookstore is scandalous. I haven't even mentioned the idea of a bar in it."

"That's just what we want!" Noelle looked over at me. "We want people talking about it. We want ladies interested. That buzz is what'll put the pressure on everyone else."

"I don't know…" I wanted a bookstore. I truly did. But I had a lot of other things to deal with at the moment.

"What's the holdup?"

"Just with Frank's death, and me being the one to find him,

and… I don't know, but my gut tells me something's up with Joe." I shook my head. "I guess I just want to wait 'til it all settles down."

Noelle clapped her hands. "You're right. I'm being insensitive. Just give me permission to mention it to a few people. I won't even include your name or the backroom idea. Just at the reunion, let me get a pulse on people's reactions."

"Sure, if you want to, but don't do it on my account. I appreciate your interest, really, Noelle."

"Speaking of Reunion Day, you're coming, right?" Noelle asked.

I shook my head. "You know I didn't graduate. I'm not invited."

"That's nonsense. Everyone expects you to go."

Gripping the wheel tightly, I stared straight ahead. "I really don't want to go, Noelle. Please, just leave it be."

"At least come as my date! I want to spend as much time with you as I can on this trip."

"You don't understand." I flicked on the blinker a bit harder than necessary. "Everyone there is showin' off how far they've come in ten years. What do I have to show off? Huh? It's just embarrassing."

"Oh, honey…"

"No, I don't want sympathy. I'm just saying it so you understand." I glanced at my friend, patting her on the leg. "I'm proud of you. You have a lot to show for yourself, moving to New York, getting your degree, helping out your parents. I'm just not like that. I'm a Powers girl, and the only thing good about that is nobody expected anything from me in the first place."

"That ain't true!" Noelle crossed her arms. "Everyone knows why you dropped out! That's nothing to be ashamed about. It ain't your fault what your mother did. You're a different person than her."

I shook my head. "I don't want to go, Noelle. I'm sorry."

Noelle sat in silence a moment. "You know, when you were in the bathroom, Angela mentioned that Joe would be back by tomorrow so he can take her to Reunion Day."

Gina LaManna

"Why should I care?" I pretended not to be interested, but the idea of talking to Joe piqued my curiosity.

"People drink a bit at these gatherings, tend to boast and brag about their accomplishments." Noelle gave a nonchalant shrug. "If someone was on the hunt for some gossip about where Angela got that new rock from, it might be a decent spot to gather some news."

"You think that rock is suspicious too?"

"Of course I do!" Noelle bit her lip. "I don't know what Joe's doing on the side, but he's feeling guilty about something. Something that must be making him a lot of money, in order for him to buy a ring that size."

I considered her bribe for a moment.

"Is it working?" Noelle asked. "Did I tempt you into going as my date?"

I had an answer ready. As I pulled up to the front of my little barn, however, I forgot all about the question. The road leading to my front door, which was really nothing more than some bent grass and crushed dirt, ended with a surprise—the door to my cozy, little home hung open.

"Wow, you left in a hurry this morning," Noelle said. "I normally don't lock my door here in Luck, but I also don't go leaving it hangin' on its hinges."

"I didn't leave the door like that." I threw the car into park and jogged up to the entrance. What little I could see through the door made my heart sink and my palms turn sweaty as all heck. "Noelle!"

She jogged up next to me, except slower, on account of her heels were fancy black ones. Under normal circumstances, I'd feel bad for getting her shoes dirty, but at that moment, I wasn't concerned with anything except the pile of destruction that was my house.

"What in tarnation?" she exclaimed. "Who would've done this?"

I began to shrug, a helpless motion, as my mind ran through the list of the town's citizens. Plenty of people didn't think too fondly of me, but I couldn't think of any that hated me enough to turn my home inside out.

"Wait a second." I turned to Noelle. "At the book club, Mack said he stopped by looking for me."

Noelle's eyes lit up in understanding. "But why would Mack tell you he stopped by if he's the one who did this?"

"I dunno," I said, my voice grim. "All I know is that my house is a disaster, and the only person who stopped by was Mack."

CHAPTER 18

Dear Diary,

A M I CRAZY? I HAVEN'T asked for any of this! I never wanted to find a dead body. I didn't want to become re-involved with Mack Montgomery, and I certainly didn't want my house to be turned inside out. Do I have a sign on my head that says Looking For Trouble or what?

I'm tryin' not to complain, Diary. I really am. But honestly, I don't understand what I did to start this whole chain of events! I only wanted my car fixed. I love my car, but I'm not sure I want her hanging around anymore. Ever since I brought her into the shop, all she's caused me is a heap of bad luck.

Love, Scarlett

CHAPTER 19

"WHAT DO YOU THINK HE was looking for?" Noelle asked, pouring me a cup of tea at the counter in her parents' home.

I dunked the tea bag up and down a few times, stalling in thought. Steam curled up from the cup, and despite the warm temperature outside, I shivered. "I don't know."

"We don't know it was Mack for sure." Noelle slid onto the barstool next to me. "It's not fun to tally up the people who don't like you, but we have to do it."

"Aren't the police supposed to be looking into it?" I said wryly. The cops had promised they'd "look into things," but I didn't hold out much hope. From what I could tell, nothing had been stolen, and the cop sent to the scene had been more concerned with Noelle being back in town than my disastrous home.

Noelle tapped her finger against the counter. "I need you to tell me everyone who might have a reason to ransack your place."

I sighed. Noelle was right. If I wanted to get to the bottom of the matter before the next century, it was up to me. "You don't mind listenin' to me? Helping me think about it?"

Noelle squeezed my hand. "I'm here, whatever you need. Check this out. My momma bought some supplies for me before I went up to New York. If I find the bastard who ruined your house, I'm not gonna be afraid to use my weapons on him."

My lips parted in surprise as Noelle unloaded a small, and very feminine, arsenal of weapons. They included a tiny, pink canister of pepper spray, a purple Taser, and a whistle that looked sturdy enough to rattle a few eardrums.

"Have you ever used any of these?" I looked up at my friend.

"No, but I'm itching to." Noelle grinned. "All I need is a reason."

"Noelle!"

"I'm just kidding, honey. But I *do* want you to feel safe. See, I'm gonna be your bodyguard until this is over. You're staying here, in my home, until we find whoever did this. You understand?"

"I don't wanna impose."

"Momma and Daddy will be happy to have you. They love you as much as I do. Now, start talking."

I lifted the steaming mug of tea to my lips, but it was too hot to drink. Just like when we were little kids having sleepovers, I walked over to the fridge and helped myself to a splash of milk. When I turned back, I met Noelle's knowing smile.

"I'm glad nothing much has changed," I said, allowing myself a small smile. "The Summers family even keeps their milk in the same place."

"With my parents out for the afternoon, we can get into all sorts of trouble, just like old times." Noelle winked. "Spill the beans before you've got to head over to Gray's."

Hopping back on the barstool, I furrowed my brow in concentration. "Well, the first suspect is Mack because he's back in town, and he told me that he'd stopped over before book club."

"He never did say what he wanted." Noelle pursed her lips in thought. "Any ideas?"

"No clue. Unless he wanted to talk about what happened last night." I hesitated. "But I'd sorta told him I didn't want to see again, and he seemed okay with that. So maybe it was something else."

"Maybe you should call him and ask. I *know* you told the cops to keep the break-in quiet, but even I know that the whole town will hear about it in an hour." Noelle shrugged. "You know Eddie can't keep his mouth shut about a piece of gossip this juicy."

I lay my head on the table. "I just wish people would mind their own business for once."

"You know it doesn't work that way down here."

I banged my head once for each sentence. "I know. I know. I know."

"Do you really think it was Mack?" Noelle reached over and rested her hand on my shoulder. "Deep down, you think he could do something like this?"

I looked sideways at her. "I don't know. I haven't seen him since he up and disappeared. Poof. Straight outta my bed."

Noelle frowned. "I know, but think. What does your gut tell you?"

"That I'm hungry?"

Noelle didn't smile.

"Fine." I sighed. "I don't think he's behind it. That man has done some stupid things in his life, but I never fancied him an idiot. Why'd he go shouting around town, right in front of the GURLZ, that'd he'd stopped by my place if it'd already been ransacked? That's just silly."

"I agree. But that means someone got to your house *after* Mack stopped by, but before you came home." Noelle bit her lip. "That's a pretty tight window. Now, either someone knew your schedule in advance, or they were watchin' your house."

"Or both," I said darkly. "My schedule isn't exactly a surprise. They hang a sign from the window of The Cozy Cafe that says Book Club Today! Any person with a pair of working eyes could've put two and two together. Plus, my car was parked out front. Purple VW Beetles aren't exactly common around here."

"I hate to mention this, but do you think it could have anything to do with Frank turning up dead?"

I gave a half-hearted shrug. "I suppose so, though I don't know *why*." I recounted the chain of events as quickly and basically as I could. "I dropped my car off at his shop a few days ago, then picked it up before church on Sunday. He told me to take it over to Joe's. I did that, but I didn't see Joe, which, now we know from Angela, is because he's away on business. Then, I found Frank's body in that closet up at church."

"And then you picked up your car from Joe's this morning and didn't learn anything new about this situation then."

"Exactly." I stared at the far wall, trying to piece together the puzzle. But it was as if someone had dumped three puzzles out on the table all at once, and I couldn't tell which pieces went with which puzzle.

"The way I see it, there's a few basic options," Noelle said. "Either someone was looking for something and it was unrelated to any of this business with Frank…"

"Which is unlikely, since everyone knows I ain't got nothing to steal."

"Then option number two is that Mack did it. I don't know what he'd be looking for, but we can't rule it out, either. Who knows? Maybe he was upset you didn't jump right back into bed with him."

I scrunched up my nose. "Yeah, I suppose, but I doubt it. Nobody's been clamorin' to get in my bed for… well, ages. If ever."

"Don't talk like that, honey. Any man would be lucky to get close enough to see your sheets. Heck, I'd love to cozy up in bed with you." Noelle winked. "Just like when we were kids, have a sleepover and gossip."

I laughed. "I don't know how you make me smile even when it seems like the whole world is against me."

"The whole world doesn't hate you. Always remember that. Sometimes it just feels like it. You just gotta tilt that chin up, stick out your stubborn nose, and smile despite everything else. You understand me, girlfriend?"

I stared at the table then glanced at my friend. "Yes," I said, clearing my throat. "Thanks, Noelle. You always know what to say."

"Now, let's get to the bottom of this. Even if it wasn't Mack out for revenge, maybe it was someone else, someone who'd be angry at you for other reasons. Any thoughts on this theory?"

"Hmm." I dunked my tea bag again, taking another sip of the soothing chamomile with a little sliver of lemon. "Well, lots of people are probably angry at me. Gray's mom, Mrs. Annie Harper, she yells at me nonstop for something every other day. Then there's Angela. She didn't seem happy with me asking all those questions about Joe, but she's got an alibi. She was with us when this happened. Unless there was a window of time over lunch? But that would've been tight. And I'm sure someone's angry about all the gossip comin' from me finding Frank's body. Maybe someone thinks I had something to do with his death…" I paused. "I'm going out on a limb here, just trying to list everyone."

"That's good, that's good," Noelle murmured distractedly. "Say, I gotta ask you one more thing."

"What's that?"

"Why do you work for that awful woman?" My friend turned toward me, her pretty eyes containing hints of a storm. "Annie treats you like garbage, and you're the best thing that ever happened to her son."

"She just has a bone to pick with me," I said. "What it is exactly has got me mystified. I ask her all the time if I'm doing as she wants with Gray, and she says, 'Yes, of course.' I get the feeling it has nothing to do with Grayson at all."

"But that doesn't make sense. You hardly spoke to her before you started nannying for Gray. What could she possibly have against you?"

I shrugged, pushing my barstool back. "That's a good question. Speaking of which, I've got to go face her."

"What if you just didn't go?"

"That's not an option," I said. "Two reasons. The first, and most important, is that I love Gray as if he were my own. That little boy has stolen half of my heart. No matter how awful his mother is to me, when I see him smile up at me, I forget all of the horrible things she's said."

"You said two reasons?"

"Well, there's this other thing called rent." I smiled. "Even my ramshackle hut that I call a home requires money for me to live there. Believe it or not, I like to eat food, which ain't all that possible if I don't have money."

Noelle grinned. "You? Like to eat? I'd never have guessed."

I playfully swatted my best friend. "You say that as if we haven't fought over the last bite of sandwich hundreds of times."

"That is one nice thing about being an adult." Noelle stood up and collected my mug from the table, dumping the tea bag into the trash. "I can buy any groceries I want. In fact, I've got a whole bag of Swedish Fish in my backpack right now."

"And you're keeping that a secret from me?" My voice nearly screeched as I leapt for my friend, chasing her out of the kitchen.

"Here! Take them." Noelle scooped up her backpack, removed a handful of Swedish Fish, and pelted them at me. "I wasn't holding them hostage. You just had to ask nicely."

"Please, can I have a Swedish Fish?" I gave a fake pout and held my hands out.

Breathing hard, laughter still on her lips, Noelle gave me a handful. Just then, the front door cracked open, and Mr. and Mrs. Summers walked into the kitchen, all southern belle and perfect gentleman.

Mrs. Summers wore a beautiful muted-yellow sundress that accentuated her dark, rolling curls. Mr. Summers was dressed in his usual uniform of perfectly pleated slacks and a crisp dress shirt. I don't know how he managed to avoid sweating through that shirt in such heat, but he defied all laws of perspiration.

Mrs. Summers took one step into the kitchen, her eyes first scanning Noelle and I, then taking in the few lone Swedish Fish on the floor. Her face crinkled into a broad grin. "Oh, girls. It's so wonderful to have you back together again. Just like it used to be. In fact, I was just telling Noelle this morning about how this house could use some new life infused into it… little feet pattering about, sleepovers with *Grandma*…"

"I need to get going," I said, wincing as Noelle shot me an evil glare. "Grayson's waiting for me."

"We're talking about you too, Scarlett," Mrs. Summers called after me. "You and any kids you have are always welcome here."

I gave Noelle a quick hug and a whispered thank-you. Then, I offered a polite nod and wave to her parents and jogged off down the front sidewalk.

I had a lot to think about before starting on the whole marriage issue. Like who had a reason to turn my tiny, little home inside out? Why me? And what were they after?

CHAPTER 20

Dear Diary,

GRANDKIDS?
Haha, that's funny. Don't you need to have a man to do things like that?

Poor Mrs. Summers. No grandkids for her yet. Not from me, at least.

Love,
A very single Scarlett

CHAPTER 21

"CAN I PLEASE, PRETTY PLEASE, play outside?" Gray clasped his skinny little arms around my calf.

I lugged him around the kitchen since he wouldn't let go. Happily, he remained sitting on my foot while I tried to prepare spaghetti for dinner. "Gray, I can't make you food if you keep sitting on my foot. Why don't you color at the table while I finish dinner?"

"I wanna go outside. Momma promised."

I looked down. Gray was more mop than child at this rate, the seat of his pants sweeping up the kitchen floor as I hauled him between the stove and the island in the center of the kitchen. I knelt down. "I'll tell you what. You can go play on the driveway, but only up until that line of chalk that we drew earlier. Do you remember why we drew that line of chalk?"

Gray nodded, his eyes serious.

"Why?"

"Because." Gray stopped to pick his nose for a second. When he was done trying to flick the booger, he looked back up at me. I swiped his hands clean with a napkin.

"Tell me why you can't go past the chalk line," I tried again.

"Because it's too close to the street, and the street is dangerous."

"Exactly." I patted his head. "So if you promise to play right near the garage where I can see you, then you can go color with chalk. But if you step one toe over that line, Gray, you're coming in here and helping me count noodles for pasta. You understand me?"

He nodded solemnly. "But maybe I can play with my Hot Wheels instead of chalk."

"Just so long as you don't step one toe outside of that chalk line."

Gray leapt up and threw his arms around my neck. He scurried to his box of Hot Wheels on the shelf, carried it outside, and plopped down right next to the garage. Waiting for the water to boil on the stove, I watched Gray zoom his cars into one another. The driveway to the Harpers' home was half a mile long, and the street they lived on was as deserted as could be, but Gray needed to learn the rules, regardless.

When the water boiled, I dumped the noodles into the pot. Gray hadn't moved an inch, still making zooming noises with his mouth. With the garage door open, I could hear him playing, which helped. I didn't like being far from him if I could help it. He wasn't my son, but he was as good as my baby. I loved him like one.

That was why the sound of a car engine had me sprinting outside as fast as if the devil were chasing me. "Gray," I called. "You come over here."

Gray hopped right up, looking curiously down the drive before coming over to grip my hand. As the car came into view, I sucked in a breath.

"I like that car." Gray pointed a pudgy little finger. "Looks real fast."

I knew for a fact that car was fast, seeing as how it had whipped by me on my walk home the previous night. That car was also expensive and dark and shiny, and Gray wasn't the only one impressed by it.

I held back a smile as Gray tugged on my arm, leading me right up to the chalk line, which I'd drawn about ten feet from the garage. Gray held out his hand like a traffic cop and gestured for the big, dark Audi to stop. His chubby cheeks pulled into a very concerned expression. "This is my play zone," he said. "No cars allowed."

The one and only Mack Montgomery threw the Audi into park

and climbed out with his hands raised. "I understand, buddy. I won't move the car one inch over that chalk line."

Gray gave a stern nod. "Good. Now, if you wanna play with me, you gotta come on *this* side of the chalk line."

"I should ask permission first from this pretty lady." Mack turned his gaze on me. "May I?"

"Why are you here?" I asked, holding Gray's hand so tightly that he wiggled to get out of my grasp. I loosened my grip, then I bent over. "Hey, Gray, can you go play Hot Wheels for a second?"

As if wanting to touch it, Gray cast a second look at Mack's car then glanced down at the chalk line. Disappointment showed on his face, but he retreated to his own miniature cars.

"May I?" Mack gestured to the chalk line separating us. "Or is this a 'Keep People Out' sort of line?"

"It depends."

"On?"

"On what you want, comin' over here and interrupting my business." I brushed my hands over the apron I'd donned to cook. "Oh, *crap*. The noodles are boiling." I whirled around, calling over my shoulder. "Fine, come inside. You have until I'm done making pasta to explain yourself to me."

"Well, if your noodles are already boiled, that doesn't leave me much time." Mack's boots stomped behind me into the kitchen.

"Then you better talk fast, mister."

Mack leaned against the door, and even though my alarm bells were going off full force, I couldn't help but appreciate the view. For one moment, I had a flashback of my wish. That one little wish I'd rested all my hopes and dreams on, the same one shattered by the man in my doorway.

I cleared my throat, but Mack didn't start speaking right away. His eyes followed me as I removed the strainer from the cupboard, then tilted the pot of boiling water and noodles so that a cloud of steam bloomed up in front of my face. In that moment, I was grateful for that steam because it gave me a minute of privacy from Mack's penetrating gaze. Even after all this time, his eyes still did funny things to my stomach.

Once the noodles were in the sink and I was no longer protected by the cloud of steam, I tipped a bit of olive oil on the noodles, sloshed the strainer around, then stuck a hand on my hip. "Are you just gonna stand there, staring at me all day?"

"Look at you, all domesticated." Mack winked.

My face must have turned the same shade as the jar of Ragu on the counter. *Had he been thinking the same thing as me?* That if things had been different, if life had worked out as I'd wished, then maybe I'd be cooking in *our* kitchen, telling *our* child to wash up for dinner, instead of staring at the man who'd broken my heart as if he were a stranger.

Since I couldn't think of a good response, I looked past Mack and shouted into the garage. "Gray, come wash your hands. Dinner's almost ready!"

The sound of *zooms* and *crashes* of Hot Wheels cars filtered through the door.

"Gray, I mean it," I said. "If you're not in here with your hands washed in three minutes, you're not getting a second story tonight. I'm not lyin', buddy!"

Mack's expression turned complicated then, and that charming, lackadaisical smile turned more serious. I'd venture to say he even had a bit of sadness, or maybe regret in his eyes, but I couldn't tell you for the life of me why.

I crossed my arms. "You heard me, Mack. You have until dinner's ready. That's three minutes, so if you got something to say, out with it."

"I didn't do anything to your house, sweetheart."

"Don't you *sweetheart* me, Mack. That chance is long gone." I wiped my hands on a towel. "Why'd you need to stop by here and tell me you didn't do anything wrong? And anyway, how'd you even know my place was ransacked if you didn't do it yourself?"

"You and I both know Eddie can't keep his trap shut. He went straight from your house to the Lucky Horseshoe, blabbin' to everyone who'd listen. Secrets here travel faster than wildfire, and you know that as well as I do, darlin'." Mack took two steps closer to me, his gaze locked tightly on mine. He didn't waver once, didn't let me look away. "And I know how your brain works. You put two and two together that I stopped over. But you can't possibly think I'd do something like that."

I put both my hands on my hips. "Yeah, but I also thought you were incapable of doing other things too."

"There was a lot going on back then." Mack's eyes flashed hard. Suddenly, I got the sense that I was playing with fire. One wrong word could cause an entire pack of dynamite to explode. "I didn't disappear because of you."

Mack reached out, his palm cupping my face as his thumb traced a gentle circle high on my cheek. I wished I could say I pushed him away right then and there, but I didn't. I just closed my eyes, letting the sensations of his touch awaken parts of my body that hadn't tingled in years. My chest rose and fell. Even though my eyes were closed, I could feel Mack scanning my face, my lips, my neck.

When I opened my eyes sometime later, my arms had magically collapsed from their defiant pose by my side, and my shoulders had crumbled from their righteous position, all stiff and high and mighty. I resisted the urge to fall back into his arms, though it sure was tempting.

"Why'd you leave?" I whispered. "Why, Mack? What did I do?"

His face took on that regretful expression again. "I had to. I'm sorry."

"Well, I'm sorry too. But an apology just won't cut it," I said. "You hurt me, Mack. I loved you."

"I love you too," Mack said, and the fact that his declaration of love wasn't in the past tense wasn't lost on me. "I did, you know that."

I swallowed. Surely he'd meant to say *loved*. He'd even corrected himself already. There I went again, assuming Mack felt the same way about me as I did about him. All that had ever done in the past was get me into trouble. Well, I was sick and tired of being played a fool.

I stepped back. "Unfortunately, that doesn't make any difference now. You have your life out in Hollywood, and mine is here." I gestured to the garage. "I'm happy. Me and Gray."

Mack looked over his shoulder, both of us watching Gray squeal with his little Hot Wheels cars across the steps.

Then, at the same time, both Mack and I called, "Go wash up, Gray."

He looked at me then, just as my eyes widened in surprise.

"Jinx," Mack said. "You owe me a Coke."

As hard as I tried, I couldn't suppress the tiny smile tugging at my lips. Instead, I waltzed right over to the fridge, grabbed a bottle of Coke, and thrust it out toward Mack. "Consider me all paid up."

He laughed. "You still owe me thirty Cokes from before. Your debt is nowhere near over."

"I don't owe you nothin', Mack Montgomery." My face had split into an embarrassing grin. Then, before I could do anything about it, Mack took a few steps across the kitchen, those legs of his in those nice-looking jeans stomping right up next to me. Then, those nice-looking arms of his in that simple black T-shirt stretched out and clasped me in a hug.

I fought him off, but not too hard. I wiggled to get out of his grasp, but he was holding on too tightly while clasping his hands behind my back. Oh, how I remembered the feel of those hands on my cheek. I'd been expecting smooth, moisturized skin from this Hollywood movie version of Mack that I'd come to know from magazines, but they'd been just as rough and well-used as I'd remembered from our high school days.

"Tell me one thing." Mack's hands slid from my lower back up to my hair. On the way up, he relieved my hand of the Coke bottle and set it on the island.

Backing me up against the counter, his hips pressed against mine just enough to make my stomach whir with anticipation, but not so hard that I could justify pushing him away. With his hands snaked into my hair, he held my head tightly to his chest and whispered against my head, "You've got to believe me."

"About what?" I asked, my voice warming a small patch of cotton on his shirt.

"Everything." Mack's hands stroked my hair, down my back, his fingers tracing tender lines across my neck. "I've never made a choice in my life that was meant to hurt you. I didn't touch your house today. In fact, I have a few words to say to the bastard who did. And I plan on finding him, since it looked like Eddie was more interested in talkin' than acting."

"Mack, you don't have to—"

"Shhh, darlin', I'm not done." Mack traced his thumb over my lips, quieting my talk with the gentleness of his touch. "When I disappeared that morning, I had to do something. Something I couldn't talk about then, and I can't talk about now. Not yet, at least. But I need you to trust me. I didn't do it to hurt you. If I could change things, I would."

"Mack, why did you open up to me, then? That night in your truck, why did you say all that, and then take me home? You made me feel all those *things*, and then the next morning you were just gone. For good. Not a word from you."

Mack's thumb slid from my lips down to my chin where he tipped my mouth up. He waited a long second, as if looking for hesitation on my part. I couldn't do anything, couldn't say anything. I froze, and when his lips met mine, I didn't pull away.

His touch was soft and tender. When he moved his hand to pull my face closer to his, a flash of excitement took over and made my knees as wobbly as those noodles.

He parted my lips ever-so-gently with his tongue, and by the time I got any sense back into my head, he was kissing me with just as much soul as that first night all the way back in high school. All of this reminded me just why I'd made my wish that night. Because until Mack Montgomery kissed me, I'd never felt anything so good, so safe, so protected, so… so wanted.

I'd thought my wish was a simple one, but boy, had I been wrong. I moved my hands up to Mack's shoulders and pushed him back with a gentle nudge. "Stop, Mack. Not now. Not here."

"But sometime?" Mack's gaze was hopeful. "Can I take you for a drink when you get off work tonight?"

"Mack…"

"Nothing has to happen. I just want to sit down and talk."

"Are you going to give me the answers I'm looking for?" I looked at him, my heart longing for one simple little word. "Just say *yes*, Mack."

"I can't."

"That's two words, and I was looking for one." I tried to hide my face, turning to the stove and shaking the strainer with so much force, a handful of noodles jumped right out of the bowl and into the sink. "It's not a good idea." I turned to Mack, clutching my hands across my aching chest. "I'm not doing it to spite you. I'm doing it to protect myself. I hope you understand."

Mack gave a succinct nod. "I'll be out of your hair, then. Just tell me one thing before I go. Do you believe me, what I said? That I never meant to hurt you?"

I inhaled, held my breath, then let it out in a rush of air. "Yes, Mack. I believe you."

He turned to go. "I'm still gonna find whoever did that to your house, Scarlett. It's the least I can do."

Unsure of how to respond, I turned back to my noodles only to find, much to my dismay, that my arms had shaken out all the noodles. Only three stragglers were left in the strainer, while the rest of Gray's meal sat halfway down the garbage disposal. "Oh no," I moaned. "There goes dinner."

"Let me play with Gray a few minutes and keep him occupied. Maybe you can salvage some noodles?" Mack looked so hopeful, I didn't have the heart to say no. The noodles couldn't be saved, but he didn't need to know that.

"I have a can of SpaghettiOs as backup. Looks like we're having that tonight. You can stay and eat, if you want."

"I don't think you want me stickin' around. I think your manners are just so good that you can't resist asking." Mack gave me that lopsided smile again. "I'll leave once the SpaghettiOs are done."

Hiding my gaze as I reached for the can opener, I nodded in agreement. Part of me wanted to tell him I'd love to have him stay for dinner, but it was for the best he didn't.

While I warmed the SpaghettiOs, I watched as Gray's eyes lit up when Mack approached, bending at the knees and extending a Hot Wheels car as a peace offering. Gray snatched the vehicle, muttered a "thank you," and proceeded to zoom the car up and down Mack's legs.

The two of them played outside as the sun began to set. The smiles on both of their faces were so bright, I couldn't tell who was having more fun, the adult or the child. The SpaghettiOs finished warming, but I shut the stove off and leaned against the counter, unable to tear myself away from the window.

Gray's contagious giggle filtered through the open door. The sound never failed to bring a smile to my face. I laughed out loud as Mack tickled the little squirt. Gray flopped back and forth, flailing his legs, laughing harder than he'd laughed in weeks. He laughed so hard that he let out a little fart, the sound of which made Mack double over in laughter himself.

"*Whoheee*," Mack said, putting the boy down. "You are dangerous."

"Can I show you my Jeep?" Gray asked, his small voice brimming with hope. "I can drive it all by myself."

Mack looked up at the window just then, and I wasn't fast enough to look away in time. "We've got to ask Miss Scarlett first. I don't want to spoil dinner for a second time."

I removed my apron and set it on the counter, strolling out through the open garage door. "It's fine," I said. "We'll let it cool for five minutes."

"Yes!" Gray yelped with delight, jumping into his miniature Jeep and starting it up. It fit his little body just perfectly, a gift from his dad last time Mr. Harper had happened to swing into town.

My throat constricted a bit as I watched quietly from the corner. Mack applauded Gray, who zoomed up and down the driveway, making noises with his mouth. For the zillionth time, I felt sorry for the boy. He needed a father in his life, not a load of apology presents.

That was the first time Gray had ever used his toy Jeep. No matter how hard I tried, I couldn't take the place of his dad. My heart pounded just thinking of how Gray had sat on the steps, his eyes looking toward the end of the driveway night after night. He'd ask over and over if tonight was the night his daddy was coming back.

And night after night, I'd had to say I didn't know.

"Let me teach you a trick," Mack said, reaching down as Gray nearly ran over his toes.

Gray looked skeptical at first, so I stepped forward, running a hand through the boy's floppy, disheveled locks. "Gray, this man here drives cars in the movies. Really fast cars. Do you know what they call him?"

Gray shook his head, but his eyes held a curious gleam.

"A stunt driver. Because he does fancy tricks. If you let him help you, maybe you can learn a fancy trick from the movies too."

Gray shot Mack a judgmental glance. "Okay, then. Show me a trick."

"Please," I added.

"Please," he echoed.

I stepped back as Mack demonstrated with the Hot Wheels car how to stop the little Jeep just before it went off a cliff.

"See this chalk line?" Mack bent over and drew another line on the driveway. "Let's pretend that's the cliff. Do you think you can try to stop before you run right off the cliff?"

Gray nodded, a determined look on his face.

"Go on then, big guy." Mack caught my eye, giving me a brief smile before turning back to Gray. "Step on it."

Gray scrunched up his little face then put the pedal to the metal.

"Brake, Gray!" I called. "Watch out for that cliff."

Mack winked at me, watching as Gray approached the line. Then, the little man stepped on the brake, twisted the wheel, and pulled up just short of the chalk line.

"Wow," Mack said. He extended a hand for a high five, which Gray returned in full force. "You're ready for the movies."

"Did you hear that?" Gray ran over to me, his legs moving so quickly he looked like the Roadrunner. "I'm ready for the movies!"

I scooped him up in a hug, cherishing every second of the little boy's arms around my neck. "Nice job, tough guy." I gave his cheek a huge, juicy kiss. "Now, go wash up for some SpaghettiOs."

"SpaghettiOs!" Gray sprinted inside, still making car noises with his mouth.

When I turned back to Mack, I caught him wiping his brow with the bottom of his T-shirt. I pretended not to notice the stunning display of abs and that nice little arrow that pointed toward his jeans. I cleared my throat and looked down.

"How did the Harpers manage to have such a nice boy when both of them are assholes?" Mack asked.

"Gray's a good kid," I admitted. "His parents aren't so bad."

Mack gave me a look, but didn't bother to argue. "I'd say it's a testament to you, Scarlett."

I blushed. "I don't do nothin' but love that kid. Well, that and try to make sure he eats his food and takes a bath, but that's small stuff."

"Sometimes, that's all it takes." Mack stepped forward, looking as if he were going to say something, but the words froze on his lips as he looked over my shoulder.

Gray whirled around the corner of the house, stopping in the doorway. "I'm hungry!"

"Let's get you some food," I said. Glancing once more at Mack, I offered what I hoped was an olive branch of a smile. "Are you sure you're not hungry?"

"I should be going." He waved. "Nice work today, Gray. Keep practicing, and you'll be in Hollywood in no time."

"No, you won't," I said, picking him up. "You're not leaving my arms, got it?"

Gray bit his lip. "Maybe you can come with."

I laughed. "We'll talk about your stardom later. Let's get some SpaghettiOs, first."

Mack and Gray waved to each other as Mack slid into his black Audi. As he gave us one last glance, I nodded. Then, I disappeared inside, with Gray on my hip, before I said something I'd regret later.

CHAPTER 22

Dear Diary,

WHY? WHY IS LIFE SO hard?
I just put Gray to bed, and he couldn't stop jabberin' nonstop about Mack. Mack this, Mack that. I swear, that boy's got Hollywood stars in his eyes now. If Mr. Harper paid that boy one ounce of attention, maybe that poor child wouldn't have to latch onto the first male figure to walk through the door. A male figure who's doing nothing but causin' me heartache.

And Mack... don't let me start on him, Diary. All those years ago, he kissed me like he meant it. Then, he went and disappeared on me for years. Finally he pops up, in Hollywood no less. As a stunt driver! I'm supposed to find out from movie credits where the man I loved ended up? Diary, what is wrong with me that I drove a man into the movie industry?

Now he's back, kissing me as if he'd never left. Holding me, playing with Gray, just as gentle as can be. Reminding me over and over again about that stupid little wish I made, all that time ago. That wish ain't meant to come true, I believe that. But all this false hope is making me exhausted.

Deep down, I guess I just don't want to believe that my wish can never come true. It's such a simple wish, Diary. But some things aren't meant to be, and I learned that the hard way once. I'm not doin' it again.

I'll write more later, Diary. I hear Mrs. Harper stompin' on in now, and she'll be screaming at me any second.

xoxx Scarlett xoxx

CHAPTER 23

"YOUR HOUSE WAS DESTROYED?" MRS. Annie Harper cornered me in the kitchen, shaking her finger so hard I worried it might fall right off. "Why didn't you say something?"

"It wasn't destroyed," I said. "Someone just broke in and looked through a few of my things."

"That ain't what I heard." Mrs. Harper looked livid. "How do you think I felt, showing up at the salon and learning from Mary Sue, who heard from Joanne, who said Eddie told her, that your place looked like a tornado had hit it? While they're staring at me, wondering why I left my baby alone with... with *you*!"

"But I didn't do anything!" I couldn't back down this time, even though my manners told me to bow my head and apologize. "I didn't do anything wrong. Someone broke into *my* house."

"You and all your shenanigans, some time or another, you're gonna get Gray involved." She shook her head, her gaze seething. "That's it. I'm not dealing with you anymore. You're fired."

"You can't fire me!" Leaning against the counter for support, I was stunned into utter shock. I couldn't process anything she was saying. "I love being Gray's nanny. I'd never do anything to hurt him."

"Well, then this is the consequences of all your poor choices. Out." Mrs. Harper pointed. "I don't want you around my son again."

"But—"

"Did you hear me?"

"You haven't paid me for the last few days! And tomorrow I'm supposed to take Gray to the doctor."

"I will *send* you money. Then I will find someone else," Mrs. Harper hissed. "You made me look like a fool tonight. I'm the last person to find out about my nanny getting in trouble? I gave you too many chances already. Goodbye, Scarlett."

"I've been with you ever since you were *sick*," I said. "What about all those years, huh? You're just going to forget about it?"

Mrs. Harper's face turned to stone. "Good*bye*, Scarlett."

With nothing left to say, I grabbed my things and made my way outside, taking the steps two at a time to avoid the sting in my eyes. I wouldn't give her the satisfaction. I jumped into my car and drove away, headed nowhere, just driving.

CHAPTER 24

Dear Diary,

M ACK TOOK ME TO THIS hill a long time ago. I don't
know why I thought it'd be a good idea to come here
now, tonight, after all that's happened.
I don't know what to do yet.
I've got to figure it all out, I suppose.
But at the moment, I can't do anything.
I don't even feel sad.
Just numb.

Scarlett

CHAPTER 25

I DIDN'T MANAGE TO PULL MY car back down the hill until the clock on my dashboard blinked two a.m. I hadn't cried, which was a small win considering the rest of the evening.

My five phases of grief got stuck on number two: anger. I'd been in denial for all of five minutes before I'd thankfully snapped out of that phase and moved right into anger.

Anger at the person who'd killed Frank and started this whole mess. Anger at whoever had ransacked my home, whether they were related incidents or not. Anger at Mrs. Annie Harper—I'd been with her since her tumultuous pregnancy, caring for her from her first trimester until her eighth month of pregnancy when Gray had come into the world a few weeks early. I'd been there the day Gray was born, and just about every day since.

The only person in the world I could think of that deserved my anger was the man or woman who'd taken my precious Gray away, the person who'd killed Frank. I'd weathered a lot of rumors from the citizens of Luck, but none of them had caused any issues in my day-to-day life. I just raised my chin, ignored the whispers, and continued on with my schedule. But this time, enough was enough. I was going to find them and set the record straight once and for all.

I turned onto the main road, heading straight for Noelle's house. I couldn't go back to my home, not since the door had been busted straight off its hinges. As I passed the Lucky Horseshoe, a bar "cleverly" named after the town, I glanced in my rearview mirror, surprised to find a set of headlights reflecting back at me.

I kept my pace up to thirty-four miles an hour, and not a hair over. Eddie would love to pull me over just to try to wrangle some gossip out of me, and I wasn't going to let him have the honors.

The car matched my pace as I passed through town, and I squinted at the vehicle. Black, or at least a very dark blue. That was the only color I could make out. That, and a shiny set of Olympic-style rings across the front.

"Mack?" I whispered under my breath.

I slowed down just a hair, a tingling sensation creeping over my spine. I was headed out of town. Noelle lived in a gorgeous house about ten minutes on the outskirts of Luck with plenty of land for horses, a back house for the live-in help, and an outdoor pool. The Summers family lived a life of luxury, that's for sure. As luxurious as our little town could support.

The car behind me slowed. Maybe Mack had heard the news from Miss Annie somehow? But why was he out driving around in the naughty hours of the morning?

I sped up, now pushing forty. There were no good answers to those questions. I had a phone. He could have gotten my number and called if he'd needed to get a hold of me.

The car tailing me sped up to match my pace.

The turnoff for Noelle's drive approached, and I had to make a snap decision to either veer right and race to the house, or keep going and see if the car behind me lost interest. Surely, it was just a strange coincidence?

As Noelle's drive neared, I made a choice the choice not to turn off. I couldn't risk leading the person behind me to an innocent family's home. I'd already gotten enough people in trouble.

But that didn't mean I was planning on being stupid. I picked up my phone from where I'd tossed it on the passenger's seat, and noticed Noelle had called me twice. I must have missed the ring in my haze on the hilltop. I struggled to hit redial while keeping my eyes focused ahead. My speed was now pushing fifty.

There was nothing on that road for the next twenty miles. Either I had someone following me with no-good intentions, or someone had decided to get out of dodge in the middle of the night. For some reason, I suspected it wasn't the latter.

"Noelle," I said in a hushed voice as soon as she answered.

"Why you talkin' so quiet? Where are you, honey? I've been calling you nonstop. I finally called Miss Annie, worried as could be." Noelle's voice was slightly breathless. "When I heard what happened, I gave her a piece of my mind, all right. I was just about to call Mack and send him out lookin' for you. I know you and him have had problems, but I also know he'd do anything for you."

I swallowed. "You didn't call him?"

"No, of course not. I talked myself down from the ledge, figurin' you was calming down somewhere like you used to do. I was gonna give you another thirty minutes before I called everyone out lookin' for you."

"Listen to me." I stepped on the gas pedal. "Someone's following me, and I think they're in Mack's car."

"What do you mean?"

"I mean someone's *followin'* my vehicle."

"Is it Mack? Are you sure he just doesn't wanna say hello? Maybe he's hoping you'll change your mind about that drink."

"My gut tells me something ain't right," I said. "I told Mack no tonight when he stopped by Gray's. I'll fill you in later, but right now, I don't know what to do. Mack seems like he understands the word *no*. I don't think it's him."

"Keep driving. I'll come find you, and don't you slow down for nobody."

"No, I'm not dragging you into this." My palms turned sweaty as the vehicle behind me picked up its pace, drawing dangerously close to the rear end of my little bug. "Here's what I'm gonna do.

That turnaround over by the MacDonald's cornfield? I'm gonna pull over there. I'm sure the car will just drive on by. If not, I'm gonna whip around quick and head towards town. Can you call the police if that happens? Get Eddie, get anyone."

"Of course. Stay on the line with me, Scarlett. Breathe. You've got this."

I stifled a small, nervous laugh.

"What are you laughing at?" Noelle sounded exasperated. "Is this one giant joke? Or are you having a breakdown, Scarlett? You're sounding a little nuts right now, I won't lie. What's going on?"

"It's not funny," I said, calming myself. "I'm just thinkin' how tonight Mack showed Grayson some of his stunt driving tricks. I wish I'd paid more attention."

"You don't need help. You can do it."

"Hang on, Noelle. The turnabout is coming up. Hold on the line." My voice turned businesslike as I set the phone in my lap and gripped the steering wheel tightly with both hands.

At the last second, I decided not to use my blinker. I yanked the car right, my wheels crunching on the gravel that formed the turnaround. The car behind me flew right on by, but their brake lights flashed on, and the car squealed to a stop. With my heart pounding, I realized there was no chance in hell that car was taking a road trip out of town. It was following me.

Stepping on the gas as hard as I could, I craned my wheel left and whipped out of the gravel, spitting chunks of the stuff behind me as my purple bug leapt onto the road. The black Audi did a quick U-turn in the middle of the road, but I had the jump on them. This time, I didn't care about the speed limit. I accelerated to ninety just as quickly as I could, hoping against all hope that Eddie would pull me over before the car got to me.

"Noelle, get the cops!" I hollered, reaching for my phone as I approached her driveway for the second time.

She asked a question in response, but I couldn't hear it.

Because at that moment, two shots rang out in the inky blackness. I was no expert, but I *was* from Texas. I knew a gunshot when I heard one. And those were two gunshots aimed in my direction.

CHAPTER 26

Dear Diary,

I ALWAYS WONDERED WHAT IT'D BE like to be shot at.

Well, tonight I found out. Wanna know something? It's not that fun. My heart is still pumping so hard, I think I need a defibrillator by my bed tonight just in case my pulse goes on the fritz.

They never did catch who did it.

Thankfully, whoever was driving wasn't good at multitasking, because he couldn't shoot and drive straight all at once. I made it back into town just as Eddie's lights flashed into view. I barely managed to stop my bug before it crashed into his patrol car, but I did. Eddie leapt out of his car with slipper clad feet, still sporting his pajamas.

I explained to him all about the chase, and at first he didn't believe me, since once I reached the perimeter of Luck that Audi had turned around and screeched off in the opposite direction. After showing Eddie exactly where my attacker had shot at my little bug, then the skid marks of two cars, I think he believed me a little bit more.

It was late and the immediate threat was gone, so any further investigation could wait until the daylight hours arrived. Noelle came and followed me home after that, and I let Eddie go rejoin his wife in bed.

But Diary, there's one thing that's bothering me.

Okay, more than one thing.

But the biggest thing that's keeping me up tonight is this: After Eddie wrote down some sleepy-looking notes and went back home, I made Noelle tail me past the hotel where Mack was staying. He'd made no secret about it, and that shiny black car of his had been parked out front in the Spot-of-Honor all weekend.

Except tonight, that Spot-of-Honor was vacant.

Diary, what does this mean?

Love,
A very confused Scarlett

CHAPTER 27

I STARED VACANTLY AT THE SLICE of toast sitting on my plate. "It ain't gonna eat itself, Scarlett." Noelle crunched into her own piece before leaning over and smothering my toast in raspberry jam, just the way I liked it.

My stomach rumbled in hunger, but the thought of toast didn't sound all that delicious right then. In fact, the thought of eating turned my stomach.

I pushed my plate forward. "What is going on here, Noelle? I can't figure it out. I'm tryin' to be a good girl, but this town is out to get me, I swear. I've got all the bad luck in this place. How come the good Lord couldn't have spread it out a bit more?"

Noelle reached over, her brows furrowed in concern, and squeezed my shoulder. "It's just a rough patch, but we'll get through it. And you've got plenty of people on your side. Like me."

I raised an eyebrow. "My whole life has been a bit of a rough patch."

"Life's more fun that way." Noelle took a giant bite of toast. "How I see it is like this: Everyone always expected us to get in trouble, so no reason to abstain, right?"

I smiled. "I appreciate your support. Really, I do. But you're the only one who believes me."

"Not true. My parents think it's an outrage, the things people are sayin' about you."

"Okay, you and your parents, then."

"And Mack."

I fell silent.

"That wasn't his car last night. It couldn't have been." Noelle sounded as if she were trying to convince herself as much as me. "He would never have shot at you. Like I said, he has done you wrong, but he cares about you. I just know it."

"Who else drives a shiny, dark car with those Audi rings on the front?" I looked at her. "You know Luck. It's full of trucks and my bug. Nobody drives that type of car, not even your family, the classiest of the bunch."

Noelle bobbed her shoulders up and down then finished her toast. She licked her fingers before continuing. "I'm sure there's a perfectly good excuse."

"Then where was he at two in the morning last night?" I asked, as much to myself as to her. "Where was his car?"

"I know one way to find out."

"What's that?"

"Come with me to the Reunion Day event tonight." Noelle reached out and gave my shoulders a little shake. "Come on!"

"Noelle, I already explained myself. I don't wanna go. Plus, now that I got fired from my job, I've got to start looking for another one. If I don't pick up a few shifts somewhere by the end of the week, I'm gonna be behind on rent again." I lay my head face down on the counter. "And I *just* got ahead."

"I'm sure something will come up." Noelle's voice was so confident, my head shot up.

"You know something that I don't?"

Noelle's eyes widened. She could be a good liar sometimes, but not to me. I knew before she said the words "of course not" that she wasn't telling the truth.

"What do you have up your sleeve?" I narrowed my eyes at her.

Before she could respond, the telephone rang as if on cue.

With a positively gleeful smile, Noelle leapt up and grabbed the phone. She muttered a "Hello" and a few words so quiet I couldn't hear. Then, she thrust the phone in my direction. "For you."

"Who knows I'm here?"

Noelle rolled her eyes. "Everyone. Eddie was on the scene last night. You can bet he stopped by the Lucky Horseshoe before he even went home to his wife, just to spread the word. I swear, that man is more of a gossip mill than the GURLZ and the knitting club put together."

I gave a shake of my head, accepting the phone with a sense of trepidation in my stomach. "Hello?"

"Oh, good! Glad I found you. This is Tiny." There was a rustle on the other end of the phone as another line, or two, clicked into place. "And Tallulah and Tootsie."

"Hello, GURLZ," I said. "What can I help you with this morning?"

"It's not so much about *us,* as about what it is you can do for this town," Tiny said. "You're a proud American citizen, right?"

I glanced at Noelle, scrunching up my nose. "Why yes, I am, as a matter of fact."

"And you've been a proud member of Luck since you can remember?"

This time when I looked at Noelle, I caught her staring back expectantly, which only gave me the sense that she knew exactly what was happening. Noelle looked away quickly, swiped the toast from my plate, and dumped it in the garbage, her cheeks turning red.

"Why yes, I'm a proud citizen of America and of this town," I said. "Now, what can I help you with?"

"The bartender called in sick for Reunion Day," Tiny said with a hoarse cough. "Can you replace him?"

"Who was the bartender?"

"You know Dan, from two towns over," Tootsie broke in. "Real sick today. I could barely understand him when he called to cancel." Then, she coughed for good measure.

Something told me Dan might not be as sick as they were letting on. "What'd you ladies do to Dan?"

"Do?" Tiny asked in a voice all too sweet for her biker-mama vibe. "Don't be silly. Everyone gets sick from time to time."

"Why are you calling me? I'm a nanny, not a bartender."

Noelle blinked, but didn't look all too surprised. I raised a finger and wagged it at her, shaking my head.

"Because you're the only one who knows the difference between a martini and a Sex on the Beach. You bartended for all those weddings that one summer," Tootsie said. "I remember because my cousin got married, and you did a right good job. I suggested you."

I hesitated. I had held a bartending gig to earn supplemental income for a few summers, but that hadn't been for a year or two. "I'm sure there's someone who'd do a better job than me. What about Mary Anne from the cafe? At least she makes drinks regularly."

"We'll pay you five hundred dollars," Tiny blurted out. "For three hours of work."

"Five hundred dollars?" My jaw dropped. "What's the catch?"

"There's no catch," Tootsie said. "What do you say?"

Noelle snatched the phone from me. "GURLZ, hold on a second, all right?" Noelle clasped a hand over the receiver and set her gaze on me. "Listen, I knew you wouldn't believe them so here's the honest-to-God truth. These ladies found out about Miss Annie going and firing you yesterday. We know it's wrong, and we're your friends, Scarlett. So Tiny might have *encouraged* Dan to take a sick day, and Tootsie might have *encouraged* the Reunion Day committee to let her take care of the replacement."

I bit my lip and shook my head. "That ain't fair to Dan."

"Dan's doing just fine. He has four other gigs lined up this week." Noelle leaned her elbows on the table. "Now, I know you're gonna be strapped for cash until you get a new job. If you take the bartending gig, you'll make rent this month and have a tiny cushion for next month, depending on your savings. That's time for you to pick up a few shifts at The Cozy Cafe or the diner. You know Mary Anne and Lulu would always take you on if you needed work."

I didn't argue because nothing Noelle said had been wrong. I *would* be strapped for cash until I could get a new job, and I suspected that both Mary Anne and Lulu, the owner of the dirty little diner with the best fried chicken and waffles in town, would let me waitress until I found something more permanent.

"Plus, look at it this way." Noelle's eyes gleamed as she dropped her voice even lower. "Nobody will ask questions about why you're there at Reunion Day since word's already gotten around. You'll have front-row seats to all the gossip. Just think, if Joe turns up tonight, you can ply him with some drinks and ask him about his relationship with Frank."

I considered Noelle's proposition a moment. "You think that would work?"

"If nothing else, darlin', I hate to say this, but you need the money." Noelle shrugged. "I'd offer to spot you the money no matter what. I always would, and you know that, but I also know you're far too proud to take a handout, even if you plan on paying me back."

"I'm not takin' your money, Noelle."

"I *know* that. That's my point." She grinned. "You're taking Dan's money. Except Dan doesn't need it, and he got a pair of baseball tickets that he's pretty excited about in exchange for a sick day, so it's a win-win."

"I don't know."

"Take the job, or else you'll be homeless. How else can I convince you?" Noelle rolled her eyes. "Stop being so stubborn already. We're just tryin' to look out for you. Help us help you."

I looked down, my lashes shading my vision and cleared my throat. "That's really too thoughtful of y'all to go to such lengths for me."

Noelle waved a hand. "It's nothing. We're just making it easier on everyone since we know you wouldn't borrow money. Plus, we didn't wanna waste the time arguing with you."

"I'll do it," I said, my throat closing up a bit as I glanced at my best friend. "I really appreciate the gesture. Y'all are too much."

"She'll do it," Noelle said into the phone. Cheers erupted over the line so loud I couldn't help but smile. "GURLZ, nice work. I'm gonna let you go now since I know y'all gotta prepare for your musical number tonight. And I have a little preparing of my own to do on Scarlett's face."

My eyes widened in alarm as Noelle clicked the End button on the phone. "I didn't sign up for that!"

"Oh, relax." Noelle crossed her arms, sizing up my face like one might a blueprint for a house. "We're gonna make you the belle of the ball. You're gonna be the most stunning thing in that room."

"Yeah, *okay*," I groaned, with an eye roll to end all eye rolls. "Good luck with that."

CHAPTER 28

Dear Diary,

WHO THE HECK IS THAT starin' back at me in the mirror? That Noelle Summers spent all day pluckin' and pullin' and curlin' and straightenin' until I can barely recognize myself. She added some gray eyeshadow in a pattern that she calls a "smoky eye," and she put so much rouge on my cheeks that I feel like a china doll.

Then, she went and tugged my hair into some semblance of a real 'do, as opposed to the frizzy mess I normally settle for. Can you believe it? My hair is long and wavy. She even fastened it over one shoulder with a sparkly clip. (Fake diamonds, thank goodness. I asked.)

To top it off, she made my eyelashes look as long as caterpillars, so long they just about tickle my eyebrows. Then she added lipstick so red it'd make the devil blush, to boot. But that's not the last thing.

She made me put on that lingerie set she brought back all the way from New York. I fought her on it. After all, I was only gonna be workin' tonight, not flauntin' my underclothes for the world to see, but she insisted it'd make *me* feel better.

She said exactly this:

"Wear it for yourself, Scarlett Powers. Ain't nobody gotta know what's on underneath your dress. You keep it your sexy little secret. But when someone smiles at you across the room, you know. That knowledge will show in your smile back because you've got a sexy little secret that nobody else is allowed to know about until you let them."

I suppose she's got a good point since at first, I felt real uncomfortable with that knowledge, but now that I'm staring at myself in the mirror I'm getting used to the idea. Especially after Noelle put me in a gorgeous black dress with a V-neck that curves halfway down to my belly button. I'm pretty sure the designer plumb forgot to make half of this dress since my back is open clear down to my rear end.

However, when Noelle put it on me, I couldn't seem to take it off. Somehow, someway, it matched those dark, smoky eyes and that blood-red lipstick. More than anything, it matched my sexy little secret. It might be sinful, Diary, but for one night I want to feel pretty. I want people to look at me and not see baby spit-up or SpaghettiOs sauce on my shirt. I want them to see a woman, a real woman. I want them to see Scarlett Powers, the vixen.

Except with my luck, folks are gonna look at me and see trouble again. But this time, I'm gonna be a different kind of trouble. More importantly, it's gonna be on *my* terms.

Now Diary, you know me. This goes against everything I'm used to, and every way I'm used to actin'. Noelle told me to fake it 'til I make it.

Do you think I'm doing okay?

Love,
xoxx A very nervous Scarlett xoxx

CHAPTER 29

"THIS TOWN IS SHUT DOWN already," Noelle said, scanning up and down Main Street from the passenger seat of my beautiful little bug. "I didn't expect things to be so dead."

"Well, anyone between the ages of twenty and forty is gonna be at Reunion Day, and the rest of 'em are staying home tonight to avoid the commotion." I shrugged. "This day doesn't come around all that often so I suppose it's almost a national holiday."

"I'm just happy it's an excuse for me to see you." Noelle reached over and squeezed my hand. "By the way, you are a *knockout*. You are gonna blow those boys' minds to the next town over. I guarantee you're gonna make another five hundred in tips, easy."

"I didn't even think about the tips," I said, smiling with a bit of unexpected giddiness. "That plus my savings would give me two months of rent and groceries. I'll have plenty of time to find more work."

Noelle grinned. "I knew you'd come around. You won't have any problem getting some info from Joe, I'm sure. He has a penchant for low-cut dresses, which is one of the reasons I stuck you in that gorgeous thing. That, plus it's *made* for you."

I glanced in the rearview mirror, still surprised by my put-together face. Noelle had even let me borrow a pair of real diamond earrings, small studs that added just the right amount of sparkle to the black, elegant look she'd created. "You are talented, I'll give you that, Noelle. New York is lucky to have you. That's for certain."

"It's nothin'," Noelle said. But even she couldn't hide the pleased expression on her face. "I'll tell you what I'm *really* excited about."

"What's that?"

"I can't wait for Mack to see you." She glanced sideways at me. "Show him what he missed all those years ago. That's one of the reasons I love my job. Stylin' clients, makin' them feel beautiful... I'm telling you, Scarlett. You're gonna 'wow' him so hard he's gonna have regret until the day he dies."

"I dunno..."

"I know." Noelle nodded. "Hang on. Speaking of that devil, ain't that his car?"

I looked to where Noelle pointed out the passenger window. I'd been so mesmerized by the sparkles in my ears that I hadn't even realized we were driving past Joe's Auto Body Shop.

Gritting my teeth, I recognized the black vehicle I'd stared at so intently the night before while fearing for my life. The car was tucked behind a row of other cars, halfway hidden behind the shop. If it weren't for those rings on the front glinting in the sunlight, I wouldn't have even noticed the vehicle.

"Sure is," I said with a terse tone. "Wonder what business he has with Joe?"

"Why would Joe be at his shop?" Noelle asked. "If he did just get back from a business trip, shouldn't he be getting ready for Reunion Day like the rest of the town? Angela seemed pretty intent on going with him, probably in order to show off that new rock she's flaunting."

I made a snap decision to pull my VW bug into the parking lot of the gas station half a block away from Joe's. "Come on." I gestured for Noelle to follow me. "We're gonna go see what's up."

"Is now really the time?" Noelle groaned. "All that effort on your hair. I'm warnin' you, Scarlett, if you start sweating, your hair is gonna frizz out to the moon."

"I just want to *peek*. I'm not doing anything wrong. I'm just checking to see if Joe's back from his business trip." I looked across the center console at Noelle, but my feet were already on the ground outside my bug. "In fact, it's my Good Samaritan deed for today. Because if Joe really is out of town, then nobody should be creeping around his place."

"And what do you plan on doing if you find someone there?" Noelle climbed out of the car. "Mack or otherwise?"

"You worry too much," I said. "We're just *peekin'*. There's nothin' illegal about it."

"You have a habit of turning perfectly legal things into highly illegal activities," Noelle grumbled.

"And you have a habit of going along with it," I whispered back. "Unless you're chickening out on me."

"I'm walkin', aren't I?" Noelle followed as I crept down the side of the road just behind the bushes lining the street.

Luckily, the area was deserted, which was a good thing because we didn't try all that hard to hide. It wasn't worth ruining our gorgeous dresses over a little, perfectly legal bit of snooping.

"Let's hurry it up," Noelle said. "You know the GURLZ will never let us live it down if we miss their performance this afternoon. We're gonna be the only ones there, and you know it. We can't leave 'em hanging."

"Look." I pointed, catching a glimpse of a shadow as Noelle finished talking.

Immediately, she quieted down and ducked behind a Charlie Brown-style Christmas tree that was so thin it wouldn't hide so much as her pinky finger. "Whoa, someone's in there."

"That's what I'm sayin'!" My voice squeaked with excitement as we moved closer. The only sounds in the afternoon lull were the crunch of our heels in gravel and the huff and puff of our heavy breaths. "Let's just see who's in there so we can leave."

"You promise? Because I didn't bring my mace."

"Don't you carry your mace everywhere?" I asked.

"People leave their front doors unlocked here. I didn't think I'd be hosin' anyone down with pepper spray out in public!"

"No matter. Just a quick peek, then we're gone."

We made quick work covering the last of the distance between us and Joe's shop. Scurrying around back, we ducked beneath windows and dashed between cars.

"This is so unladylike, Scarlett Powers," Noelle said as she unhooked her emerald-green dress from where it had snagged on a branch. Combined with her sleek black hair and pretty green eyes, she could double as one of the Disney princesses.

I opened my mouth to apologize, but Noelle turned those green eyes on me and stifled a laugh. "So unladylike… and I love it."

I reached over and clasped my hand over her mouth just as she got a fit of the giggles right behind the shop. When we got her under control, I held a finger to my lips, careful not to touch the gloss Noelle had so carefully applied.

We snuck right up under the window, our backs against the outside of the shop, our fancy heels dug into the dusty parking lot, and our eyes as big as ping pong balls.

"What now?" Noelle hissed. "Let's peek quick because I'm starting to sweat, and it would be a right shame to get pit stains on this beautiful gown. That, and I borrowed the gown from my designer friend, and unfortunately, I think she's expecting it back."

"Is mine borrowed too?" I glanced with horror at the bottom of the jet-black dress, which was dusted with a hint of sand-colored powder.

"No, can you believe it? I got it at a second-hand shop. One of them shops the movie stars and models donate their clothes to after they wear them once. I bought it thinking of you, honey." Noelle smiled, still whispering. "You can keep it."

Just as I nodded, a *crash* from inside the shop silenced us.

Very carefully, I sunk to a squatting position, then slowly arose until just the very tops of my eyes peered over the windowsill. I couldn't believe my luck. A little aloe vera plant sat on the table right near my head. I shifted so I stood directly behind it. There was enough space between the leaves for me to get a good view of the room, but at the same time, the leaves were big enough to cover most of my face.

"Can you see anything?" Noelle asked with a voice so soft I could only make out every other word.

Shaking my head, I made a gesture to indicate the room was empty. As I turned back to look through the window again, I saw a back office that I'd never stepped foot in before. The entire shop was small, so I assumed there were only a few other rooms: maybe a bathroom and breakroom, in addition to the front office where I'd chatted with Ryan or Ralph or Miguel when I picked up my car.

The crash must have come from the front office. I craned my neck around, turning my head different angles, in an effort to see inside the office. The fact was, I had two choices. I could either wait for the intruder to come to the back office, or I could sneak to the side window and try for a better vantage point.

Just then, something nudged my knee, and I nearly leapt out of my skin. When I looked down, I saw Noelle tapping me.

"You almost scared me to death," I whispered, bending over and clutching my chest. "What are you playin' at?"

"I just realized that I brought my backup." Noelle thrust a tiny black can of mace into my hand. "It was my extra one. I'm not sure it still works. It's been in here since I last used this purse, and that was ages ago."

I clasped the canister in my hand for lack of something better to do. When I popped up and took my hiding spot behind the aloe vera plant again, I sensed immediately something was wrong. A stack of papers that had been piled high on the desk a moment before was now scattered across the room. One last page drifted through the air and came to a soft landing on the floor in front of me.

I quickly scanned the room, but whoever had swooped in and rifled through the papers was gone. We hadn't heard footsteps or a motor, which meant that unless the person had magical powers, he was still around.

I bent down and whispered to Noelle. "Don't be alarmed, but whoever was in there might be leaving. They came into the room and left. Now I don't know where they are."

"You got the mace?" she asked.

I showed her the canister in my palm.

She nodded. "Let's wait a few minutes and give them time to leave in peace. If we don't hear 'em by then, we'll sneak off."

"Good plan." I leaned with my back against the shop, my leg touching Noelle's as we huddled next to one another. "Kinda reminds me of that one night we toilet-papered Josh Lewiston's house and had to hide from the cops for three hours."

"My momma was *so* mad when we waltzed in, leaves in our hair." Noelle grinned, her voice hushed. "Ah, it's nice being back with my partner in crime."

When a crunch of leaves distracted me from her grinning face, I nudged Noelle with my elbow. "Did you hear that?"

She nodded, a flash of terror appearing in her eyes. She pointed at the mace can, insinuating I should be ready.

I held my finger lightly against the trigger.

"But what if it's Mack?" she asked. "You don't want to spray him."

I opened my mouth to tell her I'd spray anyone who was after me, Mack or no Mack, but before I could do that, I saw something that scared me much worse than Noelle's upset momma after we had been caught by the cops.

Keeping my lips tightly sealed, I put one hand over Noelle's mouth. Then I raised the pepper spray with my other hand and directed it toward the corner of the shop just on Noelle's other side where a black, shiny object extended half an inch past the wall. If

I hadn't been scared shitless and on full alert, I never would have noticed it.

Ever so slowly, I tilted Noelle's head in the same direction. Tears sprung to my eyes as she bit down on my hand in surprise at the sight of the gun barrel. I tightened my lips as I tried to hold in my hiss of pain.

Removing my hand from Noelle's mouth, I held up three fingers for her to see. I folded one down, then another, leaving one finger up. Then, I put my lips against her ear and breathed as quietly as possible, "Run." I counted down the last finger.

Thankfully, Noelle and I had built up a lot of trust and a little bit of psychic ability in all of our years of mischief together. As soon as I reached zero on the countdown, she sprinted in the opposite direction of the gun. I lunged toward it, my finger depressing the trigger on the mace as I aimed the spray up and down at the person standing just around the corner.

When a male voice let out a strangled cry, I knew I'd hit my target. I took off in the opposite direction, following closely on Noelle's heels. Neither of us looked back as our feet pounded against the pavement. Lucky thing we'd had our fair share of experience running from the cops in heels—prom, winter formal, fall formal, and most high school dances, as a matter of fact.

We reached my lavender Beetle at the same time. My breath was coming in burning gulps, and a lock of Noelle's hair dangled loosely in front of her face.

After climbing inside the car like a pair of rabid dogs, I had the engine started and was turning onto Main Street before Noelle had a chance to close her door.

She slammed it shut, looked behind us, then looked at me. "Well, I guess that answers my question," she said. "I didn't know how I was gonna figure that out, otherwise."

"What question?" I looked in the rearview mirror but couldn't see a thing. Joe's shop looked exactly the same as it had when we'd arrived, with the exception of two sets of footsteps sprinting away from it. "Did you see anyone? I still don't know who it was creeping in on Joe's shop."

"Oh, I don't know the answer to that." Noelle looked amused. "I was just wondering if that pepper spray would work. Turns out, it's still good."

I shook my head, a nervous ball of energy turning into a bubble of laughter. "I shouldn't be laughing." I hiccupped as I flicked on my blinker and turned onto a side road. "I don't know what's wrong with me. That was a close call."

"You're loopy," Noelle said, unable to hide her snort of laughter. "Just like that time you drank a bottle of champagne in twenty minutes. You couldn't stop belching for twenty more minutes!"

I hiccupped again. "It was a dare, and that was a lot of bubbles!"

"So, who do you think it was?" Noelle asked a few minutes later. We had calmed down, parked outside the Reunion Day facility, and touched up our makeup. Well, Noelle touched up both mine and hers since I didn't know how to do it on a good day. At that moment, my hands were shaking so badly I would've looked like a monster in a fistfight if she had let me do my own mascara.

"I honestly don't know." I sat in thought for one last moment before opening the car door just as the first strains of the GURLZ's screeches emerged from the building. "But I'm hoping we'll find out soon enough."

"Oh, I ain't going back there," Noelle said. "I'm running out of deodorant, and I already told you my armpit concerns with this gown."

"We're not going anywhere except inside the center," I said. "Because if that man was between the ages of twenty and forty, he'll be here tonight."

Noelle's eyes brightened with understanding. "You're a genius."

"Let's just say I'll be on the lookout for a man with a bit of red around his eyes, blowin' into a tissue all night," I said. "Because I might not be a genius, but I'm a decent shot."

"What are you gonna do when you see him?"

"I haven't thought that far ahead," I said. "But I'll think of something. After all, I'm bartending in a public place. What could go wrong?"

CHAPTER 30

Dear Diary,

I F I EVER UTTER THE words "What could go wrong?" again, I give you permission to punch me in the face. Because as tonight proved, things can always get worse. Even if they're bad to start with.

Scarlett

Chapter 31

WHILE THE INFAMOUS GURLZ BAND screeched their lungs out amid the applause of Noelle and me, I set up the bar just how I liked it. I'd had enough experience during those few weddings to know the most popular drinks, the fastest way to make them, and the handiest way to arrange the ingredients. I'd also learned how to tell when it was time to cut a person off before he passed out, and I knew the appropriate array of pink concoctions that would give life to even the lamest bachelorette party. I'd even mastered the art of pouring body shots.

My most important achievement during those summer weddings, however, was learning a little cherry trick. I'd mastered the art of holding a martini spear in between my teeth, tossing a maraschino cherry up in the air, and spearing it with that little sword. Guys and girls alike had gone wild for that trick, and by my calculations it had increased my tips by twenty percent. I most certainly wasn't above performing whatever tricks I could with my clothes on to make my bank statement climb into the black, and tonight was no exception.

I easily performed my trusty little trick, but it didn't impress Noelle much. She'd seen it a hundred times.

"Guess it's like riding a bike, huh?" She reached over and nabbed a cherry for herself, then popped it between her lips with a flourish. "You never lost it. As for me, I think they taste just as good when I skip the whole juggling thing."

I grinned. "It's about the presentation, Noelle. You're a stylist. You should realize that."

"I like my clothes styled and my food simple. What can I say? I'm from Texas."

I laughed at that one, then thanked the Lord when the GURLZ finally climbed down from the stage, having just finished the two songs they were allowed, plus one extra. They tottered toward me, hands extended for the drinks I'd prepared in advance.

"For you, a filthy martini." I handed said martini to Tiny, who wore a spiky leather jacket with nothing but a sports bra underneath. I thought her body parts probably sagged a bit more than they did sixty years ago, but I had to applaud her confidence.

"And this one's mine." Tootsie, with her red beehive waving dangerously close to the bottle of wine I had sitting on the counter, picked up the frilly little daiquiri I'd blended specially for her.

Meanwhile, Tallulah picked up the lowball glass filled with pure whiskey. She didn't mess around, and I could appreciate that in a woman. Her chocolatey skin tone looked gorgeous against the light-yellow dress she wore. She was the only one of the three women who looked acceptable for the public eye at the moment.

However, once a lady got past a certain age in Luck, folks stopped commenting on her attire, myself included. I personally couldn't wait until I reached that age. Then, this town would see me waltzing around in a pair of boxers and a cozy sweater, for all I cared.

"Hurry, down these quick. I told Lou we'd be ready in one hour for him to pick us up," Tiny said, finishing her martini in one gulp and slamming the glass on the counter. "Keep 'em coming, sugar pie. I get a free drinkin' pass one night a year, and I intend on using it."

I grinned and poured her another martini, this one a bit more diluted with olive juice than necessary. When I looked up, my grin faded quickly.

The ladies took one look at my face, then saw the person I was looking at. They snatched their drinks and disappeared to the far corner of the room.

I swallowed hard, tidying up my already-tidy workspace. The sun had already started its good-night journey as GURLZ played on stage. I'd been so busy entertaining Noelle, clapping for the band, and setting up, that I hadn't realized the party was just getting started.

In fact, when I looked at my watch, I saw it was ten minutes after the event was supposed to have started. Apparently, everyone was fashionably late.

Except Frank's widow.

I scrubbed the counter some more as Frank's wife made her way into the event center, which was really nothing more than a glorified barn. The space was huge, so huge that she didn't see me right away among the tables of food lined up against the left wall, or the chocolate fountain and dessert section on my right. Strings of lights and piles of tulle hung from the ceiling, and even I had to admit that the decorating crew had done a nice job turning the barn into a respectable, bright place fit for a party.

Noelle, who'd stepped away to greet one of the new arrivals, must have seen the look on my face. She murmured something to Chet Hartman, a boy—or rather, a man—who'd recently returned home from a stint in the army, and moved quickly over to my side.

"Why are you hanging your head?" Noelle asked, putting her hand on my shoulder. "You have nothing to be ashamed about; you didn't do nothin' wrong. I know it, you know it, and deep down, this whole town knows it too. They're just passing along unfounded rumors because that's what folks *do* here."

"I should've brought Frank's widow a casserole," I muttered. "I thought about it that first night, but I had to watch Gray. Then yesterday, that whole thing about me gettin' fired happened, and I plumb forgot about it."

Noelle gave me a sad-looking stare.

I sighed. "I'm just makin' excuses, I know. I can't help feeling strange about it though, since I was the last person to talk to her husband alive, and then I went and found his body."

"An accident, don't forget. I found it too. I was there." Noelle shrugged. "You could argue I was the one who forced you to do it, bringing that lingerie set back and making you try it on right then. In fact, we're gonna get this over with."

Before I could resist, Noelle grabbed me by the hand and pulled me straight across the wooden floor, under the rafters decorated with sparkling lights, their glow fading into the depths of the lofted ceiling, and right up to Frank's widow.

I tugged against her arm, but her grip was iron-clad. By the time I even had the opportunity to feel self-conscious, it was already too late.

"Mrs. Benton, we are so sorry for your loss," Noelle said. Her green eyes were piercing in their sincerity. "Both Scarlett and I."

Mrs. Benton cut her gaze to me with a sadness in her eyes, but before she could say anything, Noelle was already talking again.

"I'm just lucky Scarlett was there when I stumbled on the body," Noelle said. "It was the most horrible thing. Frank was such a great guy, and I'm sure he made for a wonderful husband. I'm sorry I was the one to find him. I'm not sure I'll ever get over it."

My jaw dropped open.

Noelle shook her head. "I've had nightmares ever since that day, and my heart hurts just thinkin' what you must be going through." Finally, Noelle took a breath, giving Mrs. Benton a chance to process the twist of events.

I cleared my throat with the intention of setting the story straight, but Noelle dug her nails into my palm so hard I thought I might need stitches. I shut up, but only because I was biting my lip to stifle a cry of pain.

"But I thought… hang on, it was you who discovered Frank?" Mrs. Benton turned to Noelle. "I thought it was Scarlett."

"Well, I hate to be disrespectful during this time, but you thought wrong." Noelle leaned conspiratorially toward the widow. "I'm not gonna name names, but did you hear it from Eddie? Because we all know not to trust a word outta his mouth."

"But he was the policeman on the scene…"

"Nobody was at that scene when Frank was found, God bless his soul. Just me and Scarlett, and we know the sad truth. Don't we, Scarlett?"

At Noelle's painful hand squeeze, I managed a nod.

"Oh, my, well…" Mrs. Benton looked a bit shaken. "I just assumed…"

"We don't like assumptions here, now do we." Noelle gave a pleasant smile, though her green eyes remained firm. "The truth is all that matters, right?"

Mrs. Benton raised a hanky to her nose and blew into it. Although judging by the empty sound coming through her nostrils, she was just stalling for time. When she finally tucked her handkerchief away, she gave a more affirmative nod in Noelle's direction. "I suppose you're right. Well, Noelle, I'm so sorry you had to see that. I can't imagine the fright you had."

Noelle nodded along as Mrs. Benton fondly discussed her late husband, making the appropriate *mmms* and *ahhs* that the conversation required.

When there was one second of an opening, I jumped right in and seized the chance to pay my respects. "I'm so sorry for your loss, Mrs. Benton. Like Noelle said, it must just be horrible for you."

"Thank you." Her words were curt, her voice calculated. "I appreciate it."

"Would you like a beverage?" I asked, gesturing to the bar behind me. "I'm working tonight. Maybe something light?"

"How about a red wine?" Noelle suggested.

Mrs. Benton eventually nodded, and I disappeared behind the bar and poured her a glass. I served a few customers while I waited for Noelle and Mrs. Benton to swing by for the glass, noting that the party was picking up pace. The big Reunion Day sign flapped in the breeze out front, the barn doors were open, and the night was beginning to cool as the sun dropped below the horizon.

Eventually, Noelle came over to the bar.

"She's coming right behind me. She just got stopped by the pastor real quick," Noelle muttered in my ear. "I think that went well."

"Why'd you do that?" I asked. "You didn't have to lie for me."

Noelle shrugged. "This town tends to forgive me for things that they don't let you get away with, and it's unfair. Look at how it went tonight! When I find a body, it's an unfortunate accident. You find a body, and you're a murderer. I don't understand this place." Noelle threw her arms up. "I don't know how you stay here!"

"Well, I appreciate that. You didn't have to. That is the kindest thing anyone's ever done for me."

"You've bailed me out of jail six times, and I've only bailed you out five, so let's call it even." Noelle winked. "Are you okay back here for now? I wanna go chat with Chet a bit more. That *boy* came back from the army a *man. Mm-hmmm.*"

I laughed and handed her a spritzer. "Go on. And take this drink for the road."

Noelle glided off, her emerald gown sweeping across the floor, her shoulders on proud display, and those black locks beautiful as they hung down her back. More eyes than mine followed her across the room, and I didn't blame a single one of them.

"She's a pretty girl." Mrs. Benton appeared next to the bar, startling me out of my people-watching moment.

"Yes, beautiful." I swiped up the glass of wine I'd poured and handed it over. "And a great person."

Mrs. Benton blinked, nodding in agreement. "Shame she's not married yet. You know, Chet is a good boy."

"I'm sure he is." I turned back to the bar and mixed a tequila sunrise just because I wanted something to do with my hands. I also didn't want to spill the beans about Noelle having gone on a date up in New York. She'd said it was nothing serious. "Noelle will settle down when she's ready."

"It'd be nice if she found someone 'round here, moved back to settle down."

I added the grenadine to the sunrise, making it more sugar than alcohol since I was so distracted. "Yes, that'd be nice, but it's her life. If she wants to live in New York, I support that too."

"Scarlett, I wanted to apologize."

"What?" I jerked the grenadine bottle so hard, the entire drink clattered into the sink, the glass cracking in two.

"I'm sorry how I treated you back there. I didn't realize Noelle was the one who found the body, and… well, I'd just been hearin' the rumors around town. It was easier for me to believe the rumors than to take a second look at the situation."

I shrugged. My family got a bad rap in this town. It started a few generations ago with my great-great grandma. Some say she was cursed. Others say it was bad luck. A few were convinced that all Powers girls were just born bad apples.

If you ask me, it was more bad luck than anything else. The last few generations of Powers ladies had been a string of single women with no long-lasting men around to speak of, and we drifted in and out of town with the tides. Now, I was the only one left. "There've been rumors drifting around Luck since the day my mama brought me back here. That's just the nature of life. I've learned to deal with it; you don't have to apologize."

"Noelle's right. I shouldn't have assumed." Mrs. Benton looked over to where Chet very lightly touched Noelle's shoulder. She bent in half, laughing at something he'd said. "Noelle pointed out after you left that you'd been hurt by the rumors. I just wanted to say I'm sorry."

I dumped the broken glass into a special container. "Well, I appreciate that, but really, you're the last person who should be apologizing. You've been through a lot."

Mrs. Benton looked down, twisting the handkerchief between her fingers. Her mouth worked real fast, as if she had something to say but couldn't get the words out.

I stepped closer. "Are you all right?"

She looked up at me, her eyes shining with unshed tears, her medium-sized figure looking weathered and beaten down. "I loved him."

"Oh, Mrs. Benton, of course you did." I opened my arms and, to my own surprise, she fell right into them and clasped me back hard. I patted her shoulder. "I am so sorry."

She pulled back after a moment of sobbing. Luckily, I'd tossed a towel over my dress when I'd cleaned up the spilled drink, so her puddle of mascara had landed on the towel and not my new gown.

"I'm sorry to ruin your dress." She sniffed. "I swear, we're the only town in the world that wears *ball gowns* to Reunion Day."

I gave a slight shake of my head, glancing out at the crowd. "I think you're right. We're also the only town that has a reunion for all grades every ten years because we don't got enough people to fill a yearly one."

She gave a watery smile. "You and Noelle are great friends, huh?"

I smiled. "The best."

"You're lucky. Hold onto her." Mrs. Benton looked across the crowd, searching for someone I couldn't find.

"I plan on it." After I refreshed Mrs. Benton's wine glass, she took a sip and set it back down. Then I made up my mind to go out on a limb. "I have one more thing I wanted to tell you."

She raised her eyebrows, taking a healthy sip of the red liquid. "Go on, child."

I was only ten years younger than she was, but I continued anyway. "I did speak to Frank on the morning... er, before church."

Mrs. Benton's eyebrows furrowed. "I heard that. Picking up your car? Frank told me he was expecting you on Sunday. He said he'd had your car done the day before, but something came up, and you couldn't get it."

"Exactly. But it wasn't quite done. Turns out he sent me over to Joe for a few more fixes. What I wanted to tell you is that he said he had plans to take you out for a real nice dinner. Steak maybe, and treat you to something special." I bit my lip. "I don't know the occasion, but I just thought you should know how much he cared about you."

She sucked in a shaky breath.

"I'm sorry to be bringing this up, but I thought you would want to know he was thinking about you that morning. He loved you and wanted to treat you right."

Mrs. Benton reached out, taking my wrist in her hand and squeezing it tightly. "Thank you for tellin' me. I really appreciate that." She looked wistfully into my eyes. "I just don't understand *why*. Why would someone do that to my Frank?"

"I hate to be insensitive, but I was gonna ask you the same thing. Was Frank acting suspicious lately? Anyone hanging around his shop that shouldn't have been?"

"Who wants to know?"

I lowered my voice. "I've sorta been workin' with the police on finding the answer to the same question. Not official business, of course. But since I was there that morning, I've just been asking around a bit and trying to see if I can help them find whoever had it out for Frank." I didn't bother to clarify that by "working with" the police, I meant that I was more a "person of interest" than an "investigator."

But I *had* worked with them. I'd answered their questions about why I'd been in the church basement stumbling across dead bodies. Like it or not, judging by the state of my house at the moment, I was inadvertently wrapped up in the whole business, anyway.

With a hesitant sigh, she eventually gave in and nodded. "I don't know of any enemies Frank had, but what bothers me is all that business he was sending to Joe's. We were trying to redo our kitchen, and I swear he sent at least half the cars that came to his shop over to Joe."

"Were they arguing again?" Everyone knew about the rivalry. It wasn't a secret around town.

"Not like before." She shook her head. "They worked out some sorta deal and actually seemed like they were getting along great. Don't get me wrong, I had no trouble with Frank sharing business with Joe, but it should be a two-way street, don't you think? If I had to guess, Joe sent Frank one car to every three Frank sent his way. Just don't seem fair."

As if to punctuate the point, Joe's wife waltzed up to the bar at that very moment. Angela, dressed in a white gown with a diamond necklace, called out for a wine spritzer. I nodded, but before I could respond, her gaze fell on the woman next to me.

"Oh, Mrs. Benton, how are you doing?" Angela, whether she realized it or not, rested the hand with her brand-new, sparkling rock over her mouth. "I'm surprised you came here, darlin'. How are you holding up?"

Angela's concern seemed genuine to me, but I stayed out of the conversation, making a spritzer with my head down.

"Thank you for the casserole," Mrs. Benton said. "It was real delicious, one of the best. I appreciate you thinking of me."

"Like I said before, anything that Joe or I can do to help you out with the shop, finances, more casseroles, you just say the word, and I'll be over in a jiffy." Angela stepped around the bar and gave Mrs. Benton a hug. "I can't imagine what you're going through."

"You're doing too much, Angela, but I appreciate it." Mrs. Benton scratched her forehead, her expression overwhelmed. "I won't be dealing with all of that until things calm down, but I promise I'll call you."

"Spritzer?" I handed over the wine glass, sensing Mrs. Benton had run out of things to say and was looking for a way out of the conversation.

"Oh, thank you." Angela looked surprised that I'd remembered her drink. "Well, I'll let you two continue. I just wanted to check in and offer my help in any way I can."

Once Angela disappeared, Mrs. Benton turned to look at me. "I can't make sense of that woman."

"What do you mean?"

"She seems genuine. She says all the right things." Mrs. Benton gave a slight shake of her head. "But something is funny about it, though I can't put my finger on what. Then there's that huge diamond. Where's she getting that money?"

"Well, yesterday at book club she mentioned that Joe bought it for her."

"But my Frank and her Joe had made some sort of a deal in order to stop their ongoing feud." Mrs. Benton frowned. "I don't know the details. I'm not sure it was never anything more than a gentleman's agreement, to be honest, but the gist of it was that if one of them started doing way better than the other, they'd start sharing business."

"It sounds like they *were* sharing business, just... not in the right direction." I crossed my arms, leaning against the bar as I tried to figure everything out. "Then again, Frank did say he wanted to take you out to a nice dinner, so maybe..."

I trailed off at the look on her face. Comparing a steak dinner to a rock the size of Angela's was like comparing a decent shirt from the Goodwill to Dolce and Gabbana couture.

"I see your point," I said. "But why would Frank be giving away all that business? Unless maybe he was forced to?"

"What do you mean?" Her eyebrows knitted together, and I could tell I'd grabbed her attention.

"Well, what if there was some sort of... I don't know, blackmail involved. Could Joe have had something on Frank that forced him to give away a portion of his business?"

Mrs. Benton tapped a finger to her lips. "If there was, I didn't know anything about it. It was business as usual, as far as I was concerned."

"Was he acting strange these last few days?"

"Maybe a bit quiet, but that's pretty typical of him lately. Though on Sunday morning he did seem excited, but I don't know about what. He just said he was lookin' forward to my fried chicken that afternoon, and I didn't really bat an eye." Mrs. Benton gave a sad smile. "My fried chicken *is* something to get excited about. I'm just sad he didn't get a chance to eat it."

I bowed my head once more, feeling Mrs. Benton's pain more than I'd expected. "I'm really sorry."

"Just do one thing for me." She stepped closer, the faint scent of her perfume swirling around us, smelling a bit like laundry day and fresh linens. "If you can find out who did this to Frank, do that for me."

I nodded. "My house was ransacked the other day. I'm sure you heard from Eddie." I looked up, not seeing any disagreement in her gaze. "Like it or not, I'm involved, though I can't figure out why. I promise you, I'll do whatever I can to help find whoever did this to your husband."

With a watery blink, she gave me a grateful nod. "You have a reputation for trouble, Miss Scarlett, but I'm starting to think this entire town has you pegged wrong. You're a treasure. I hope you know that."

That time, the warmth inside my stomach had nothing to do with the glass of wine I'd been sipping on the side. Luck liked its stereotypes. The townsfolk liked pegging people into perfect little categories, and I'd had the unlucky fortune to be born into a trouble-shaped hole with a trouble-shaped peg.

"Your words mean a lot to me." I gave Mrs. Benton one more

refill. "I can't promise you that I cook a good casserole, but if that's what you need, then you just let me know, and I'll do my best."

"These hips don't need any more casseroles, but Frank needs closure." She cast me a meaningful glance before stepping away from the bar.

I reached out and grasped one of her wrists. "One more thing."

"Yes?"

"About the blackmail… might that be something you think Joe was capable of?"

"I'm learning not to assume things anymore," Mrs. Benton said, her voice lowered. "But I'm telling you, business wasn't good enough to buy a diamond that size. And I'm also wondering what sort of *business* drew him out of town on Reunion Day."

I looked around the gymnasium, noting that, true to her word, Joe was still suspiciously absent from Angela's side.

"And Angela?" I asked on a whim.

"What about her?"

"Do you think she knows about it?"

Mrs. Benton's eyes darkened as she glanced at the woman waving her rock at anyone who would look at it. When Mrs. Benton looked back at me, she paused for a second, and the expression disappeared. She cleared her throat. "Now, Scarlett, it wouldn't be right for me to start rumors I know nothin' about."

CHAPTER 32

Dear Diary,

WITH EACH STEP FORWARD, I open up six more doors that all lead back to where I started. Why would Frank be sending business like that over to Joe's if it weren't blackmail? And if it *were* blackmail, then what did Joe have on Frank?

Even if Joe had unearthed something embarrassing about Frank, was it embarrassing enough to donate enough "business" for the man to buy his wife a diamond ring the size of Rhode Island?

Diary, I'm confused. Then on top of it, there's Angela wavin' that ring around like it's the American flag. Is she that proud of her husband? If not, then what does she know that I don't? And where is that husband of hers? If I could just talk to Joe for three minutes…

Shit. Diary, here she comes. Heather Holloway. I was hoping that maybe she'd suffer a mysterious allergic reaction this morning and be too sick to show up. As usual, this town holds nothing but bad luck for me. Because here she is, waltzing in like a young, beautiful queen of England. I know jealousy is a sin, Diary, but that woman tempts even the strongest of wills. I should know.

She tempted Mack Montgomery right out of my grasp the first time around, and she ended up dating him first. For a long time.

Now, she can have him. I'm not getting involved this time. She can have her heart broken, and see how she likes it.

Love, a sort-of-fuming Scarlett

CHAPTER 33

"GIVE ME A DIET COKE with a splash of vodka," Heather Holloway instructed as she sidled up to the bar.

It was as if her eyes had laser beams that had focused on me the second she walked in the door. I'm sure the fact that I was tethered behind the bar working, just like all the help she employed on her ginormous farm, had thrilled her. But I wouldn't let her bossiness ruin my day.

"Sure." I kept my eyes averted, knowing that those piercing blue glaciers of hers could freeze my heart over and poke a knife between my ribs with one glance. Instead, I focused on adding extra ice to her glass, splashing in just the right amount of vodka—not too much, because we all knew Heather counted calories obsessively—then began adding the Diet Coke.

"God, can't you do anything right?" Heather leaned over the bar, picked up the glass, and threw it into the sink. "I said a *little* bit of vodka, not half of a bottle. We're not all lushes like you."

Gritting my teeth, I picked up the two glass halves from the sink and deposited the broken pieces into the same box where I'd set the pieces of the tequila glass a few minutes earlier. I had barely used a *hint* of alcohol, not enough to get her calorie-counter on the fritz.

"Sure thing, Heather." I told myself over and over that it wasn't worth a fight. I avoided her more days out of the year than not, and that was a win.

"Shouldn't you be calling me Miss Holloway?" She examined manicured nails. "Since you're the *help,* and all."

I swallowed. "Sure thing, Miss Heather Holloway." Maybe I could wear this girl down with sweetness. But I couldn't resist the slight jab of including her first name.

Her eyes flashed at me, but I was already busy making her next drink. That time, I didn't even bother to put in vodka. She wasn't watching anyway. Frankly, she didn't deserve the fun of getting a little bit tipsy. Straight Diet Coke for her.

Except, as I moved to press the diet button on the soda gun, my finger "slipped," and I hit the regular. It was as if the devil himself had grabbed hold of the soda machine and added real Coke to her glass instead of that diet crap.

Heather leaned over. "That's *enough.* God, what did I tell you?"

I couldn't resist. As I handed over her glass of real, sugary Coke, I winked.

Heather's eyes widened, then she let out a tortured "ughh" before snatching the glass from the counter and striding across the room. When she took her first sip of the drink, I felt an embarrassing rush of pleasure at the sight of her surprised face, looking like *wow, this is good!* Then with shifty eyes, she glanced around the room before guzzling the rest of the glass.

"You're welcome," I muttered under my breath. "The pleasure of real sugar."

"Hey darlin'," said a new voice. The voice belonged to a man hanging over the counter with cigarette smoke drifting out of his mouth and filtering across the bar.

I wrinkled my nose. "What can I get you, Art?"

The man's greasy hair swung onto his forehead as he spoke to my chest. "Can I get a beer to start off with? I'm gonna save the fun stuff for later."

"Okay." I grabbed a pint glass from the bar, but instead of filling it with Bud Light from the tap, I poured straight water, seeing as he was already drunk. "Already" drunk was putting it lightly. Art had probably never stopped being drunk from the night before.

He took the glass as soon as I set it on the counter and swigged the clear liquid, not even noticing the lack of alcohol. He smacked his lips then examined the nice V of my dress again. I crossed my arms over my chest.

I'd done my good deed for the day, substituting H2O for booze. I'd practically started Art on the road to detox, helping to prevent him from getting too unruly and embarrassing himself again. A few more glasses of water, and he might manage to stumble only half the time he walked. But if he kept ogling my body in that way, I might just undo my good deed with a punch to his schnoz.

"Why you never dress like that on a normal day?" Art slurred.

"Are you having a nice conversation with my chest?" I took a dainty sip of my own wine, my fingers gripping the glass so hard, it nearly shattered. "You know, if you want our conversation to go two ways, you could always talk to my face."

Art dragged his eyes upward as if the effort was beyond difficult. "Your face?"

"Yeah, this thing." I waved a hand in front of my face, but it seemed a foreign concept to Art. "Two eyes, nose, mouth… you know."

As Art took a moment to study the human face—a novelty item to someone as chest-focused as him—I glanced over his shoulder. My stomach plummeted as I noticed two things at once. The first was Mack's presence. He must have made his appearance while I was distracted, serving my new pal, Art.

Besides Noelle, Mack was probably the most anticipated return for everyone in town. Noelle had "gotten out" and into the glamorous life, while Mack had simply disappeared. The mysteries surrounding his sudden departure from town had only become more strange when he'd turned up in Hollywood years later. All the female heads in the room twisted in his direction, their gazes lingering, surveying the seemingly oblivious Mack.

The one person who Mack wasn't oblivious to, judging by the closeness of their bodies, was that brat, Heather Holloway. She clung to Mack's arm as if he might blow away to greener pastures if she let go for one second. Her pretty pink lips were all too close to Mack's cheek, while her pretty blond hair brushed against his shoulder. Those pretty pink nails of hers clawed at his arm, while her ice-blue eyes held his attention.

I swallowed hard, wiping up a nonexistent spot on the counter.

"You like him?" Art asked, swiping a hand across his mouth.

"What?" I looked up to see him glancing over his shoulder at Mack. Then he turned back to me with an expectant look. "No, of course not," I said hurriedly, dismayed that my reaction was obvious even to a person who was so drunk he'd mistaken water for beer.

"You know, I'm available."

I narrowed my eyes at Art. "I don't *like* Mack, and I'm not interested in you. Now, beat it."

Still, I couldn't help one last glance at the happy-looking pair in the center of the room. Yes, they had a history. No, it wasn't my problem. Yes, I should hate Mack at the moment. After all, he might have aimed a gun at me back at Joe's shop. I just had to get close enough to his eyes to confirm. So why did the thought of Heather and Mack cozied up together make me sick?

"I like your lips." Art's eyes nearly crossed as he stared somewhere between my nose and my neck. "Maybe I can kiss'm."

"Maybe not." I couldn't keep my eyes off Heather and Mack. I was getting myself so worked up I was seeing stars. I was almost thankful when Art started making a racket again, just so I didn't have to watch the reunion between those two.

Art raised the water to his lips, chugged it, then slammed the glass so hard on the counter that it cracked in half. Sighing loudly,

I started to clean up the third shattered glass of the evening. If we kept up that pace, we would be swigging straight from the bottle by nine o'clock.

As I dropped the two halves of the glass into the rapidly filling discard container, Art reached over the bar and clasped his grimy little hands to the sleeves of my dress. He yanked so hard my sleeves nearly ripped right off, and my secret undergarments were almost a secret no more. He thrust his lips toward me, aiming for my face but hitting my shoulder.

I recoiled so violently, I nearly shattered another glass, but this time, I managed to set it in the sink before it hit the floor. Remarkably, even louder than the pint glass hitting the metal sink was the sound of my hand cracking across Art's cheek.

"Get your filthy hands off me, Art." I couldn't help the words blurting out of my mouth. I wish I could've dealt with things more quietly, but that was just my natural reaction. Besides, he had it coming. While I didn't get enjoyment out of embarrassing a drunken fool, I also didn't want to be molested while doing my job.

Before I could calm down, two hands much larger than my own yanked Art up by the collar so hard I heard one of his cowboy boots clatter to the floor as his feet left the ground. How Mack had covered the distance so quickly, I had no clue. But the stunt driver now had Art pinned against the wall next to the bar. Mack's face was so close to Art's that I wondered how he could breathe with the amount of cigarette smoke lingering on Art's clothes. It was enough to set off fire alarms.

"Why don't you keep your hands off her?" Mack's words were so quiet I thought only I could hear them, but when I looked up, the entire venue had fallen as silent as a tomb. It was so quiet that Mack's words echoed as if he'd shouted them.

I tried to sneak a sideways peek at Mack's eyes, but he was leaning in too close to Art, and I could only make out the side of his face—that angry curve of his lips, the muscle twitching in his jaw.

Well, that, and I could make out the nice-looking arm muscles that held Art's blimpy body against the wall. Along with all the other women in the room, I could also make out the well-defined nature of his rear end, which flowed nicely upward into a tapered waist, and just as nicely downward into a set of lean legs.

But I pretended none of that mattered. After all, I should still be skeptical of Mack and his intentions. Letting my mind wander to his body would only lead to dangerous places I'd been before. If crazy meant doing the same thing over again and expecting different results, well, maybe I was less crazy than this town believed because I didn't intend to repeat my former mistakes.

A part of me wanted to go to Art's aid and encourage Mack to set him down. Another part of me felt warm inside for no good reason. I knew Mack wasn't doing this for me, personally. Mack would have yanked Art away from any female he'd laid his hands on. Say what you want about our rumor-infested, gossip mill of a town, but the men of Luck watched out for their women. The good boys, at least.

While I considered how to ask Mack to set Art back down, he did it on his own. Art slumped to the floor as Mack let go. Then, Mack looked down as if there were a pile of cow dung near his shoes.

"Go home, Art. You hear me?" Mack squatted, his arms folded as he looked Art right in the face. "I don't wanna see you back here tonight. In fact, I don't wanna see much of you at all the entire time I'm home. Got it? And if I hear you're laying fingers on the ladies of Luck, I'll be back. I promise you."

Art scampered unsteadily to his feet, then made his way toward the door in his own pile of stink, wiping away a bit of blood around his nose. I wasn't sure how that had gotten there, but Art's eyes were so bleary I bet he would've fallen all on his own at some point during the evening.

"Mack," I called, wanting to thank him before that brat Heather got her pale arms all over him once again. "Mack, wait." I leapt around the edge of the bar and walked quickly after Mack.

But he walked faster than I could, weaving his way through the crowd as if he'd learned from Moses how to part the Red Sea.

"Mack!" I hollered one more time, loudly enough that any souls in the room who weren't already paying attention swiveled their gazes to me.

But Mack still didn't stop.

He marched right on out of the auditorium, past the Reunion Day banner flapping under the night sky with the stars reflecting off the shiny white paper. I stopped in my tracks, watching him go.

I simply couldn't bring myself to chase after a man who didn't want to be caught.

CHAPTER 34

"WHAT HAPPENED?" NOELLE RUSHED UP to the bar with lipstick smudged on her cheek and her hair in disarray. "Are you okay? I heard there was a tussle."

I raised an eyebrow as I looked at her. Despite my upset feelings toward Mack at the moment, I couldn't help feeling the twist of a grin on my lips at Noelle's adorable display of concern. She looked like a guilty teenager who was sneaking in a little after midnight with a turtleneck pulled over her neck to hide a hickey. "Where have you been? I thought *everyone* had seen what happened."

"Not everyone," Noelle hissed. Lowering her voice, she leaned toward me. "Chet took me outside for a walk. We were gonna talk."

"Yeah, you were *gonna*." I leaned on the bar, shooting a *yeah, right* sort of look in her direction. The one good thing about the events of the evening was that people didn't feel the need to refresh their alcoholic beverages, which meant Noelle and I had a bit of privacy around the bar. "What, did he get lost walking outside? Because it looks like his lips found your face. All of your face. I mean, maybe I've been doing kissin' wrong because you have lipstick up by your eyebrow. I ain't *never* kissed so much that my lipstick slid up to my eyebrow."

"What?" Noelle's face turned horrified. She picked up a silver serving tray and began examining her face in there. "Oh, my. Sweet baby Jesus, I need to go die now. Can you believe I walked all the way through that crowded room with lipstick like a rainbow on my forehead? I'm finished in this town, Scarlett. I am so embarrassed."

"At least you didn't run after a man screamin' his name, only to have him keep on walking out on you." I shrugged. "Frankly, I'd trade places because at least you got to do some kissin' before the embarrassment. I didn't even get the good stuff first."

"Oh, honey." Noelle set the wine glass down and turned a pair of sympathetic eyes on me. Somehow, she'd managed to remove all the errant lipstick, and her face looked just as pretty as ever. Even the slightly disheveled nature of her hair looked chic, where on me, it would've looked like I'd jammed a few forks in the toaster. "I thought you and Mack had made up. I didn't realize he walked away from you."

I shook my head, refilling my own wine glass. "Made up? What gave you that impression?" I didn't have a buzz yet because each time I tried to enjoy my glass of vino, someone kindly came along and interrupted me with their nonsense. "I guess I don't really know what we are, the two of us. All I know is that Art, that drunken fool, tried to make out with my face from across the bar. You know, now that I think about it, I could see that ending up in lipstick over my eyebrow, but for entirely different reasons."

Noelle gave me a cut-to-the-chase glance. "What happened?"

"Mack just stormed over here and kicked Art out." I remembered the brief whiff of his scent as he'd swept past me, the flex of his muscles as he'd slammed Art's body against the wall, and the anger simmering in his facial expression. I took another sip of wine. "But he wasn't doing that for me. You know Mack. He would've done that for any lady."

"Maybe," Noelle said, sounding unconvinced. "But he did it for you, which means he was lookin' out for you, at least. I'm telling you, I know all this looks bad for Mack, but I just can't find it in myself to believe he'd ever hurt you."

"I don't think so," I said, my voice turning soft. "I don't think he'd hurt me. Maybe I don't know why he's back in town, or why he's appearing in all these places shortly before there's trouble, but I don't think he wants to hurt me."

"Then why the long face?"

"Because, Noelle. Not wanting to hurt me and wanting us to be friends are two separate things entirely. Plenty of people don't want to hurt me, but that doesn't mean they wanna talk to me, either."

"Where is this coming from?" Noelle reached across the bar, removed the glass of wine from my fingers, and put both her hands on my shoulders. Then, that girl shook me until I begged her to stop. "Get a grip on yourself, Scarlett. I know you have a lot on your mind, but you're not thinking clear."

"I am thinking clear. It's just that the thoughts are confusing."

"He wanted to take you out on a date. You said no." Noelle tilted her head sideways. "You know me. I'm always Team Scarlett. I'm always on your side. But have you ever thought maybe *he* is hurt from your rejection?"

"He's not hurt!" I retorted, the words coming out before I could even think about whether or not they were true. "He had his chance. Why'd he leave if he wanted his chance?"

Noelle looked down. "Like I said, I'm Team Scarlett. You wanna go out with him, I support you. You want nothing to do with him, well hell, I'll support that too. But this in-between thing has got to stop."

"How do I stop it?"

"You want to know why he left?"

I bit my lip, then after a moment, gave a nod.

"Then ask him." Noelle's words were firm, but her eyes were soft. "Go after him and sit down for a drink. If he answers your questions, good. If not, you have your answer. Either way, you stop this waffling back and forth."

I nodded, wondering how Noelle had the ability to make things sound so simple when in my head, things were a confusing, jumbled mess of false clues, unexplained disappearances, and unresolved issues.

"I suppose you're right," I said with a sigh. "Darn it, Noelle. I didn't think I'd be taking advice from you tonight, seeing how you're slinking around with that Chet boy." I leaned in, noting the sparkle in her eye. "So tell me, how was it?"

"We didn't do nothin' like that! Gosh, Scarlett." Noelle swatted me. "We just went for a little walk outside, down past the hotel across the street and into the gardens at the end of the road. The flowers were bloomin', and it was beautiful."

"Right. Like you were lookin' at the flowers."

Noelle laughed. "He's a nice boy, Scarlett. We just kissed a few times. There's no harm in that."

"There ain't nothing wrong with that. And you know I don't make judgments about pretty much anything." I crossed my arms. "So what about this man you've gone out with on two dates back home? You gonna dump him now?"

Noelle looked a teensy bit guilty. "That one hasn't even kissed me yet. We're not exclusive or anything like that. We went for coffee once, and then drinks the next week. It's nothing serious."

"And what is Chet?"

"Chet is… unexpected," Noelle said, her eyes focused on something I couldn't see in an alternate world. Maybe she was concentrating on the high of love; I didn't know much about that.

"You didn't answer my question. Are you gonna dump this guy back home?"

She shrugged again. "I probably won't have to. We went out two weeks ago, and I've texted him twice, once right after, then once just before I left town. I know, I know, maybe it seemed needy. But I just wanted to see him one last time. Maybe get that goodbye kiss I'd been anglin' for."

I looked at my stunning best friend, already knowing what she'd say before she came out and said it.

"He didn't respond." She cleared her throat. "Dating is strange up in New York. It's like nobody believes in manners anymore."

"I'm sorry, Noelle." I reached out, sensing that she was hiding more hurt than she wanted to show. "Any man who doesn't text you back is an outright idiot. I'm saying that as a blanket fact. You're funny, you're smart, and you're the most beautiful thing I've ever seen, and I'm not just saying that because you're my best friend."

"But there's a lot of funny and smart people up in New York."

"And you're the best one." I reached out and gave her shoulder a squeeze. "Trust me, I just know that for a fact. And anyone that doesn't realize it is a prick with their head up their ass. You hear me?"

She smiled. "I don't believe that's true, but it makes me feel better, anyway."

"I'm glad you had a chance to get some kissin' in down here," I said with a smile. "I would sure hate to see you torn up over a man who doesn't deserve your second thought. Just remember that, okay?"

"You're the greatest." Noelle stepped around the bar and pulled me into a hug. Her expensive perfume smelled airy and elegant as she held me tightly. I secretly hoped some of it would rub off on me and cover up my Dollar General spritz that was scented like Sweet Pea.

"Explain one thing to me, though," Noelle said, wrinkling her nose as we pulled apart. "If you two didn't make up, then why did you give him the keys to your car?"

"What? I didn't!" I reached for my clutch next to the bar, opened it, and showed Noelle the contents. "They're right here."

"Huh."

"Huh, *what?*"

"Well, either he borrowed them for a minute, or he broke into your car since I remember you locking it. You beeped the horn twice, and you know that always drives me nuts."

I narrowed my eyes. "Mack, the man who just stormed out of the bar was in my car?"

She pursed her lips. "Well, he wasn't driving it around or anything. He just had his head stuck inside the front door. That's why I came back in here, to get the juicy details of your newly made-up friendship, which was why I was surprised to hear all of this."

I bit my lip. "That ain't right, Noelle. Mack broke into my car, and there are only two main reasons people break into cars."

"Only two?"

"They either wanna steal something like the radio, the car itself, or a purse." I paused, looking up at her. "Or else they're lookin' for something."

"But what would he be looking for?"

"I don't know, but I intend to find out. Can you watch the bar?"

"I'm coming with you."

"You already said it, Noelle. He doesn't want to hurt me. It's high time I talk to him and find out what's going on." I handed her the martini shaker and stepped out from behind the bar. "Plus, the car is in a public area with people coming and going at all times. Nothing could possibly happen to me."

Noelle looked dubious. "Well, keep your phone on you. If you're not back in five minutes, I'm coming out to find you. I'm only letting you go because you're parked right out front, and there's lots of people going to and from their vehicles."

"I'll be fine," I said. "We're at a Reunion Day. What's the worst that could happen?"

CHAPTER 35

Dear Diary,

WHAT DID I *TELL* YOU about me saying that phrase? I give you permission to give me a nice, solid clock to the face. Give me a shiner. I deserve it. Never in a million years am I gonna ask what could possibly go wrong. Because the answer, in my experience, is always EVERYTHING.

Before I went outside, I filled Noelle in on all the information I'd learned from Frank's widow. Unfortunately explaining it one more time just opened up more questions I hadn't thought up the first time. Like, even if Joe was blackmailing Frank, why would that be a reason for Joe to kill Frank? If anything, Joe would prefer Frank alive in order to keep that extra business coming his way. Unless, maybe Joe got a taste for the extra business and decided that he wanted to eliminate the competition completely.

See what I mean? So many questions, and no answers. Then there's Angela. What's with her flauntin' that rock on her finger so hard? It was as if she bought it herself; she's so proud of that thing. And where is Joe tonight? He should be here with her. She said so herself. This business trip of Joe's smells fishy, but until I find him I have no clue where he was headed. Ryan slash Ralph didn't seem to have a clue either.

Don't even get me started on Mack. I hadn't confirmed that he was the one at Joe's shop poking around where he didn't belong, but my gut feeling told me he was a valid suspect. Also, Mack *must*

150

have seen Frank sometime before he died in order to pick up that shiny black Audi. Then, Mack had conveniently "stopped over" right before my place was ransacked. Now, he was going through my car? If he's lookin' for something, why doesn't he just ask? I'm not hiding anything.

My head is about to explode. Diary, I am sitting on a huge house of cards that's ready to topple over, but I can't put my finger on exactly which card I need to slide out in order to make the entire web of lies collapse.

I suppose I can start by paying my car a visit and seeing if Noelle's information is correct. I can ask Mack why he keeps breaking into places around town. The man's not a petty thief. He's got plenty of money from Hollywood, I'm sure, so what is he playing at?

The next step is Joe. I need to find him.

Love,
Scarlett

CHAPTER 36

FTER CONVINCING NOELLE TO LET me go check on my car while she watched the bar, I made my way through the hungry crowd of folks descending on the food table. A few of them took hesitant steps toward the dance floor, migrating in groups of twos and threes as the music picked up the pace. The bobbing, awkward dance moves gave me some added cover as I snaked my way through the sea of bodies.

Mack had left ten minutes before. If he'd gone straight out to my car to rob it, or more likely to snoop around, then he would be long gone. If he wasn't breaking into my car, then there had to be a perfectly logical solution that he could explain in person. Even Noelle had agreed Mack wasn't a danger to my health—at least, not my physical health. Mental and emotional health were an entirely different conversation.

I caught a glimpse of that brat Heather standing with the same sidekick she'd had all through grade school and into college. Heather had been the queen bee of the popular girls her entire life. The fact that she was still rich as God meant she'd kept her title.

She sneered at me as I strode past her, but I pretended I didn't notice. When Mack had stormed away from me ten minutes prior, Heather had waited only a second before chasing after him, shooting me scathing glares over her shoulder. But that didn't matter because either she hadn't managed to catch Mack, or he hadn't wanted to be caught. Or both.

Striding under the Reunion Day banner, I spotted my car in

the corner of the lot. It was parked in the first row, which was plenty visible from the front entrance. Even so, it was dark out, and the trees surrounding the parking lot seemed foreboding instead of charming, and the light from the stars had turned eerie instead of romantic.

I hesitated, wondering if I should have had Noelle walk with me.

Just as quickly as that thought popped into my head, I tried to un-think it. I wasn't going to let some outsider back in town for Reunion Day scare me away from my own vehicle, even if his name was Mack Montgomery. Plus, there were still plenty of couples mingling around the parking lot. Most of them had their lips locked on one another, but a few of them looked to be loners. Surely, their presence would keep anyone—Mack or otherwise—from doing something stupid, like breaking into my car.

I clicked the unlock button and strode to the car, scanning the parking lot out of the corner of my eyes.

Nothing.

I breathed a sigh of relief as I reached the lavender door of my bug. My grasp on the familiar handle felt comforting in the dark of night. I pulled open the door, poked my head inside, and took stock of the interior. As far as I could tell, nothing had been touched. In fact, I'd just cleaned the car out before I brought it into Frank's for repair, so everything was actually straightened and in place for once.

After popping open the glove compartment, the center console, and checking every other cubby, I found nothing missing or out of place. I straightened as a feeling of relief took hold and the stress slipped away from my shoulders. I'd been nervous for nothing.

I walked around to the rear of the car and popped open the trunk.

Just as quick, I wished I'd left it shut.

CHAPTER 37

Dear Diary,

I JUST TOLD YOU I WANTED to talk to Joe. Well, I don't want to talk to him anymore.

Scarlett

Chapter 38

Joe's business trip hadn't ended well. In fact, it was the last trip he would ever take, except for a ride to the morgue. His unseeing eyes stared up at me from the depths of my recently cleaned trunk. I clasped a hand to my mouth to hold in a gag.

But I couldn't hold in that gag for long. For lack of something better to do, I slammed the trunk shut. I stumbled over to the bushes, trying to keep quiet, but I was unable to hold in the contents of my stomach. I relieved each and every thing from my dinner into the bushes. It was as if the universe was telling me I wasn't meant to drink an entire glass of wine that night.

I stood up, swiping a hand across my mouth. Glancing around the parking lot, I thanked my lucky stars that nobody had noticed my foray into the bushes. Thankfully, the bushes were pretty big, and I had tried hard to keep quiet. The couples holding hands and traipsing across the parking lot were oblivious to me, and to the dead body renting out space in my trunk.

Shock must have grabbed hold of my insides right then and there because I didn't even think of all the logical questions, such as: Why was he there? Who'd put Joe in my car? If Joe was dead, then what did that mean for Frank? Because as much as I'd tried not to assume anything, a part of me would have sworn that Joe had taken part in Frank's demise.

Then all at once, a thought popped into my head out of nowhere that caused all other thoughts to vanish. Maybe the killer was still hanging around. My skin prickled with goosebumps as I scanned the dark woods. I took a step forward.

Was the killer inside? Inside the reunion?

I took another step away from the bushes. Had I served the murderer alcohol tonight, or maybe even brushed my hand against theirs? Had I murmured a greeting as I'd handed over a sparkling spritzer? My stomach roiled at the thought that someone might still be wandering around, gossiping and dancing with the rest of the crowd while the body of a local citizen lay dead in the trunk of my car.

Either the shock wore off all of a sudden, or it gave me the kick in the tush I needed to get going. I snapped out of my haze and figured I needed to *do* something. I debated running inside, grabbing Noelle, and calling the police. Although for some strange reason, I didn't want to leave the car. I was going to stay right there and guard Joe until someone could take care of him in a respectful way.

My fingers fumbled when I dialed Noelle's number, so I was glad I had her on speed dial. She picked up right away. "Noelle? Noelle, I need you to come outside—"

Before I could finish speaking, the scent of something fruity and light filtered up to my nostrils right before a hand clamped down over my mouth.

"Scarlett, are you all right?" Noelle asked over the phone line.

I tried my best to respond, but the most I could do was bite down on the hand covering my mouth—a man's hand, judging by the size of it. I unleashed all the fury I had in my body with that one little bite, and I was proud to say I drew blood.

"Scarlett, answer me," Noelle demanded as my attacker groaned loudly.

I tasted metal as I struggled to respond, but the man didn't loosen his grip in the slightest. Instead, he started hauling me back toward the woods. At the same time, all those thoughts swirling around in my head started to blend together. The edges of my vision became a little foggy, and I couldn't seem to get the right words to come out of my mouth.

The blackness hovering around my consciousness grew stronger. I think the phone slipped from my grasp, but since I couldn't feel most of my body, it was hard to be sure.

"Scarlett!" This time, Noelle's voice pierced the night air instead of coming through the phone.

I raised a hand, trying to wave, but my arm didn't listen to my brain. It didn't move at all. I couldn't figure out which direction her voice had come from.

The scent of fruit and flowers got stronger then, as did the fogginess.

I closed my eyes.

Maybe it would just be easier to sleep...

CHAPTER 39

See, Diary?

THIS IS WHY I TOLD you to slap me if I ever said things couldn't get any worse. I'm tempted to say this is the low point of my evening, but I'm not stupid. Because if I say, "Things can't get any worse," right now, I reckon the universe will see that as a challenge. And the universe always wins.

Diary, I don't know what I did wrong to piss off the universe, but it sure had it out for me tonight. Because even though I didn't ask if things could get worse again, they did anyway.

Scarlett

Chapter 40

W HEN I OPENED MY EYES, I was alive. I'm pretty sure at least, judging by the headache in my skull. I was pretty sure dead people didn't suffer from aching noggins.

Assuming I wasn't dead, then I'd woken up in some sort of hotel room. As I regained snippets of memories—a hand over my mouth, Joe's dead body, Noelle's cries as I was hauled into the woods—the entire story started coming back to me. My mind flashed to the hotel across the street from the reunion center, and I wondered if my attacker had dragged me across the street.

That scenario begged a few more questions: How had a strange man hauled me all the way across the street without someone noticing? Were people really that oblivious?

I raised a hand to my forehead, but the pounding made it difficult to think.

"Drink this." The male voice startled me, and I flinched hard, immediately trying to sit up.

The ground beneath me was soft. I couldn't sit up, so I lashed out with my legs at the voice. I didn't come into contact with a human, but I did wind up tangled in a pile of bed sheets.

I lunged forward, then cried out in pain when one of my arms met resistance. I realized I'd been handcuffed to a bedpost, and I'd yanked against it so hard my arm had nearly flown right out of its socket. As I fell back, I closed my eyes, not wanting to see the man who'd kidnapped me then cuffed me to a hotel bed. "If you wanna kill me, just get it over with, already."

I sensed a large, hulking figure at the end of the bed. I purposefully hadn't looked at him yet. I was afraid I'd crumble in fear if I saw the man's face. I hadn't recognized his voice. When he'd spoken, his words had been so low, so close to a whisper, that I could hardly understand them. Then again, I was in so much shock, I hardly recognized my own voice.

To my surprise, the man gave a short laugh. "I ain't gonna kill you, Scarlett. Though I do have to admit, you're difficult to get a hold of—wiggly little fighter, you are."

My eyes shot open. "Mack?"

He raised an eyebrow at me from where he was perched lazily in a chair at the end of the bed. Kicking his feet up nonchalantly on the desk, he looked for all the world like a model in a home furniture magazine. It was just wrong how a man could be so good-looking that he made me have naughty thoughts, even when I lay there, kidnapped at his hands.

"Drink this." He handed me the glass again, which was a cup of water with a colorful token at the bottom emitting a bubbly fizz. "It'll help with the headache."

"Hold on a second. You think I'm 'hard to get a hold of'?" I blinked. "You kidnapped me. Was I supposed to make it *easy*? Let me go, you perv." I yanked at the hand cuffed to the bed as if to emphasize my point.

He watched, his gaze patient. "I did it for your own good. And don't be stubborn. Drink up. I promise you it'll help."

"How do I know you ain't gonna drug me again?"

"It was a very mild sedative." Mack's expression flashed with an emotion that looked like discomfort. "I didn't want to, I promise you. But like I said, you're a fighter, and I couldn't take the risk that *they'd* see us."

"Who's they?"

He ignored me. "I had to get you here, lock you up, and then go back out there for a bit. I couldn't risk you makin' a sound."

"Well, I didn't give you permission to *mildly tranquilize* me. Now that I think about it, I also didn't give you permission to handcuff me in a hotel room."

"I'm not a perv."

"If the shoe fits." I slammed the glass onto the table next to me, wishing I had both arms free so I could cross them. Since I didn't, I settled for glaring at Mack just as hard as I could. "I'm not drinkin' it."

"Drink it."

I reached a hand over and tipped the glass on its side so the water soaked right into the armchair next to the bed. "I'm *not* drinkin' it."

The glass continued to roll off the edge of the dresser, and I lunged for it, forgetting I was still handcuffed. My cuffed arm held me back, and the glass rolled right off, hitting the floor hard.

There went dropped glass number four for the evening. How high would the number get before I could just go to bed and pray that none of this had been real?

He sighed. "I used to love how stubborn you were, but right now it's wearin' on me, sweetheart."

"Then start explaining."

"I *can't*. I told you that," Mack said. "I just need you to cooperate."

With a hugely sarcastic eye roll, I pasted a goofy grin on my face and gave him crazy eyes. "Why sure, Mr. Mack. I'll blindly cooperate with the man who has been sneakin' around this town ever since he came back—for the first time in ten years—and who just recently drugged me and kidnapped me away from the scene of a murder." I shook away the sarcasm, my voice ringing with a bit of hurt. "What, did you think I got *stupider* while you were gone?"

"I never once thought you came close to stupid," Mack said. His voice was soft, dangerous. "I think you're the smartest, stubbornest woman I know, but I also think you have a problem trustin' me. You don't have to know every single detail."

"You're right!" My voice rose. "And I'm not asking for every detail. I'm just asking for some of 'em."

Mack fell silent. He kicked his feet down from the desk and spun around to face me. As he rested his elbows on his knees, he sized me up through narrowed eyes.

"I'm part of this… this *thing,* whatever it is." Shifting uncomfortably under his gaze, I continued. "I just want to understand. And frankly, I'm still waiting to hear one good reason I should trust you."

"There's not a thing in this world I can say to make you trust me." Mack stood, the fight in him softening as his gaze flashed over me, and a new desperation appeared in his eyes.

"Well, then what do you expect me to do?"

He took his time walking around the bed. He came to the side where my hand was cuffed, and with the gentleness of someone holding a newborn baby, he rested his hand on my cheek and stroked his thumb over my lips.

"I intend to *show* you," he said before bending his head. His lips brushed mine, but instead of locking for a kiss, he brought his hand up to my shoulder. Ever so gently, Mack hooked his finger on one of the sleeves of my beautiful black gown, which was a bit wrinkled from wear and tear, and straightened it back up on my shoulder.

The sleeve had slid down, and I hadn't even noticed. With him so close, I could smell the fresh mint of his breath, and I wondered if he could hear the pounding of my heart.

Then he looked me in the eyes, his lips hardly a whisper away, and he murmured in my ear, "Just give me some time. I need a chance. I need more than a minute to show you how I feel, sweetheart."

I almost said "no" right off the bat, wanting to demand further explanation before I'd even consider taking the time to talk with him. But Noelle's words came back to me—her absolute belief that Mack didn't want me hurt. I took one long, shaky breath before I raised my head and nodded. "Fine."

"Really?" Mack's eyes widened, and his back stiffened as he stood up straight. The look on his face reminded me of a child surprised on Christmas morning. "You mean that?"

His expression was so adorable, I couldn't help but laugh. "Yes, I mean that. I'll talk with you, but can you uncuff me first?"

He winced. "I'd like to…"

"But?"

"Let's play a game," he said. "I ask you one question, and then you ask me one. Once we've asked three questions each, then I'll uncuff you. Hopefully by that time, you'll understand what's happening here, and you won't try to run off and do something dangerous."

I bit my lip, but then again, it didn't take me long to figure out that I wasn't exactly in a position to argue. "Fine. Three questions?"

He raised an eyebrow.

"Oh, stop it. That doesn't count. Who's going first?"

This time, he laughed.

"That doesn't count either!" I abruptly shut my mouth before I could ask another question.

"You go first," he said. "Three questions, starting now. So make 'em good. Or don't. It's your choice."

I swallowed hard, taking time to consider all my options. On one hand, three questions seemed so limiting… *only three?* I had hundreds I wanted Mack to answer. At the same time, three questions was an overwhelming number. What three questions, out of hundreds, deserved the highest priority?

I coughed, then I bit my lip, and eventually I couldn't think of anything else to do in order to keep on stalling. So I went ahead and asked the broadest, most all-encompassing question I could come up with. "What happened here tonight?"

Mack didn't flinch and didn't bother to move. For the first time since I woke up, I realized that his eyes had just the slightest red tinge to them. *Pepper spray?* If so, he must have done a good job of rinsing his face because he didn't look too bad. Either that, or my aim wasn't as good as I'd thought.

"Well, I don't know all the answers to that," he drawled slowly, strolling back to his chair at the end of the bed. He sat down, kicked his feet back up on the desk, and reclined. When he continued speaking, it was to the wall. "This is how I see it. We came to the reunion, you found the dead body, and we ended up here."

"Mack." My voice had a heavy warning lilt to it. "Don't start with me."

"That's an answer."

"Then don't expect much from my answer."

"What's your wish?"

His question threw me off, and it took my brain a few seconds to rewire. Thankfully, my mouth didn't blurt out any answers that time. "My wish is for you to tell me a better answer than that load of bull."

Mack laughed, the sound soft and amused. He threw a glance over his shoulder at me. "You're not fun to play this game with, sweetheart."

"How many women have you played it with over the years?" I asked in a wry voice. "Actually, don't answer that. I'm not wastin' my question on something as silly as that."

Mack didn't answer. Even though he was following my instructions not to answer, I sorta wanted to know. However, I had too much Texas pride to waste my question on something as trivial as Mack's dating life. I was dealing with some life-and-death issues here, so any other conversations would have to wait.

"Why'd you ask me to play this stupid game if you didn't plan on answering any questions?" I shrugged. "I'm not technically in a position to argue, but if you think this is going to be a one-way conversation, you're wrong. I'll sit here all night, handcuffed to the bed. Don't think I won't."

"Oh, I know you will." Mack steepled his hands in front of his lips. "Like I said, I've never doubted your stubbornness."

I let out a long sigh.

"Tonight," he started. This time, his voice turned hard, and his words were clipped and emotionless. It was almost scary how fast he'd changed on me. "Tonight, let's see. I'm guessing you figured out it was me over at Joe's shop pokin' around."

"I suspected, but I didn't know for sure. Can you confirm or deny?"

Mack's eyes flashed up at me. "What is this, an interrogation? That counts as a question."

"Does not," I retorted. He didn't argue, so I assumed he was okay with my decision. I also took that as a *yes*.

"You so kindly pepper-sprayed me," he continued. "I didn't realize it was you out back at first. That's the only reason I had the gun out. When I saw you whippin' away in that purple little bug of yours, I realized my mistake. I'm sorry I had my gun out. You know I'd never hurt you."

"Who did you think was hidin' out back?"

Mack didn't seem to notice that was an extra question, so I didn't push my luck by clarifying that it did not, in fact, count as one of my three.

Instead, his eyes seemed to glaze over, seeing something invisible to me. "Not you," he said. "That's for sure. I thought it was someone else."

"Someone dangerous," I whispered. "Else why would you be walkin' around with your gun drawn?"

Mack glanced at me, his expression the only confirmation I needed.

"That's enough," he said. "I'm gonna finish answerin' your initial question now, since I wanna play this game fair. What happened tonight? Well, after you cruised away from Joe's, I left too. I got ready for the party, and then I came here. You know what happened inside by the bar…" He trailed off, and the image of Mack lifting Art against the wall flashed into my brain again.

I nodded. "But I don't know what happened outside of the venue."

"You're getting better at this game," Mack murmured. "Since that wasn't a question." He cleared his throat. "Well, I left after that idiot Art put his hands on you. I went outside and took a quick peek at your vehicle. I was just getting ready to leave and go home when you came outside. Then you opened your trunk and found Joe. I had to act quickly. I didn't have this part planned. That's why it's a bit rough around the edges."

"By rough around the edges, do you mean having to knock me out and handcuff me to the bed?" I asked wryly. "Speaking of, who the heck *are* you that you walk around carrying knock-out potion on your person? That's not normal. You're starting to scare me."

"Good." Mack's comment sounded like a joke, but when I looked at him it was clear he meant exactly what he said. "You should be scared of me. The smartest thing you've done your whole life is say no to me this week. If I were a different person, a better person, I wouldn't have even asked you out. If I were a stronger man, I would never have stepped foot back in this godforsaken town where I knew I wouldn't be able to resist you."

"You're allowed to come home," I said quietly. "I just don't want to see you leave again. That's why I've been sayin' no. That, and my pile of unanswered questions."

"You don't understand." Mack stood up, fury brimming beneath those brilliant eyes of his. The dress shirt on his back tensed as his muscles flexed. He stood up, his hands balled into fists as he paced back and forth at the end of the bed. "The reason I had to come back is because of *you*, Scarlett. I can't stay the hell away from you."

I didn't know what to say, so for once, I kept my mouth shut.

"It's selfish of me. My work, my job—I *can't* get close to you." Mack stopped his pacing and shoved a hand halfway through that disheveled hair that looked so touchable. "But I can't seem to stay away. I told myself I'd leave you alone, I'd avoid you... and what's the first thing I do? I come over and ask you out on a date. It's like my body can't listen to my brain."

"What do you do?" I asked. "What has you so up in feathers about dating me? You're a stunt car driver. Is it because I'm not pretty enough for Hollywood? Not polished enough for those red carpet events of yours? If that's it, you can tell me. I *know* all those things. I belong here in Luck, not out in the wild, wild, west of La-La Land."

Mack looked as if he wanted to say something, but he didn't. He just bit his lip and watched me, so I kept right on talking.

"That's your domain, that sparkling city. Not mine. It doesn't hurt my feelings. I prefer sundresses to ball gowns, and small towns to a buslin' city. I prefer pecan pie to those kale smoothies, or whatever the diet *du'jour* is out there. And mostly, I prefer real people to fake ones." I shook my head. "People here in Luck can be mean. They can be snippity and uppity, rude and cruel, spiteful and even dishonest. But the one thing they're not is fake. I'd rather know where I stand with these folks here in Luck instead of thinking I have friends in that glamorous place, only to find out that when the going gets tough, my so-called friends are nowhere to be seen."

He watched me, his eyes following my every movement.

I took a deep breath. "Because at the end of the day, these people here in Luck will stick up for me because I'm *one of 'em.*"

My thoughts immediately flashed to Noelle and all she'd done for me. I thought of her parents. I thought of Gray's little hand clasping mine as we read through one of my made-up stories, one in which he'd colored in all the pictures as we cuddled late into the night. I thought of the GURLZ—Tiny, Tootsie, and Tallulah—who'd threatened Dan, the bartender, just so I could score a few bucks to make ends meet. I thought of Frank's widow, who'd given me a second chance despite having every reason not to listen to what I had to say.

I thought of Mack, who even after I'd turned him down more times than I could count, shook some sense into a handsy drunk on my behalf. And I knew that I was speakin' from my heart. I complained about that town, but I didn't belong anywhere else.

"I'm off my soapbox now." I offered a small, slightly embarrassed laugh. I wasn't ashamed of anything I'd said, but it did sort of just blurt out in one big stream of thoughts. Since Mack still wasn't talkin', the silence in the room started to feel a teensy bit awkward.

He cleared his throat. "My turn."

"Hold on. I think as part of question number one, you need to explain one or two more things." I raised a finger—a finger not attached to my handcuffed wrist. "I appreciate your honesty, first of all. I knew you were at Joe's, and I knew you were at my car. But I still don't understand why. And one more thing I'm not clear on is whether or not you knew Joe's body was in my trunk. Or if that was you chasing me in that car the other night."

I was pretty proud of myself for phrasing none of those things as questions, but Mack didn't even seem to notice.

"Chasing you? I'm chasing you, Scarlett, but not in any sort of car. However, I didn't know Joe was in your trunk, which was why I had to react in the moment," he said. "I was just lookin' for something in your car... not to steal, but to keep you safe."

"That makes no sense! How is breaking into my car keeping me safe?"

"The same way handcuffing you to the bed keeps you safe."

"Well, I don't know how that one figures, either. Or why you have that 'knock-out' potion on your person at all times."

"Here's your answer: I keep the sedative on my person because of my job. I needed to lock you up to keep you safe, so *they* didn't find you. And the reason I broke into your car is because *those* same people think you have something of theirs. I didn't think you stole anything, but I had to make sure."

"What do you think I have? What is your job?" To hell with the question count, this was getting strange. When Mack didn't seem inclined to answer, I clarified for him. "So, let's go over this once more. You're saying there's some people after me—probably the same people who killed Joe, and even possibly Frank—and they think I stole something that belongs to them?"

"More or less."

"What? If I had something valuable, I'd sell it. I'd rather pay my rent than hang onto something worth money."

"That's what I thought."

"But you didn't trust me?"

"I just wanted to make sure. That's my job."

"There you go again with that *job* business. What does a stunt driver care?"

"You've had your first question more than answered." Mack crossed his arms. "Now, it's my turn."

"Fair is fair." I leaned back, biting my lip.

"What's your wish?"

"That's honestly your question?"

"You've talked about that one little wish so damn often, I'd like to know what it's all about. And also, did you think I forgot about our pact?"

I looked down. Of course I thought he'd forgotten the pact. He had bigger, better things on his mind than a little promise we'd made at the end of our high school years.

"You thought I forgot." Mack shook his head. "You told me that night, that one night, you told me that you'd tell me your secret wish at our ten-year reunion. Well? We're here."

I remembered the night we'd made our pact as if it were yesterday. Though in retrospect, my tiny little wish seemed stupid.

And impossible. I had no clue why I'd ever thought it had a chance of succeeding.

"You know, if you'd just stuck around that next morning for all of *five minutes,* I would've told you." I swallowed. "It wasn't a secret, not until you made it one."

"I couldn't!" His eyes shifted from mine. "I *couldn't* stick around."

"Let me guess. You're gonna blame this one on your job too."

"Yes, as a matter of fact, I am."

I looked up. "Well, you're blaming one secret on another, so I'm not sure what you want me to say."

Again, Mack looked like he was on the verge of telling me some real information, but then he pulled back at just the last moment. "You really would have told me that day?"

"Yes." I shrugged. "I almost told you that night, but it would've been too quick. But if you'd have asked the next morning, I would have told you. I wasn't ashamed of it. I'm still not ashamed of it. I'm just embarrassed that I ever thought it had the chance of coming true."

"If you're not ashamed, then tell me now."

I almost shouted it out right then, just to get it over with, but I composed myself. And I thought for a moment. "Fine."

Mack looked at me, his eyes scanning mine.

"Here is my wish. I always wanted to own a bookstore," I lied. Well, it wasn't a lie. I *did* want to own a bookstore, but that hadn't been my wish ten years ago.

Mack blinked in surprise.

I shook my head, glancing down at the bedspread. "I used to write these little stories. At first, it was just to keep myself entertained, but in recent years, I've been doing it for Gray. I love it. I don't want to get paid for any of them. I just want people in this town to have access to books. People like Gray, so they can grow up reading. Experiencing all sorts of worlds without having to ever leave Luck."

"There are books here…"

"Yeah, about five of them, total. We don't have a library, and not a single bookstore. Either people bring back books from traveling, or maybe order them online, but what about a place where people of this town can go to read? Enjoy a coffee maybe, and just browse…" My voice turned a bit dreamy as I imagined it, but I shook myself out of the reverie just as quickly as it started. "Anyway, it's stupid. See?"

"It's not stupid." His voice sounded a bit throttled, hesitant almost. "I think it's generous. And I think you'd be the perfect person to own a bookstore."

I waved my un-cuffed hand. "Whatever, it ain't happening. I don't have the money, and this town won't give me the funds. It's a shame, but I've come to terms with it."

"But—"

"That's it," I said firmly. "Now, I want to know what you do for a living. Really."

"Then I want to know your wish, *really*." Mack's lips straightened out into a thin line. "I thought we weren't lyin' to each other."

"I do want to own a bookstore!"

"But that wasn't your wish."

"That's because my wish was insane. And stupid. I always knew you were gonna leave this town. And just as sure, I knew I'd always stay. So, that meant my wish was impossible."

"What was it?" Mack took a few steps, drawing so close to me that my breathing suddenly turned difficult.

"I wanted a happily ever after!" I shouted. My declaration came out loudly, as if all those years of keeping it a secret had been simmering those words, getting them ready to pop right out. Once my wish was out there, the words just kept right on coming, and I couldn't do anything to stop them. "With you, okay? Do you understand?"

Mack's face didn't give away a single clue as to how he was feeling.

"See? Now you understand why it was so stupid. I had a crush on you for all those years, then we had that one night... that one, perfect night. I *knew* it'd have to end. I knew it was too perfect. But that didn't make it hurt any less when you left the next day." The words tumbled out, hard and fast and honest. "But for that one night, for about eight hours, I thought that maybe it would be possible. I even let myself *hope*. And that's where I got myself in trouble. See, hope's a bitch. It can really bite you on the ass, especially when that hope is founded on a wish."

"Scarlett..."

"You don't have to say anything. You asked; I answered. That's it. I came to terms with the fact that I wouldn't get my 'happily ever after' a long time ago. With you, or with anyone." I raised my one free hand then let it drop to my side. "I've come to terms with it. I have... well, I *had* Gray. I have Noelle. I have the GURLZ. I have book club. I'm happy enough."

Mack seemed stunned for the next few minutes. When he finally did speak, it seemed difficult. "Happy *enough* isn't something I can live with, not when it comes to you."

"Well, it's nothing you can do anything about, so let sleeping dogs lie."

"But—"

"That's enough. I told you the honest-to-God truth, and now I want to know the honest-to-God truth about you. What you do for a living, for crying out loud, that has dead people turning up all around you?" I pointed a finger at him. "And before you say anything, I'm just gonna remind you that I have no one to tell, and even less reason to blab. So I don't want any of this 'I can't tell you' bullshit. You can either tell me the truth or just leave me here alone. Got it?"

Mack remained quiet as a bug, just sizing me up. I matched him, eye to eye, even though I would rather have crawled into a hole. I sat there, meeting his gaze, feeling as if someone had taken all my clothes off and made me stand naked in front of a crowd. I'd bared my most hidden secret, my one little wish—the one that had been keeping me going for all these years—the wish that now had to die.

Because I could feel it deep down in my soul. This was the last chance Mack would ever get. It was the very last strand of vulnerability I had inside. If he broke that tiny, fragile thread, there was just nothing I could do about it.

Mack shifted. Then, he walked over to the door, and I thought he was just about ready to walk right out of that hotel room. At the last minute, he leaned his head against the wall. Then, he closed his eyes. I watched his struggle, wishing I could help him. But it was his decision to make.

Finally, one of those sighs that rattle the soul emerged from him. It rattled his body from the inside out. I could see it, starting from a forbidden chamber in his heart and coming out in a guttural cry through his lips.

I hated to see him like that. I really did. But I knew what that sigh meant. It meant he was gonna talk.

"Scarlett…" Mack turned around, and his eyes were clear. I knew that feeling. Making a decision, even if it was the wrong one, was better than being in limbo. "I'm gonna tell you the honest-to-God truth. But remember, you asked for it. Once I tell you, there ain't no going back. Love it, hate it, I don't know what you'll say, but I know you won't forget it."

"I won't say nothin'." I raised my eyes, hoping my expression was a gentle one. "You can trust me. I just want the truth."

"The truth is this." He sighed. "I want to ask you to go out with me and have a drink. That's the truth." A shadow of a smile flicked across his mouth. "In this game, my first question was for you to tell me your wish. My second question was for you to tell me your *real* wish. My third question is this: Will you have a drink with me? Just one?"

"You can have another question. The second one doesn't count. It was my fault for lyin'."

"I don't need another question. I really only needed one. The rest was just gravy." Mack took two paces closer and held up a finger. "Now, I'm going to tell you exactly what I do for a living."

"Is what you do really that bad?"

"That's what you have to decide," he said. "Because I want you to know the whole truth, every last bit of it, before you answer me yes or no. I believe in what I do, but not everyone does. If you say no, it won't hurt my feelings. But I think it's important for you to have all the information before you make any decisions one way or another."

Mack's grim expression sent a chill down my spine.

"Fine." I crossed my arms. "Talk and don't leave anything out. Start from the beginning, please."

CHAPTER 41

Dear Diary,

I WASN'T SURE IF I WANTED to find out what Mack did for a living. Part of me liked the mystery of not knowing, because with mystery, there's always potential. Part of me liked the wonderin', the dreamin', the belief that maybe Mack had reasons that would make our history fall into place, and let everything make sense. Part of me didn't want to find out the truth.

But I couldn't have lived with myself if I told him to stop. I needed to know the truth, Diary. I swear to you, I would never have gotten a full night of sleep if I hadn't heard him out.

And now, I've heard him out.

Diary, do you want to know something?

I still don't know if I want to say yes or no to his question.

Because even though everything makes sense now, I'm not sure if that's for the best... or the worst.

Love,
Scarlett

CHAPTER 42

ACK STARTED SPEAKING JUST THEN. He looked at me, and I could tell the words coming out of his mouth were the truth. "That one night, and the morning after when I left..." He sighed. "Scarlett, I knew a week before that night we spent together that I was going to have to leave."

"Why did you do that to me, then?" I cried out. "Why'd you stay the night if you *knew* you were gonna disappear without a word the next morning?"

"If you want the truth, you have got to *listen*." Mack's expression was no-nonsense. "It's hard enough as it is for me to say these things, and if you keep interrupting, we're never gonna get anywhere."

I closed my mouth, gave a begrudging nod, and sat back against the pillows.

"I did it because I loved you." Mack looked at me, watching, waiting for my reaction.

I only had time for one reaction. My head shot up, a look of surprise on my face. Before I could say anything, we were interrupted by someone else entirely. Or rather, something.

A *bang* sounded from outside the room. It was so loud my eardrums rattled.

I threw myself against the sheets as fast as I could, but my handcuffed arm tangled with the sheets, and I yelped in pain. At least I think I did, but I couldn't hear anything. If I'd thought that "mild sedative" had left me with a headache, well, that was nothing compared to the aftereffects of a gunshot ten feet from my skull.

By the time I realized what had happened, about ten more things had happened. That first bang had been a gunshot, blazing its way through the door. Luckily, it lodged in the wall next to the hotel bathroom, and not in any human flesh, mine nor Mack's.

Mack had disappeared. At least, I thought he had until I saw a movement in the corner behind the door. The movement turned out to be Mack gesturing for me to hover even lower on the bed. I slouched, but thanks to that handcuff, I couldn't do much better than that.

I tried my hardest to remain quiet, despite my heart pounding so hard I could feel it in my ears. All my efforts to remain silent flew out the window when a hand flung the hotel room's door open. Either the intruder had a key, or Mack hadn't locked it. Probably the former. When a gun appeared in the hand opening the door, I couldn't help it. I yelled, and I yelled loudly.

"Mack, look out!" I flailed against the bed, going nowhere. "Mack!"

But Mack didn't need my help. He had a gun raised, waiting, training the end of it on the person stepping through the door. But he didn't shoot yet.

I struggled against my bindings, wondering if that would be the moment I would die. I didn't want to die. I still didn't know what sort of business Mack did that made guns appear around every corner. Although, he *had* said he loved me. Maybe I *could* die a happy girl. Then again, I'd be happier if I didn't die at all.

What was he waiting for? Time seemed to slow down, but all those thoughts flashed through my head in under a second. By the time I looked back at the door, that hand had turned into a full body... a man's body. And that man had Mack cornered, a gun to his head.

Mack dropped his gun and raised his hands above his head in surrender.

177

"Where are they?" the man growled. "Give them to me, or you die."

Before I could use my brain, my mouth began working for me. I needed to do something. I needed to distract the man.

"I don't have them," Mack said. "I don't have what you're looking for."

"Liar," the man snarled.

"I have them, not him," I shouted, as the gunman's trigger finger tensed. "I have what you're looking for. It's *me* you want, not him."

That moment of hesitation when the man looked up, that brief instant when he glanced away, was all Mack needed. Mack lashed out, his leg sweeping the intruder from his feet, sending his body clattering to the floor. In the next second, Mack had wrestled the gun from the man's hand, slammed the door shut, and pinned the intruder tightly to the grimy carpet.

"I need to borrow those cuffs," Mack said to me, reaching into the back pocket of his fancy dress slacks and removing a few small keys. He tossed them across the room so they landed within my reach. "Can you unhook yourself?"

"You didn't ask nicely." I tried to keep my hands from shaking as I grabbed the keys from their landing place on the bed. "What if I want to keep them as a souvenir?"

"I'll handcuff you to the bed anytime you want." Mack looked over toward where I was working to uncuff myself, and he had the guile to wink as I set myself free.

Rubbing my wrist, I hurried across the room and dropped both the keys and the cuffs into Mack's outstretched hand. Then, I walked to the door, opened it a crack, and peeked out.

"Get away from there!" Mack called, fastening the man's hands behind his back. He grabbed a cushion from the nearby armchair and shoved it over his attacker's face as a temporary silencing device. "You tryin' to get yourself killed?"

"I just wanted to make sure no more of 'em were coming," I said. "I've been surprised by guns and shooting enough in the last few days. Just once, I want a heads up *before* the gunshot is fired."

Mack glared at me, then at the man lying still beneath him, then back at me. "Anyone out there?" His expression said he didn't want to ask, but he couldn't resist the opportunity.

"Coast is clear right now." I shut the door. "How about I stand as the lookout while you ask him questions."

"How do you know I want to ask him questions?" Mack's eyebrow rose, his expression mystified.

"Do you want to or not?"

"Two minutes. Stand outside and look pretty, then if—"

"Look pretty?"

"Well seeing how you're already gorgeous, just stand outside, I guess." Mack looked exasperated. "Because that way, if someone with a gun comes, you give one knock on the door and then just walk right on by them. They'll never suspect a woman lookin' like you would be involved with a guy like me."

"A guy like you?"

"I'll explain later. Just *trust* me."

I swallowed, thinking I had a lot of comments to follow that one up. Instead of wasting more time, I gave one look at the guy wriggling on the floor with the pillow over his mouth, and I decided that if I didn't get outside quickly, the guy might not be able to breathe very well. Then, he wouldn't be answering any questions.

Stepping outside and closing the door, I straightened up my dress. I smoothed down the front, pulled up the straps, then set to putzing with my hair. I no longer had my phone on me, and my handbag was still at the bar... if nobody had stolen it.

Judging by the darkness seeping through the windows at the end of the hall, it was still nighttime, and the distant *thump* of a bass made me realize that I couldn't have been knocked out for very long if that was the sound of the Reunion Day dance party.

Mild sedative, my ass. We'd have to talk about his way of making me listen to him later. For now, I wasn't doing any talking. I was doing the "looking." The hallway stayed quiet for the next minute or so, with the exception of one lady opening the door to the hallway, then muttering "wrong floor" and turning around.

I did my best to tuck some flyaway hairs behind my ears and flatten out the frizz that had sprouted up with my adventures. Unfortunately, without a purse or a phone I couldn't do much. Plus, my hands felt useless without my usual devices to hold their attention. I strolled halfway down the hall just so I could catch a glimpse of myself in the mirror.

Yikes. No self-respecting Texas gal would walk around during Reunion Day looking like she'd been dragged through a pile of sticks and leaves then bounced around a bit before getting shoved into a fancy dress. At least the gown looked relatively unscathed, despite a slight smear of mascara under my eyes, a touch of lipstick on my front teeth, and a little twig sticking out of my hair.

I set to work, making myself as presentable as possible without the help of Noelle. Normally, I wouldn't care all that much, but something about knowing Mack was right behind that door spurred me into some serious action. I shouldn't really care what he thought about my appearance, especially in a moment like this, but I had time to kill.

Leaning closer to the window, I bared my teeth like a lion, licked my finger, then rubbed my front tooth vigorously to get off the smudge of lipstick glaring back at me. Just as I was rubbing away with all the elbow grease I could muster, I heard the light *click* of a hotel door behind me.

I straightened up, my spine snapping to rigid attention as I spotted Mack behind me. Whipping around, I ducked my chin to hide the blush on my cheeks from being caught grooming myself instead of looking out for the bad guys.

"I didn't know *lookout* meant starin' at yourself in the window."

Mack crossed his arms over his chest, somehow looking like a picture out of a magazine, even after a gun had just been shoved up his nose. His dress shirt still had crisp iron lines, and his pants were pleated and showed off those gorgeous legs of his.

Meanwhile, I'd been sleeping through the last few hours, and I looked as if I'd been in a fight with a treehouse and lost. What was his beauty secret?

"Well, we all can't look as put together as you after fighting off guys with guns," I said, trying and failing to look tough. "At least you knew this guy was coming… at least, it seems like you did, since you're carrying a gun yourself."

"Carrying a gun ain't that unusual down here, sugar."

"No, but…" I tilted my chin up. "So? You still knew he was coming."

Mack took two steps toward me, putting one hand on each of my shoulders and loosening my arms from their pretzel position across my chest. "You look gorgeous just how you are. Yes, even with lipstick on your teeth." He pulled me in closer, first tucking some of those flyaway hairs behind my ear, then giving me a kiss on the forehead. Before he pulled away, he spoke softly. "We've gotta get out of here."

Mack hooked his arm through mine then marched me down the hallway.

"This is the weirdest date I've ever been on," I said as Mack cinched an arm tighter around my waist. "You are one strange man, Mack Montgomery."

"I didn't know this was a date, but I'll take any excuse I can to take you out. You know what they say. Desperate times call for desperate measures." Mack glanced over at me. "As a matter of fact, that's a good idea. You just pretend to *like* me, as if we're just a couple staying at the hotel, heading out on the town for a nice dinner. If we're lucky, the receptionist won't ask questions."

"I'll do my best," I muttered. As we passed the door from which we'd emerged moments before, I noticed a Do Not Disturb sign on the lock. "What did you do to him?"

Mack ignored my question. "We've gotta get out of here. We've got until housekeeping finds him tomorrow morning before people start asking questions."

"Get away?" My heart started pumping. "Mack, I didn't *do* anything. I'm not 'getting away' anywhere. Not with you, not by myself, not with anyone."

We'd reached the lobby by this point, and the concierge at the front desk hardly glanced up. He was looking down at his computer already as he called out, "Have a wonderful evening, Mr. and Mrs. James."

"James is now your last name?" I whispered, trying to ignore the burning sensation on my face from the front desk man assuming we were a married couple. "They don't usually remember names."

"They do if you leave a good enough tip." Mack led me outside, and the crisp air jolted me even more awake. The breeze ruffled Mack's hair, causing it to stand on end in cute little tufts. "They're also a lot less likely to open their traps if people come asking questions. Plus, even if they find out my name is fake, they'll just assume we're having an affair."

"You want people to assume we're having an affair?"

"Pick your poison, babe. Affair or kidnapping?"

I blinked. "I can't believe I'm in a situation where those are my two best options."

"They're not your *best* options."

"What are you talkin' about?" I asked. "You have another option you're keeping a secret?"

"We *could* just have an affair, and then it wouldn't be a lie."

I spun around as we stopped walking and turned away from Mack. We stood right next to a weeping willow tree the hotel had planted for landscaping purposes. We were shielded from the road, the drooping branches providing us plenty of cover. The moonlight glinted off a small little brook bubbling nearby, giving a "classy" sort of ambiance to the hotel—one of the only overnight facilities in town. Either visitors stayed at the hotel, the B&B, or with a family member.

"What did you mean when you said we have to get away, Mack?" I felt cold without his arm slipped through mine, but I couldn't bring myself to go back to him just yet. I had to know where we stood, all joking aside.

He held his distance, and those eyes of his scanned me up and down. Goose bumps prickled my skin under his gaze, and I'm certain he noticed them. "Just think about it, Scarlett. What do you have here? What is holding you back? We could run away, you and I. Escape from it all."

I swallowed and considered it. "That's not possible, Mack."

"Why not?" His eyes glimmered, excitement bubbling from the inside out. "Just think. I have money, Scarlett. Resources. We can change our names, disappear, you and me. We can give it a go, for real."

"Mack…"

He stepped toward me, his hands reaching out tentatively. One of his fingers ran down the side of my bare arm. "You're cold. Come here."

I shook my head, unable to speak.

"Come here. Huddle for warmth. I promise I won't tell anyone."

This time, I couldn't shake my head. It just hung there as the weight of everything that had happened hit me like a sack of hay. My shoulders shook, some of those stubborn tears sprang into my eyes, and eventually, I just let my body tip forward into Mack's arms. Again. As my head hit his chest, I found myself wondering why every time my body collapsed, Mack was there to catch me.

"It's okay." Mack's voice soothed me as his fingers stroked my hair. He murmured words that didn't make sense to my ears, but they calmed me down, regardless. "It's okay."

I stood there with my head on his shoulder for I don't know how long. Wind whispered through the weeping willow, and the hiccupping of the brook provided an easy, calming background track, allowing my mind to work through the events of the night.

First, I'd found Joe's body, which was not only shocking, but confusing. Then, Mack had drugged—or *sedated*—me, then another man had a gun. Was that the same man who'd killed Joe? Or the man who'd killed Frank? Or the one who'd shot at me?

On top of it all, Mack was asking me to run away with him. I'd spent so long trying to get over him that his request just overwhelmed my senses. It was the straw that broke the camel's back, per se. I'd steeled myself against the town rumors, and adrenaline had pushed me through the trauma of finding two dead bodies in one week. But the steel around my heart was weak when it came to Mack.

And last but not least—what, or who, were we running from? What did they think Mack had in his possession?

"Listen, I want to explain everything to you, but we need to get somewhere safe." Mack set his palm on my cheek, holding my face so I had no choice but to look back into his eyes. "I'll tell you the truth. Just trust me one more time. Let me take you somewhere private where we can talk."

"That's not the first time I've heard that line from you." I forced a smile onto my face. "We've managed to find a few private places before."

Mack's eyes lit up. "So that's a yes?"

"I don't think I have a choice," I said, "seeing as how people seem to think I have something of theirs that I know nothing about. And they're pretty determined to get it."

Mack grabbed my hand, led me to the hotel parking lot, and looked around.

"Your car's there." I pointed to the black Audi right in front of him. "I'd offer to let you use mine, but there's a body in the trunk. Speaking of, we should call the police."

"I already did," murmured a distracted Mack. "Aha. Here we go. This is Eddie's truck. He's so drunk, he won't be driving anywhere for at least forty hours."

"You're stealing a cop's personal car?" I raised my eyebrows. "That doesn't seem smart. And we've done a lot of non-smart things lately."

"Think of it this way." Mack crossed his arms. "We're keeping him safe by borrowing his car. He won't be able to drive anywhere. And I'll have it returned by morning. Hell, I'll even take it through the car wash."

I frowned for a second. Then I looked up. "Well, if that's the case, can you borrow my car too?"

CHAPTER 43

Dear Diary,

I COULDN'T BELIEVE MY EARS. MACK remembered our pact. Back before we'd had that one night together, that one night that gave me hope for my *one little wish,* we'd been acquaintances. We'd talked every now and then. Not much, seeing as how he was dating that brat Heather Holloway for most of high school, and she'd slap him upside the head if he so much as nodded at another girl.

But for one week, the week leading up to that one night... we'd been friends.

We'd snuck away every night and talked. I'd never slept so little or been so energetic. We talked 'til six in the morning, then drifted to sleep for an hour before we rose at seven for school. I'd never been happier.

Our secret place had been the drive-in movie theater ten miles outside of Luck. Well, not *inside* the theater, but just outside of it. Mack had a car back then, and if you tucked it just right in the back corner behind a row of evergreen trees it was practically invisible. In fact, it was such a good hiding spot that we could watch movie after movie for free, and when they closed up the theater, they never thought to check just outside of the gate.

It was our secret little hiding place, a cozy little nest where we could talk for hours. Hold hands. Laugh and dream about the future. But never kiss. We never moved beyond hand holding, a bit of him touching my arm, or me resting my head on his shoulder. I watched twenty-one movies that week, though I couldn't tell you the name of a single one.

Now, ten years later, we were right back to where we started.

Not much had changed.

He tucked the beat-up truck behind those same evergreen trees. We watched another romantic comedy that I've already forgotten the name of, and we still didn't want to be found, just like the good old days.

Except this time, we were running for our lives.

Scarlett

Chapter 44

"I F THIS DOESN'T BRING BACK memories, I don't know what does." Mack shut the car off, our view of the big screen only slightly obscured by the far-reaching pine branches. The same old guard from our high school days still patrolled the perimeter of the drive-in theater once every hour. As long as we remembered to shut off the ignition when he came near, we were good to go. Mack sighed, leaning back against the seat and looking over at me. "Peace and quiet."

"Yeah." I meant to say more, meant to say something intelligent, but I couldn't come up with anything good. I was too distracted by the combination of nostalgic memories and recent memories, events that had left me with adrenaline coursing through my veins. It was an odd combination, one that mostly made me tired. One that had me contemplating running away from it all.

"You won't run away with me," Mack said, his voice resigned. "I know it, but it was worth a shot."

"I don't think you want to run either," I said after a moment. "I don't know why, since it seems like you've been running for a while now, but I get the sense that's not what you're after this time."

"It's not for the reasons you think," Mack said. Before I could respond, he continued. "I know you don't know *what* to think. If you still want to hear what's going on, I owe you an explanation."

I reached over. Some of the fight had gone out of me. "I don't know what to say. I'm curious. I want an explanation. I want to know why everyone's after us. But if you really don't want to talk,

I decided that I'm not gonna be the girl who forces you to spill the beans. Tell me if you want, or don't. I just want things to go back to normal. I want to go to book club, nanny for Gray, and go to church on Sundays. That's it, Mack. I'm a simple girl. No tricks."

"Do you remember when I broke up with Heather?"

Of course I remembered. I could tell him the exact date, as a matter of fact. I remained silent, working on a response that wouldn't sound so desperate. "Yeah, I remember. What was it, about a week before you graduated high school?"

He nodded. "That morning. And that evening was the very first night we came here."

I remembered that too, but I didn't want to give away the fact that each and every day of that week was seared into my mind. I'd almost developed a photographic memory for that one week, and that week alone.

"Did I tell you why we broke up?" He glanced over at me.

I shook my head. "You said you broke it off, but that was pretty obvious. She was upset for weeks."

"She wasn't upset because we broke up. She was just mad I did it first. I shouldn't have waited so long."

I frowned. "It seemed like you guys liked each other a lot. If I'm gonna be honest, it still seems like she's not over you, based on tonight's performance."

Mack blew a strand of hair out of his face. "Yeah, well, our parents liked us together back then, and I think they're all still holding out hope that we'll get married now."

I looked out the window. "Ah, I see. That makes sense."

It made all too much sense, in fact, which brought up a whole 'nother reason my little wish was stupid. I wasn't the caliber of girl that dated someone like Mack Montgomery. Heather Holloway had the pedigree to date someone like him, not me. I'd be lucky to capture any man at all, not to mention one with a job, let alone a man who'd treat me nice.

"No, it doesn't make any sense," Mack said. "It's my job to determine who I love, not my parents'. As far as I'm concerned, I've only ever loved one woman. I've also only ever told one woman 'I love you,' and it was the wrong girl."

My breath hitched in my throat, and I hated that he could still have that effect on me after so long. I didn't even know if he was talkin' about me. He certainly hadn't hinted that he loved me back then.

"Do your parents know you're in town?" I looked over at that handsome man, every inch of him familiar despite our time apart.

Mack's parents, I knew, lived forty miles away, somewhere in between Luck and a much bigger city fifty miles further. Like the Holloways, they were filthy rich.

However, unlike Heather, Mack had managed to grow up without the stink of money tainting his essence. When I was growing up, I had thought Noelle's family had lots of money, but compared to Mack's family and the Holloways, Noelle lived in a shack.

I'd driven by Mack's parents' place just one time. It was a plantation fit for a movie with a long driveway covered by a canopy of well-groomed trees. That's about all I could see of it from the road, but rumor had it, they had an entire team of help to care for all of the rooms inside. I'd even heard someone say they had an entire second house for the help to live in just out back. But I'd never asked, and I'd never seen it, so that was all hearsay. That family was Texas royalty, and according to tradition, their son should marry a beautiful Texas princess. That princess was Heather Holloway.

"I'm sure they know," Mack said, his jaw tense. "But we don't talk anymore. So if they do know, it's because they heard it from someone else."

"Like the Holloways," I said. I knew I was egging him on, but I couldn't help it.

"I don't love Heather," Mack said. "I never did, looking back. I thought she was pretty enough, but she never sparked anything inside of me. I never felt anything lookin' at her. Not the way I do when I look at you, Scarlett."

"Mack…" I looked down. "We can't be together, all right? I've come to terms with it. Me dreamin' about ending up with you is like Cinderella dreamin' she'd be dancing with the prince. Maybe it happens once in a blue moon, but not here. The glass slipper doesn't fit. Look at me."

Mack looked, and he looked, and he looked, and he looked. "I told you I don't talk to my family anymore. I don't care what they think."

"No, but someday you'll have kids, and your mother and father will be grandparents to those children. Every child deserves to know their relatives." I tried to keep the bitterness out of my voice. I knew from experience what not having a family did to a child. It wasn't pleasant. "And when you get married, you'll want them to be there. Mack, you and I aren't ever gonna happen. So can we please just figure out what's going on here so you can go back to Hollywood, and I can find myself some honest work?"

Mack looked as if he didn't want to talk about anything except that family of his, so I raised a hand and rested it against his face. I looked into his eyes, feeling my own sting with tears. My heart wanted him so badly, but my mind knew it couldn't happen. I only hoped he understood.

He cleared his throat, breaking his gaze from mine. He pulled my hand from his cheek, clasping both my wrists in his palms. "I broke up with Heather for my job. My parents wanted me to stick around here in Luck when I graduated to take over the family business, maybe go into politics. They wanted me to rule this godforsaken town just like they have their entire lives. But I didn't want that for myself."

I squeezed his hands, silently begging him to continue.

"I wanted to get out. I wanted to travel. I wanted to do something meaningful with my life." Mack's expression turned wistful, and I got the sense he wasn't even in the car with me anymore. He was daydreaming about things I'd never seen, places I'd never go. "The last thing I wanted was to sit on a pile of money with my nose in the air and my thumb up my ass."

"You're right," I murmured. "That doesn't sound comfortable."

Mack flicked his eyes to me, and the sound of his laugh was easy on my ears. "That must be why my parents look so uptight all the time. They're uncomfortable."

I laughed too, thankful the tense mood was broken. Now that Mack and I had both realized we couldn't be a couple, maybe we could just go on and be friends again. It had worked well the first time until we'd screwed it up by makin' it more than a friendship. I wouldn't make that same mistake again.

"Two weeks before I graduated high school, I got a phone call." Mack's expression turned complicated. I couldn't read his emotions anymore. "It was all very clandestine, very covert. Mysterious. Exciting. Everything my life wasn't up until then."

"What do you mean? You were popular in high school. Athletic, wealthy… what more could you have wanted?"

"Freedom!" Mack's voice turned sharp. He took a few deep breaths, calming down before he spoke again. "All those things—power, money, popularity—seem good, but they come at a price. A very high cost. I had to live my parents' idea of a successful life. That meant becoming an all-star football player. It meant keeping my status up as boyfriend to 'that Holloway girl.' It meant getting in line for the family business. I had no choices left to make."

Never having been rich myself, I'd never stopped to consider the downsides of having money. Of which there were many, according to Mack. I'd been broke as could be most of my life, but I'd never had someone telling me what to do, when to be home, or what to be when I grew up. At times, I'd wished I had. Although the way Mack described it, the whole thing sounded claustrophobic.

"This job, they were promising me everything I didn't have,"

Mack said. "Travel. Danger. Money of my own. The opportunity to change the world."

"What are you talkin' about, Mack?"

"Government agency work," Mack said. "But none of the acronyms you know. This branch isn't open to applications, if you understand what I'm saying."

"I *don't* understand."

"This group sends recruiters all around the country, recruiters meant to scout out potential applicants from the general population, based on a huge long list of criteria." Mack paused. "Turned out, I was the perfect fit. Athletic, reasonably intelligent, looking for a way outta dodge."

"But what is this group?"

Mack turned to me, his eyes hard. "Let's call them a 'national security team,' since they don't have a real name. They wanted me to work as a field agent for them. They promised me all those things, Scarlett, and they delivered. They gave me dangerous work. They gave me enough money so that I don't have to worry about working for some time now. They gave me chances to change the world, and I took them."

"But... what about Hollywood? You're a stunt driver."

Mack cocked his head sideways. "There comes a time when even the best agents want out. I went undercover as a stunt driver in Hollywood for one of my last missions. Turns out, I was good at it. Took a few lessons, and by the time I'd completed my mission, I had three more movies lined up, thanks to some of my contacts." Mack shrugged. "I took the opportunity. Entertaining job, enough money to be comfortable, a flexible work schedule. What more could I ask for?"

"And this... this *agency* just let you go?"

Mack's face tensed. "Not quite."

"Are you running from them, Mack?" I felt light-headed all of a sudden. "Is that who's after us?"

Mack swiveled his head to look at me. "No, Scarlett. It's not like that."

"What is it *like,* then?"

"They don't just *let* you go, like you said." Mack's voice sounded resigned. "As much as I wanted out, they wouldn't let me. So, we worked out a deal. I'd go part time. Right now, I freelance for one-off missions. When they found out I was from Texas, they sent me down here to investigate something. That *something* is what's after us."

I swallowed. "Do I get to know what this *something* is?"

Mack hesitated. "I don't want to get you involved more than you already are."

"That's stupid," I said. "I'm already involved. Keeping me in the dark is more dangerous. If I know what I'm involved with, at least I have a chance to understand. You're using me as bait, Mack. At least that's what it feels like."

Mack turned to face me, his movements so quick they shook his explanation into place. Things started making sense. Things like why Mack might be carrying a gun on him at all times, and why he'd have a "mild sedative" in his pocket. Things like why and how he'd taken down the intruder with a carefully aimed swipe of his foot. Things like why he'd been gone for so long, and why he'd vanished from the face of the earth for over five years before resurfacing in Hollywood as a stunt driver. It made sense, but it didn't help me straighten out my feelings.

"Let me tell you something, Scarlett." Mack grasped me firmly by the shoulders. "The reason I walked away from you tonight after ripping Art's filthy hands off of you is because I didn't want anyone in that room to think there's something between us. If I had stopped when you called me, they'd have noticed. Something is going on down in Luck. Two dead bodies in one week? That ain't the average mortality rate around here for a middle-aged, healthy male. Someone is watching, and I couldn't take the risk they'd put me and you together."

"I wouldn't know what you're talkin' about, since I'm still not exactly sure *what* your job is or why these people are out to get us." My voice was laced with sarcasm.

Mack rested one hand on his forehead and shook his head. "Let me explain it this way. I work for the United States of America. But you won't find any paperwork saying that, which is why you've gotta trust me. We're the FBI's booty call, Scarlett." Mack looked up at me, and those eyes of his were so different I could hardly recognize him.

They were eyes that knew things I could never understand. I shivered. "Booty call?"

"The FBI, CIA, you name the acronym." Mack gave a tense smile. "They call us in the wee hours of the morning when they're caught in a compromising position with their pants down and they need someone to finish the job. They call us just before dawn, just before all hell breaks loose, and it's our responsibility to complete the mission, no matter the cost. Much like a booty call, we don't exchange names. No numbers. Just cold, hard cash for a job well done."

My mouth couldn't seem to form a proper response, and my brain wasn't helping out.

"You don't have to say anything," Mack said. "I don't expect you to know what to think, not yet."

"And… and you're down here on a mission?"

Mack nodded. Again, he hesitated. "I can't tell you details, but there is a man in this country that has his hands in all sorts of black markets. Some worse than others. My assignment is to find him. In order to get to the top dog, I have to start at the bottom."

"And you've followed his trail to Luck," I said as things started to click into place. "And either Joe or Frank, or both, were somehow involved."

Gina LaManna

"They were the bottom layer," Mack said. "They were smuggling diamonds out of Joe's Auto Body Shop. The reason you're involved is because they used your car as a transport vehicle. Let me guess, your car didn't need repairs from Joe, but Frank sent it over anyway?"

I nodded. "Ryan slash Ralph couldn't figure out why Frank had sent it over since the car only had a smudge on it, but Joe was out of town, so he ended up just giving me the bug back. Shortly after that, I started finding bodies. And shortly after that, people started chasing me."

Mack pursed his lips. "You discovering Frank's body must have been a coincidence. I think someone was trying to set you up, but they couldn't have guessed you'd find the body. I'm guessing Joe got greedy, offed Frank, and then tried to frame you."

I chewed on this. Maybe, just maybe, I could see it happening.

"Joe would've made sure you were the last person to talk to Frank. He knew you'd go to church, so he dumped the body there. Then, he could start a rumor to fuel the flame with your name in the mix, and the town would take it away."

"That's all a theory," I said. "And we won't be able to find out now since Joe's dead too. You think that someone found out Joe offed Frank, then killed him as retaliation?"

"I don't think it was retaliation so much as a power move. The guys in small operations like this take orders from the guys above. Once one of the low men on the totem pole starts making their own decisions, decisions like offing their partner, the big dogs upstairs get nervous. What's the easiest way to take care of troublemakers?"

"Shut them up," I said, a tremble wracking my body as I said the words. This whole thing had escalated quickly from a small-town murder to a nationwide web of black-market lies.

Mack nodded.

"And my car? What... what is it about my car?"

"I'm guessing that whoever was sent to kill Joe stuck around long enough to hear your name wrapped up in the rumors. Chances

196

are, dumping Joe's body in your vehicle was the easiest thing for them to do. They already had a 'fall guy' in the form of you. By the time everyone pulled their heads out of their asses and realized you hadn't done a thing wrong, they'd be out of town."

"Damn."

"That's about right." Mack turned to look at me. "How are you holding up? This is a lot of information."

"As strange as it sounds," I said, pausing to figure out how to express my jumbled thoughts, "I suppose it makes more sense than anything else you might've told me. I believe you, Mack. I do. And I trust you. But I don't know what to do now."

"Well, I do have one more question to ask you before we finish up talking." Mack reached over, grabbed my hand, and looked at me. "Sometime, when this is over, will you have a drink with me?"

I thought of all the reasons I should say no. And there were hundreds of them. Millions, even. But that didn't stop my body from responding with its own answer. "Only if you're buying. And I want more than one. I think I deserve it."

"I'll buy you the whole bar." Mack grinned. "You know, I have one more thing to explain."

"You have a lot more than one," I interrupted. "But I suppose you've gotta start somewhere."

Mack laughed. "That week we had together... as soon as I got the call from the agency two weeks before graduation, I knew I was gonna take that job. They told me I couldn't have any attachments. They said I had to leave everything—mentally, emotionally, and physically—back home. I'd already been looking to break up with Heather, but frankly I didn't have the balls to do it. The best thing that job offer did was give me the strength to break up with her."

"Why didn't you just disappear on Heather?" I looked up through my lashes, dreading the answer I'd been waiting ten years to hear.

"It's a funny thing," Mack said. "When you find out everything you love is going to be taken away from you in a week, it makes certain things crystal clear. For me, that meant I couldn't waste a single minute more with Heather. I wanted to spend that time with you."

I remembered that golden week just as sparkly now as it had been back then.

"I knew logically I shouldn't do it. I knew it would hurt both of us, but I couldn't stay away." Mack cleared his throat. "I didn't let myself kiss you that whole week, couldn't allow myself to touch you until the very last night because I knew if I didn't disappear the morning after, I would never leave. Ever. Leaving you was the hardest thing I've ever done, Scarlett, and I am sorry. With all my heart, I am so, so sorry."

I looked down, surprised to find a splotch of wet shining from the lap of my gown where a single teardrop had landed. "It's okay, Mack. I understand."

"I loved you back then, Scarlett, even though I didn't tell you." He reached over and brought my face close to his. "If you give me the chance now, I'd like to prove it."

I let my lips hover above his. "You get us out of this alive, and I'll let you buy me that drink, Mack Montgomery. We'll take it from there."

And then with a kiss as light as a secret, he sealed his promise in a way that told me he meant it.

CHAPTER 45

Dear Diary,

I THINK I STILL LOVE HIM.
God help us both.

xoxx Scarlett xoxx

CHAPTER 46

"**A**RE YOU SURE WE SHOULD be here?" I whispered across the console of Eddie's truck. As Mack drove, I looked out the window at Ryan's house, wondering if it would be a good idea to keep poking our noses in this business. "You did say that you already called the cops about Joe's body, right? I'd hate for him to just be lying there unattended."

"I called them," Mack said. "They have a backup crew on tonight, though, from thirty miles away since it's Eddie's night to drink and be merry. They'll need your car for a few days to process everything, I'd guess."

"Isn't it a bad idea that we left the scene of the crime?"

"Yes, it's a terrible idea. I wouldn't recommend it for the normal person."

"Remind me why we did it, then."

"Because we aren't the normal people, Scarlett. We'll answer all their questions in the morning, cooperate and apologize, but hopefully by then we'll have some new information." Mack looked out the window, turned the headlights off, then opened his door. "I wasn't gonna let us be sitting ducks for whoever's watching. I don't like to be reactive. I'm more of a *take action* sort of guy."

"I'd never guess," I said wryly, hauling myself out of the truck and making the small jump to the ground. The state of my dress continued to deteriorate, and I wondered if it wouldn't be a mere thread by the time the night was over. "What are we gonna say?"

"I'm just gonna explain to Ryan and his wife that you were

worried when you didn't see them at the event tonight, and you can agree. If you wanna chime in, just tell them you asked me to stop by their home on the way back to check on everyone." Mack cocked his head, looking at the house. "Then, I have a few questions for Ryan if he's around. A few things I need clarified."

"Do these clarifications have anything to do with what you found at Joe's office today?"

"You know, they just might." Mack winked at me. "So, shall we?"

I slid my arm through his extended one, and together we marched up to the front door like a happy couple after a night of dancing... minus a few stray twigs attached to my dress, and stress levels higher than a patient headed to open heart surgery.

The door to Ryan's small, ramshackle home was opened on the first knock by a woman with mascara streaked down her face. Her hair looked as though it had been in a fancy updo at one point in the evening, but now it fell in ragged curls by the side of her face. A bit of lipstick streaked her cheek, and her eyes were red-rimmed and tearful.

"You!" Ryan's wife pointed a finger in my direction. "I can't believe you have the *balls* to show up here tonight after what you did."

I glanced first at Mack, who gave me a calming squeeze around the waist, then back to the woman with her finger in my face. "Lana, what are you talking about?"

"Don't play dumb with me, Scarlett Powers. You Powers girls have always been trouble, and the whole town knows it. Now, where's Ryan?"

"What?" My jaw might've dropped open, but I didn't feel it. I was too busy feeling shocked. "What are you talking about?"

"He said he was just gonna *stop by* your place earlier. Had something to tell you or whatever. That was four hours ago. Where is he?" Lana's voice shook, her shoulders trembled, and she looked on the verge of collapse. "I had a suspicion he was steppin' out on me, but with you? What in tarnation was he thinking?"

On a different day, I might've been offended that I wasn't good enough for her Ryan, but today I was too busy trying to put the puzzle pieces together to care. "I never saw Ryan at my house. I haven't seen him since I picked up my car."

"Can we come inside?" Mack stepped forward, sliding his arm from where it'd been hooked over my elbow. He extended a cautious hand toward Lana's fragile-looking figure, waiting for her approval.

She hesitated at first, but Mack had magic hands that could soothe a skittered horse. Eventually she nodded, leaning on Mack as he helped her to the couch. Once we were all situated in the living room, I nodded at Mack to take over the questions.

"Mrs..." Mack hesitated.

"Lana." She sniffed, eyeing him. "Call me Lana."

"Lana, let me explain something." Mack leaned forward, his elbows on his knees, his fingers steepled together over his lap. "I don't know Ryan all that well, but I do know that he's not stepping out on you with Scarlett. Frankly, he'd be stupid to step out on you at all. Look at you in that pretty red dress. Were you planning on going to the Reunion Day event tonight?"

I watched in awe at Mack's gentle handling of the woman. It seemed to be working, seeing how even a woman in the midst of anger and sadness could be wooed by a hint of flattery.

She nodded again, her tears falling slower, the anger less fierce in her eyes as she held Mack's gaze. "Yes sir, I had my hair all done up by Betty, and I picked this dress out special. Ryan was just gonna stop over by her place, even though I said he should just call her. Or wait and talk to Scarlett at the event, but he insisted it was important."

"Well, we came here tonight because Miss Scarlett was workin' the bar at the event," Mack said. "She noticed that yourself and

Ryan weren't there, and she asked me to stop by real quick and just check up on you to see if everything was okay."

"Why does she care?" Lana asked, speaking as if I weren't there. Obviously, she wasn't convinced I wasn't trying to steal Ryan.

"Because she's nice, and she's a neighbor," Mack said. "That's all. She's been with me the entire evening, over at the event hall, setting up the bar. I promise you that she hasn't seen Ryan."

"I haven't seen him since I picked up my car from him, and he was kind to me," I said. "I was just returning the favor of checking on y'all, since he helped fix my car up."

Lana looked mildly appeased, but she still had no interest in talking to me. Her gaze turned to Mack. "Well, now what happens? Where is Ryan?"

"Like I said, we thought he'd be here." Mack turned to me, his gaze brooding. "Do you have any idea what he wanted to tell Scarlett that was so important it couldn't wait?"

Lana rested a set of freshly manicured red nails against her matching lips. "I don't know."

"He didn't mention anything?" Mack asked. "Think. It might be important."

"Is Ryan in trouble?"

I looked down, which apparently gave too much away.

"Is he or isn't he in trouble?" Lana pressed.

"He's not. I just had a few questions for him," Mack said. "Any information you have might help."

"What are you, the cops?" Lana asked. "I said I don't know."

"Here's the deal." Mack leaned forward, his words sharp, and his gaze sharper. "I think Ryan's life might be in danger. I don't think he's stepping out on you, and I don't think he would've missed seeing you in that pretty red dress. But I do think we need to work quickly."

For the first time, Lana's disgruntled expression turned to one of fear. "My Ryan? In trouble?"

I wondered why her first guess had been that Ryan was stepping out on her instead of asking around to see if he was okay, but it wasn't my place to judge.

"Here's what we're gonna do," Mack said. "You're gonna tell me everything you know about what Ryan had to tell Scarlett. Then, we're gonna leave and go look for him, and you're gonna call the police." He crossed his arms. "Tell them everything that you told us, just don't tell them that we were here."

"But—"

"If you want your husband found, and found *safely*, this is the best way to do so," Mack said. "It'll take twenty minutes for the cops to get here, and another thirty for them to question you. Even then, they might decide there's nothing suspicious going on. I don't believe that, and I don't think you do either. Am I right?"

Lana's fingers played with the fabric of her dress. "He wouldn't have missed our date tonight. I made him his favorite bleu cheese burgers."

"See?" Mack crossed his arms. "So, tell me, Lana, what do you know?"

She bit her lip. "I honestly don't recall all that much since I was busy curling my hair, but I got the sense that he'd just realized somethin', like a lightbulb went off in his head. Something about the other man that works at the garage... the one who doesn't speak English."

"Miguel?" I supplied.

"Sounds right." Lana lifted her shoulders. "But that's it. He had to let you know something about him, and I'm guessing it wasn't something good. I don't know *why* he had to tell you, but he insisted. I told him to call Joe first, but he wouldn't do it."

Mack looked over at me, his eyes dark. Then, he glanced back at Lana. "We're going to head out. Thank you for your help, ma'am. Now, call the police, tell them exactly what you told us, and if you could leave out the small fact of our visit, it'd be much appreciated."

"Do you think he's okay?" In a startling motion, Lana stood up and grabbed Mack by the front of his shirt. "Tell me my husband is okay."

"I'm not in the habit of making that kind of promise," Mack said, his expression stoic. "I can promise you we'll do everything in our power to find him and get him back to you safe."

Lana's eyes flicked between the two of us in a rapid, wild motion. "Please," she whispered. "Please find him."

I reached for Mack's wrist, pulling him toward the door as Lana followed us. "Lana, if you can trust anyone in this town to get your husband back safe, it's Mack. Remember, we don't even know if he's in trouble yet."

"He is," Lana said. "I can feel it. Please help him."

We stepped outside, Mack touching my hip with one hand while he shut the door firmly with the other. I didn't speak until we'd reached the car, and even then, Mack put a finger to his lips until we were inside with the doors locked, cruising away from Lana's home.

"What do you think?" I eventually broke the silence because I couldn't hold it any longer. "Of Ryan? Miguel?"

"I don't state my theories until I have evidence to confirm them." Mack sealed his lips tightly, his mouth a firm line I knew that I couldn't budge.

Of course that didn't mean I wasn't going to try. "Come *on*. With your... uh, career, you have to have some ideas."

"I have plenty of ideas, but not enough facts." Mack glanced at me. "I don't operate on assumptions, gut feelings, or theories. I operate on facts."

I detected a hard edge to Mack's voice, one that sounded all too natural. Then again, he'd spent long enough working in the realm of his "business" that I shouldn't expect anything different. He wasn't the cute boy from history class anymore, or the football star with the prom queen on his hip. He was Superhero Mack, out to save the world and not get any recognition for it.

Suddenly, the thought made me feel small and insignificant. While Mack had been off saving the country, one mission at a time, I'd been cleaning up one SpaghettiO at a time, tucking Gray into bed one night after the next. I'd loved Gray all of those years, raised him as my own, only to have him ripped away all thanks to a rumor.

I was filled with a sudden hate for Annie Harper, a rage so blinding that my hands shook.

"Are you okay?" Mack asked.

I hadn't realized my fingers had clenched themselves into fists. "Let's just find whoever's responsible for this." Because now, more than ever, I wanted to put a name and a face to the shadow who'd taken away everything that mattered to me.

"Do you have a suggestion as to where we should start?" Mack asked, his eyebrow raised. The way he asked the question, I got the feeling he already knew the right answer. He just didn't want to be the one to say it.

"Well, I suppose it'd make sense to start with the one person who links everything together." I turned my eyes out the window. "Me."

CHAPTER 47

Dear Diary,

WE'RE COMIN' HOME NOW, BUT I don't think I want to since I don't really think I'll like what we'll find there. I'm crossing my fingers it's nothin' bad, but with bodies dropping like flies around here, I'm not sure we'll be in luck. No pun intended.

Seems like my little car is cursed. Everyone who touches it ends up dead.

I loved that car, but it might be time for a change in vehicles. Maybe when Mack leaves, he'll donate his Audi to the "Save Scarlett" fund.

I'm just kidding. I don't know what to do anymore, Diary. It feels wrong to joke, but if I didn't do something to keep my spirits up, my eyes would just be a leaky faucet, and that wouldn't help anyone.

Anyway, we're here, Diary. And we're going inside. I'm just hoping that I find an empty home. For the sake of everyone—Lana, Ryan, and even myself. Because if I can't find out who is behind this mess, there's really no hope of me getting my nannyin' job back. Even though I can't stand that woman who calls herself Gray's mother, I can't stay away from my little man.

Fingers crossed,
xoxx Scarlett xoxx

CHAPTER 48

"SHOULD WE CALL THE COPS before we go inside?" I asked.

Mack shook his head. "We don't know anyone's in there at all. Still just a theory."

"But..." I hesitated, knowing I didn't have a phone on me. I was willing to bet Noelle was cussing a blue streak, not having heard from me in a few hours. She might even have found my phone along the edge of the parking lot, discarded in the bushes when Mack had pulled me away from Joe's body.

Or maybe the police had found it. They had to know Joe was dead. The party was probably dissolved. If Lana had called the police like Mack had said, then they'd already have a hint we'd stopped by anyway, since I didn't trust her to keep a secret about our visit. Even if Lana *had* kept her mouth shut about Mack and me, the cops would already be looking for me since Joe's body was in my trunk.

That's not saying anything about Noelle, who would also be looking for us, once she stopped going wild about my disappearance. Maybe Mack was right; someone would be there soon enough looking for me, so why waste the precious amount of spare minutes we had left calling the cops? Better to digest whatever was inside before we had company. Plus, I had Mack by my side. Mack was a professional.

I looked up at that steely gaze, and matched it with one of my own. "I'm ready."

Mack looked across Eddie's truck, and I realized if nothing else, Eddie would probably be sobering up at the news of Joe's death. Once he was sober, he'd be looking for his car. Was there anyone in this town *not* looking for me? For Pete's sake, this was getting ridiculous. All I'd done was get my car serviced. From now on, I was taking the bus.

"I think it's best if you wait here," Mack said. "Sit in the driver's seat, keep the car ready to move."

"I think that's not gonna happen." I crossed my arms. "I'm going in with you."

"I've spent years training for moments like this."

"Well, I'm angry enough to turn someone to stone with my eyeballs."

Mack stared at me, and I watched him struggle with how to respond. Eventually, he gave a wry shake of his head and a quirk of his lips. "I've worked with men who have less composure than you."

"Is your agency hiring?" I smacked my lips. "Because I'm out of a job, and the way things are going, I will be for a long time. In a town named Luck, seems like I've got all the bad portion of the stuff."

Mack laughed. "Fine. But do you have a gun?"

"Not really." I hesitated. "Unless you've got an extra one you wanna loan me?"

"Here." Mack shifted in his seat and reached down his leg in a way that was oddly captivating. From somewhere near his ankle, he removed a small, pencil-like black object. "Dart gun. It'll stun anyone for thirty minutes max. That way, even if your aim is terrible, you won't kill anyone."

"I appreciate your vote of confidence." My voice was heavy with sarcasm, but I pocketed the dart gun anyway. Thirty minutes of stunned silence was better than nothing. I could do a lot to an unconscious person in thirty minutes. For example, thirty minutes gave me enough time to tie a person up, draw a mustache on his or her face, and call the police. The options were endless.

"I'll put in a good word for you with the agency," Mack said, that ghost of a smile dancing around his lips again. "Resume: Sarcastic under pressure. Fearless. Has mastered the art of distraction."

"Distraction?"

As an answer, Mack reached over, and his fingers ran up and down the lengths of my black shoulder straps. He toyed with the fabric, traced the neckline, and by the time I wrapped my mind around what was happening, he'd leaned in close enough to kiss my neck.

And he did just that. He kissed my neck, just below my ear, before whispering softly against my skin, "You're gorgeous, Scarlett. We'll get through this. Stay strong."

My skin trembled with a shiver that started on my neck and snaked its way down to my toes. I couldn't think of a good response, so I just offered a nod then pushed the door open. I stepped from the car before I could let the tenderness of his words sink in and ruin my hard-earned shield of sarcasm.

As we approached the front door of my restored barn, the place felt strangely foreign. I'd only stayed at Noelle's for a night, but even so, a mist of trepidation hung in the air. My normally cozy home was tainted by a breach of trust... someone going through my personal items.

The moment would have been ten times worse, however, if I hadn't had Mack by my side. His tall, lean frame stepped with confidence toward the door, and his hand held a gun just beside his hip. I hadn't seen when he'd made the gun appear, but I wasn't surprised by its presence. In fact, it was oddly comforting.

Mack turned to me as he rested one hand on the broken front door. His gaze met mine, and he raised an eyebrow in question.

I gave a nod to signify I was ready, and he pushed the door open.

CHAPTER 49

Dear Diary,

I DON'T KNOW WHAT I EXPECTED to find in that house. I didn't really feel anything. I didn't think much either. I just acted. I followed Mack, I gripped my dart gun, and I ignored the creepy crawlies slithering over my skin. Something didn't smell right here, Diary. As much as I didn't want to take one more step inside that house, I did anyway.

Scarlett

CHAPTER 50

"Ryan?" Mack's voice was soft, gentle, and even, despite the hard lines on his face.

None of the boyish charm was left in his smile, and the mischievous sparkle in his eyes was gone. Even his hair, which I'd normally call disheveled, seemed rifled to attention—messy, yes, but not in that chaotic way that was so endearing.

There was no response, so we moved further into the house. It was a simple place with only two floors. My bedroom was upstairs, along with a bathroom and a small nook in the corner that was perfect for reading. The nook was my favorite place in the entire house.

Downstairs, the layout was plain—a functional, mid-sized kitchen, a bathroom, and a dining room that blended into the living room. The first floor had an open layout. Once we stepped past the entryway, there would be no cover whatsoever.

After a few head nods, whispers, and hand gestures, we got into a position that would allow Mack to step out first, while I covered him with my tiny dart gun.

Mack held up three fingers.

"Three," he mouthed.

Scanning the first floor, I noted the upturned furniture and scattered papers caused by someone rifling through my things. This place didn't feel like home. Although it was familiar, it wasn't my sanctuary anymore. My privacy had been invaded, leaving me with a slimy feeling.

"Two," Mack whispered.

I held up my dart gun just as I heard the slightest shuffle of movement coming from the living room.

Mack put down his pointer finger, signaling it was time to move. And move he did. As fast as a cheetah and as sleek as a panther, he sidestepped into the room, gun drawn, sweeping the place. My heart pounded in my chest, and I broke into a cold sweat as the silent moments ticked by.

I wanted to call out, but I kept my mouth shut. I couldn't hear anything.

Then, I heard another shuffle and a groan.

"Mack?" I hissed. I couldn't help it. "Are you okay?"

"You can come out here," he said with a firm voice. "Keep your eyes open."

I stepped from around the corner, and clasped a hand to my mouth as I saw Ryan, bound and gagged, on the floor in the center of the living room.

I rushed toward him, covering the short distance in three steps. To my surprise, Mack didn't argue. I glanced up, waiting for permission to rip the tape off Ryan's mouth.

Mack's eyes flicked around the room, his breathing even, and his gun drawn.

"Ryan, are you okay?" I asked. He had a black eye and a splotch of blood under his nose. Other than that, he looked unharmed, minus the bindings around his ankles and wrists, and the tape on his mouth.

"Are you here alone?" Mack asked Ryan, his even voice breaking the tense silence.

Ryan hesitated, looked at me with pleading eyes, then shook his head.

I didn't care what Mack said. Ryan's gaze, the one he'd given me just then, was pure terror. Somewhere in my gut, I found myself believing that Ryan was as guilty as I was in this whole mess, which meant he didn't know anything at all. So I ripped the tape off his mouth.

"You're not here alone?" I parroted. "Who else is here? Miguel?"

"Miguel is dead." The terror was back in Ryan's eyes. "Leave. Scarlett, you have to leave." His voice shook, though his volume was just above a whisper.

"Miguel is dead?" My words came out louder than I'd anticipated.

"*Leave.* I'm bait, Scarlett. You've got to get out of here." Ryan looked up at Mack. "You've got to go. Now."

"Bait?" I asked in confusion. "But who are you bait *for*?"

"Scarlett, let's go." Mack's voice was just as sharp as I'd ever heard it. "Move."

"Not so fast," a voice drawled, coming from somewhere above us.

I looked up and saw my beloved reading corner had been taken over by someone who hadn't been invited into my home. That someone had brought a kidnapped man in there, might have been responsible for the murder of two or three other men, and was pointing a gun at my head.

Unable to tear my eyes from the man who'd claimed my house as his own, violated my privacy, and ruined my life, I stood motionless. I opened my mouth to speak, but I couldn't do it. No words came out.

But the man spoke for me, though his gaze was fixed on Mack. "Hello, son." Dressed in a finely tailored suit, he had a head of white-gray hair and an expression of calculated politeness. As he leaned on the railing of the small balcony, he held a gun pointed downward. "Nice of you to bring a date to the party."

CHAPTER 51

Dear Diary,

MACK'S FATHER IS RUMORED TO be many things. He's been called a legend. A king. The most powerful man south of Chicago. I'd never had the pleasure of meeting him face to face, seeing how he doesn't deal with trivial creatures like myself.

Until now.

I wish he'd go back to his mansion and leave us all alone, but he's not going anywhere. It's clear by the way he's pointing that gun at my head and talking to his son. It's clear by his sharp eyes and piercing gaze that he's in far too deep to shake hands and walk away now.

He's playing to win.

But then again, I ain't playing to lose.

Scarlett

CHAPTER 52

"**S**IR? WHAT ARE YOU DOING?" Mack gave a brief shake of his head, as if trying to rattle the puzzle pieces into place. "Why are you in Scarlett's home?"

"You know, I expected you to be brighter than this, Mack." He gave a disappointed tilt of his head. "I thought that's why they chose you for the job. *They* thought you were intelligent. I might have even thought they were right. Although now, I can see I was mistaken."

"What are you talking about?" Mack scrutinized his father, and as my eyes flicked between the two men, I saw a frightening resemblance between them.

They both had blue eyes, a full head of hair, and an expression that had the power to intimidate and charm, all in one swoop. But where Mack's expression could soften and glow with happiness, his father's face seemed more groomed, as if every wrinkle had its appropriate place, and God forbid, his laugh lines should show. Where Mack's hair fell any which way, his father's hair was combed into perfect little rows, as if he'd spent hours getting it just so.

Mr. Montgomery laughed, the sound hollow, as if it had been practiced over and over again so that it wasn't too loud, and it wasn't too quiet. "You thought I'd let my son run away after high school and not look into his disappearance? What do you think money is for, if not to buy the information one needs?"

I glanced at Mack, watching his reaction. His gun was pointed somewhere between the staircase and his father, not directly on a target, though his fingers tensed and untensed around the butt of the gun in agitation.

"And I suppose you think your little agency was 'so covert' that no amount of money could buy me the information I needed to find you?" He took a few steps toward the staircase, his gun still trained on me. "Well, son, I tried to teach you this early in life. Money is everything: Power. Success. Happiness. Wealth. You had it all, and you gave it up for your little dreams, your desires to do good in the world."

Mack kept his mouth shut, though anger simmered behind his irises.

"Now son, you've had your fun. I've let you have your fulfilling career, given you the chance to realize that 'doing good' doesn't get you a whole lot in life." He paused. "So, let's get rid of these two, and you can come join the family business, once and for all."

"Are you nuts?" Mack took one step forward, but his father took two steps down the stairs, his gun coming ever closer to my head.

I remained crouched in the middle of the room, next to a silent, shaking Ryan.

"Who put you up to this?" Mack asked.

Mr. Montgomery let out a bark of laughter that almost seemed genuine. "You've played around long enough, Mack. I needed you to come home. So I organized this little 'issue' here in Luck. I bought myself a meeting with your boss—what's his name, Lucas?—to get the information I needed."

I could tell by the way Mack didn't correct his father that the information was probably accurate. "Lucas wouldn't give any information away."

"No, you're right." Mr. Montgomery frowned. "He didn't, but a source close to him did. Someone you work with at your little agency told me you'd been called in for a special assignment. You know this special assignment I'm talking about, don't you?" He blinked. "I heard all about your desire to get out of the business and go play around in Hollywood. And I knew you had this one-off contract left to take care of, to go after someone called…"

Mack ground his teeth together, his jaw tense, but he didn't respond.

"The Master. Is that it?" Mr. Montgomery asked.

Mack's eyes flashed at me, and I knew it was true. The Master—or whoever was behind the name—had to be the man at the top of the food chain. The man Mack was working to catch. The man he'd told me about outside of the movie theater.

"After I had that information, the solution was simple." Mr. Montgomery stepped down a few more stairs, the gun wobbling with each step. "Where would you start? With the low men on the totem pole. The weak links, just like I taught you. So if I set up a little side business down here, a little diamond-smuggling gig, let's say, it wouldn't take much for you to put two and two together. All I had to do was pay my source at the agency to pass along the rumors to you that this diamond business down in Luck was linked to The Master. That's it. You'd come down here to check things out, desperate to finish your assignment and get out, and ignore the convenient fact that the chain started in Luck."

Mack didn't meet my gaze, and I could tell he was working through issues I knew nothing about. A brief glimpse of a different emotion, maybe hurt, crossed his face. Had Mack been betrayed by a co-agent? Misled by someone he'd trusted, leading him right into the hands of his father and a trap?

My heart suddenly twisted in pain. Not only was Mack's father threatening him with a gun, but everything Mack had been working for the last week was a sham. The diamond-smuggling business was all a hoax. Or it might have been real, but it had nothing to do with The Master. It was all a stunt set up by Mack's father to get his son home.

My own fingers started to shake, and I hauled myself to my

feet. Mr. Montgomery took the last few steps down the staircase and stood just a few feet from me, his gun aimed at my chest.

"You set this all up?" I asked. "Do you realize that you've killed two people, or possibly more? You've ruined my job, and even more, you've tricked your son. Do you realize what you've done?"

"Fully, Miss Powers." He gave a succinct nod. "I did it knowingly too. And if you expect me to whimper and beg forgiveness, you're mistaken. The best don't rise to the top without making some difficult decisions."

"You've never had a problem doing that." Mack's voice was a snarl. "Business first since day one, no matter the cost."

"Better my way than yours," Mr. Montgomery said, looking at Mack for the first time in a few minutes. "Because I don't make emotional decisions. I knew you'd be back here in a heartbeat if you had an excuse—a chance to save the town with your heroic actions. I knew you'd come back for a girl, Mack. I just didn't realize it'd be this one."

A blind rage built up inside me as I thought of Heather Holloway with her hands on Mack tonight. I thought of poor Mack, and what growing up in this man's house must have been like. Suddenly, not having a family didn't seem so bad after all. At least my father wasn't pointing a gun at anyone.

"I think you've underestimated your son," I said. "Because he's more courageous than you any day. With no control over him, you can't stand to see him happy and successful, to see that he can make his own money, have his own life, and use his freedom however he likes."

"Scarlett, stop." Mack raised a hand. "The man won't listen to reason. Let it drop."

"You know, I really envied the fact that you had a father, Mack." I was still looking at Mr. Montgomery. "I was jealous of your home, your wealth, your fancy things. But after meeting your father, I wouldn't touch a penny of his money."

"You're a worthless thing, anyway," Mr. Montgomery said in a bored voice. "I'd kill you myself before I'd let Mack take you into my home for Thanksgiving, let alone marry you. So if you have any fantasies in that head of yours, you might as well get rid of them now."

Mack raised his gun and pointed it at his father. The three of us had an odd triangle of weapons going, and my little dart gun wouldn't hold up against either of them. Not to mention I'd never used the thing, and I'd hardly trust my aim.

"Here's the deal, Mack," Mr. Montgomery said. "A person with emotions like yourself... well, you won't shoot me. You don't have the guts because I'm your father, and no matter how psychopathic you think I am, you won't be able to forget I raised you." He shook his head. "As for me? I'm stronger than you. I'll shoot the girl. So lower your gun and listen to me."

"Listen to him, Mack," I murmured, trying to keep my voice calm despite panicking on the inside. "Please, it's okay."

"Good boy," Mr. Montgomery said as Mack lowered the gun to his waist. "Now, here's what's going to happen. Miguel has taken a permanent vacation from his short-lived career at Joe's Auto Body Shop. However, tomorrow, enough evidence will turn up that will point the finger at him being the mastermind behind the whole smuggling business in town." He paused to take a breath, his gaze steady and even. "There'll be receipts saying that he set up the drop, he fostered communication with the sellers, you name it. There'll be notes surfacing that allude to Joe getting greedy and killing Frank. There'll be enough evidence for the town to realize that Miguel didn't like Joe acting on his own, so he took care of that problem and stuffed Joe in this girl's trunk. Then the girl and Ryan here, they'll be unfortunate casualties in a bad situation. You can be the hero, Mack. Just say the word."

My stomach roiled at the calmness of his voice and at the

thoroughness of his plot to entrap Mack back into whatever this family business was all about.

"Even if that's how your plan went, I still wouldn't ever come home," Mack said. "You have to understand that."

"I was afraid you'd say that." Mr. Montgomery let out a sigh. "We'll work something out."

While trying to figure out what exactly he meant, my mind leapt from one conclusion to the next. However, before I could offer a theory, the sound of a tiny little motor came zooming through the door. I knew before anyone what that noise meant. Unfortunately, I also knew I couldn't do anything to stop it.

Mack turned his head, and I could see by the sag in his shoulders that he knew the sound too.

By the time Mr. Montgomery turned toward the entryway, the visitor had already arrived.

Gray stood in the entryway, blanket in one hand with the edge dragging the ground, and a book in the other hand—one of the books we'd made together. A look of excitement beamed from his face. "Scarlett, can you read me a book? I can't go to sleep."

"Not now, Gray. Is Mr. Newton watching you?" I asked, trying to keep my voice even.

Gray nodded. "He saw your light on and told me I could drive my truck over for a story."

I closed my eyes at the image of Gray riding his little vehicle across the lawn to my place. It wouldn't be the first time Mr. Hal Newton had let him do it. In fact, it was a fun game we liked to play. Mr. Newton kept a spare little car in his garage just for days when Gray stopped by; days when I was busy, but Mrs. Harper needed to run out for a minute to the grocery store or run another quick errand. Hal would check to see if my light was on, then send Gray over in the car and watch from the window. Once Gray arrived, Hal would give me a call to make sure the boy had arrived safely. Hal thought it would teach Gray independence.

True to form, the phone rang at that very moment. *Hal.*

"Answer that," Mr. Montgomery said. "And tell whoever it is that things are just fine."

I took a few steps across the room, thanking my lucky stars for the brief movement. I picked the phone up from its place on the wall, told Mr. Newton that Gray had made it safely and that I would read him a story, then hung up. I'd debated trying to sneak in a hint that something was wrong, but I couldn't risk it. Not with Gray standing there.

Instead of going back toward the center of the room, I stood near the entryway and scooped Gray into my arms. "Be still, child, all right? I'll read you an extra story tonight if you keep quiet."

Gray nodded, then started humming and flapping the book around.

"Well, this is unexpected." Mr. Montgomery twisted his lips slightly. "I'll tell you what. Mack, you come with me now, and I'll let the boy live."

"Let them all live, and I'll go with you."

Mr. Montgomery ran his tongue over his lips. "And risk them getting the police involved?"

"They won't get the cops involved," Mack said. "Right?"

Ryan nodded vigorously, and I nodded, as well.

"Good. Let's go, then. I'm glad we could come to an agreement." Mr. Montgomery surprised me with his agreeableness. He nodded. "Mack, shall we?"

Mack glanced my way, his expression full of apology. I tried to show him with my eyes that I didn't think any of this was his fault, but I could only say so much without using my words. I took a few steps back, giving the two men a wide berth to leave. Gray rested his head on my shoulder, snuggling in tightly.

As Mack watched, something clicked in his eyes. He looked at Gray, who'd stuck a thumb in his mouth and was humming a nonsensical tune, then he looked at me as I rubbed Gray's back.

Before I could say anything, he spun toward his father, gun raised, finger ready to shoot.

But he was too late. His father had acted already, his gun aimed at a new target. With a terrifying smile, Mr. Montgomery tensed his finger for a brief moment before pulling the trigger.

Not one, but two gunshots erupted.

And not one, but two bodies fell to the floor.

CHAPTER 53

Dear Diary,

I'M NOT THE RUNNING-AWAY TYPE. If I was, I wouldn't have stayed in Luck all these years. I'd be up and gone, disappeared like Mack who took off to save the world. At that moment when Mr. Montgomery pulled the trigger, I ran like a bat outta hell. Whatever it took to keep Gray safe, I'd do it.

Immediately when I saw that *thing,* that decision click in Mack's eye, I knew what was happening. As two guns were raised, I used my momentum to launch both myself and Gray toward the door. Attempting to shelter him the best I could, I clapped a hand over Gray's face. I'm pretty sure he couldn't see a thing through my fingers. He could hear, that's for certain. We all went half-deaf at the sound of the double shot, but I couldn't do anything about that.

I didn't go back into that room until I heard a groan. My heart tore in two. I wanted to go to Mack, to make sure he was safe. But what if that's what Mr. Montgomery was waiting for, his gun itching to fire another shot the second I stuck my head around the corner?

I clutched Gray close until I couldn't bear to listen anymore.

Then, I pinky-sweared with that boy, begging him to wait quietly in that corner upon the threat of never reading him another bedtime story. I felt bad using fear to keep my little man quiet, but you know what they say—desperate times call for desperate measures, and I was desperate.

Then someone screamed.

Diary, I don't wanna see who is laying on that floor.

Scarlett

CHAPTER 54

RAISING MY LITTLE DART GUN, I scanned the room for something, anything, I could use to help me get around that corner without ending up getting shot. But my entryway was too bare, and I couldn't find a thing to use as a shield. However, there *was* a pot hanging in the kitchen that gave me a perfect reflection of the living room. Although the figures in the reflection were wobbly and distorted, I couldn't make out a gun pointed at me. That would have to be enough.

I took one final look at Gray and raised a finger to my lips. Zipping his own lips, Gray pretended to swallow the key. As I inhaled a deep breath, I poked the very top of my head around the corner of the wall, not exhaling until I was certain that nobody was lying in wait.

The scream had come from Ryan, judging by the rest of the options. He lay on his side, clutching his arm to his chest. I hurried around the corner, taking in the rest of the scene.

Mack, thank goodness, looked unharmed, except for the fact that his face was as white as a sheet, and his posture was stiff and mechanical. He stood over his father, looking down at the man.

"I shot my father," Mack said, his voice thin. "I shot him, Scarlett."

It took two seconds for me to join Mack. Both of us looked down at the powerful, old man. His gray hair was slightly ruffled, and his powerful face was peaceful as he lay still.

I bent down and felt for a pulse. After a few seconds of clasping at his cold wrist, I got one. "He's alive, Mack. Call the police. Get an ambulance."

Mack hesitated, as if he almost didn't want the ambulance to show up.

"Mack, call the ambulance," I said again. "We need one for your father and for Ryan."

At Ryan's name, Mack glanced over to the mechanic on the floor, who was still conscious, his face contorted in pain.

"This hurts like hell," Ryan said, his teeth gritted. "Call the ambulance."

"Are you okay?" I asked Ryan.

"Oh gee, I'm great. Except I've been shot in the arm and kidnapped. Not to mention the fact that I am bleeding all over your floor."

"Mack," I said more firmly. "Call the police."

Finally, Mack snapped to attention and went to the wall phone. He punched in the three little numbers on the landline that connected him to the police. While he explained in short, terse terms the nature of the situation, I focused my attention on Mr. Montgomery.

I found the bullet wound quickly. The bullet looked as though it had gone straight through his left shoulder. Seeing how he had a pulse and was still breathing, I figured he went unconscious from the pain. I grabbed a blanket from the couch and pressed it to the wound, shouting for Mack to do the same to Ryan.

Thankfully, Mack turned on his business mode and operated with quick, efficient movements. He had Ryan's arm bandaged in a matter of minutes then came over and helped me with his father.

"Mack, you had to do it," I said, resting a hand on his shoulder after both men's wounds were stable, the bleeding controlled as much as possible. "Your father was going to kill me and Gray. He wasn't gonna let us go."

Mack nodded.

"Look at me." I waited until Mack met my eyes. "There's no way he'd have let two loose ends go so easily. You had to do it. Your father will live. I promise you. Then, the justice system can take over."

Mack gave a short laugh. "The justice system that *he owns?*"

My blood ran cold. "But he's responsible for the murder of at least two people, maybe more. There's no way he can get away with it."

"What worries me is that if he hadn't pointed that gun at you and Gray, I might not have had the guts to do anything about it," Mack said, ignoring my concerns. "I wasn't going to do it. He was right."

"Mack…"

"I wouldn't have shot him. Not until he threatened a child." Mack shook his head. "All these years, and I still can't stand up to him."

"Stop it," I said, my voice firm. Tears pricked my eyes. "You saved us, Mack. You did what you had to do. Do you hear me?"

He looked at me then with an expression so hollow and so pained, I wondered if he'd ever be able to feel joy again.

I threw my arms around his neck, hating his father more than I ever had, even more than when he'd pointed that gun at my face. Because that man had destroyed Mack from the inside out.

This time, I managed not to cry except for a few stray tears that leaked onto Mack's shirt. When I pulled back, I kissed him on the cheek with as much love as I could muster.

Mack might have warmed the tiniest amount, but then he looked back to his father, and the color disappeared from his face again… until he cleared his throat and turned to me.

"You're right," he said, as the fog cleared from his eyes. His voice was crisp and businesslike, but instead of making me feel safe, the transformation was worrisome. Already, I could see Mack pushing away any thoughts, emotions, or repercussions of shooting his father, shoving the event into a dark closet in the back of his soul. He cleared his throat again. "It was necessary. Now, time for cleanup. Here's what needs to happen: You take Gray to Mr. Newton's house. Take care of him, get him to his mother, do whatever you have to do. I'm going to wait here for the police."

"Mack," I said, my words strained. "Please."

"Go, Scarlett." He turned unseeing eyes on me. "Go now. The cops can talk to you later."

I squeezed my eyes shut for a minute. When I opened them, Mack remained still, watching me through lidded eyes.

I took a few steps backward. Mack continued to watch as I scooped up Gray and moved my legs just as fast as I could toward the main house.

And I prayed as hard as I could that there wouldn't be another shot when I left.

CHAPTER 55

Dear Diary,

It's over. I still can't believe it.

The cops showed up that night, and we explained everything that'd happened.

When all three eyewitnesses—myself, Mack, and Ryan—all told a similar story, the cops were forced to take the accusations against Mr. Montgomery seriously, despite his prominent position in society. It helped that the man wasn't awake to defend himself.

Even though all three of us pointed fingers at Mack's father, explaining how Mr. Montgomery brought the gun out first, how he'd shot Ryan even after agreeing to let him go, and how he'd confessed to getting rid of Miguel, the cops were cautious to believe us.

Because no matter how this situation plays out, it'll be high-profile. It'll be explosive. It'll make the news. And any cop with an ounce of common sense realizes that it'd be career suicide to be heard accusing Mack's father of any wrongdoing without firm proof and the promise of life in prison for the man. As of now, Mack's father is expected to make a full recovery. He's expected to go to jail. Will he?

We shall see.

At least Ryan is fine; the shot hardly nicked him. He'll need a sling for a few days, but he'll have full use of his arm within the month. On top of that, he offered me free car repairs for the rest of the year. Looks like I can finally get my alignment fixed without breaking the bank.

As for Miguel, they found him—alive, thank the Lord. They also found all of the notes Mack's father had promised would be there. They'd already been put in place, the chain of events that would point the finger at Miguel ready to be set in motion like a chain of dominos tipping over, one by one, until the entire thing collapsed. Except this chain of dominos would've collapsed on the wrong person if we hadn't stepped in to derail it.

They pulled Miguel from the trunk of a car, from one of those vehicles sitting in the lot behind Joe's shop. If I had to guess, Mr. Montgomery's minions were probably planning to take him out of town before they killed him. Maybe to the river in the next city, or an empty plot of land miles away. Either way, I was bettin' that if Miguel hadn't been found right then, he wouldn't have been found at all. At least not while he was still breathing.

There's a lot that still needs to be answered. Who chased me that night in the Audi? Who ransacked my home, and what were they lookin' for? And most of all, who else was involved? There was a chance that Joe and Frank were the only ones involved in the scheme, but some part of me wonders if anyone else knew about it. Angela, maybe? What about Miguel? I was willing to bet most of these questions could be answered by Mr. Montgomery, but since the man wasn't talking I was left wondering, at least for now.

I suppose life doesn't always get wrapped up in a pretty little bow. I should know, of all people. And I have my theories. I'm nearly certain that Mack's father was behind the car chase—either scarin' me away from his son, or trying to get me out of the way. The ransacking could have been another scare tactic. Or Mr. Montgomery might have organized it for the sole purpose of adding fuel to the fire of rumors swirling around my name. Only time will tell, and maybe not even then. For now, I'm just happy that more people weren't hurt.

Diary, it's a real shame that lives had to end over something like this. It's real unfortunate that my car was used in the scheme, and that my name got attached to the terrible things going on around town. It's a shame Mack lost any trace of a father he'd thought he had. At least Gray hadn't seen much of anything. We talked about it after, and he seems to be okay. For that, I'm thankful.

I'm thankful for my life, I really am. But I don't know what's gonna happen next. I don't have a job now, and I don't see Miss Annie hiring me back anytime soon. Maybe Mary Anne will let me wash dishes or serve food at The Cozy Cafe for a little bit, but that's not long-term. That's called a pity job. At least I collected some money from my bartending gig, though I was a bit short on tips. I suppose that's what happens when I'm kidnapped halfway through the job.

On the positive side, Noelle stuck around for a few more days. After the kidnapping, she filled me in on everything that'd happened from her point of view. How she went from angry to nervous when she found my phone outside of the Reunion Day festivities. How she went from nervous to scared when the police showed up, then completely terrified when they uncovered the dead body in my trunk.

Thankfully, all of that vanished the second we saw each other. She'd run towards me with a hug as powerful as a grizzly bear, and everything had gone back to something resembling normal. Noelle let me stay with her family for some time, and the Summerses took care of me real nice. They pampered me, fed me, and let me sleep undisturbed, which was good, except for the occasional nightmare that'd have me waking up in sweats.

Now, it's the Sunday after Reunion Day, and we haven't learned much of anything in the past week. It's been a blur these last few days, with no small amount of thanks to the Summerses and their help. They shooed away nosy reporters and lookiloos stopping by for a peek.

I haven't seen Gray yet, which isn't surprising, but I've heard rumors that he doesn't have a replacement nanny yet. That gives me a tiny amount of hope since Miss Annie's got to be going wild without help.

But my biggest disappointment of all is Mack.

He did it again.

I told myself I wouldn't get upset when he disappeared this time. I told myself I wouldn't get duped into falling for him again, just to have him vanish into the night.

Oh, well. It's my fault.

You know what they say.

Fool me once, shame on you.

Fool me twice, shame on me.

Well then, shame on me because it hurts just as much the second time around.

Scarlett

CHAPTER 56

"I DON'T HAVE TO GO." NOELLE hugged me tightly in her bedroom on that Sunday afternoon, a beautiful Sunday afternoon filled with sunshine and balmy temperatures. "I can stay. I've told you that a hundred times."

Despite the picturesque temperatures, I couldn't bring myself to enjoy the day. I was too busy trying not to feel sorry for myself. For her, I pasted a smile on my face. "You have to get back to New York. I know that. You already stayed three days longer than you planned."

"I don't want to leave you." Noelle clasped my hands in hers, and those green eyes watching me were filled with concern. "It's your first night back in your place. Are you sure I can't stay and spend it with you?"

"You already have your flight booked," I said. "Don't worry, I'll be fine. Your family was already too generous to hire those cleaners for me, and to let me borrow Sandra."

"Sandra offered to do it," Noelle said. "You are family here, and she loves you to death. Really, it's nothing."

The housekeeper for the Summerses had directed a cleaning crew over at my tiny little home and gotten everything in tip-top shape. I'd done a walk-through the day before and had been absolutely wowed with the results. Fresh flowers lined every spare surface, and the pleasant scent of a lemon twist hung sharply in the air. Every inch had been scrubbed, vacuumed, and dusted until

234

it was in better shape than it had ever been. Seeing my house that clean almost made this whole ordeal worth it. Not quite, but almost.

"I'll miss you." I met Noelle's gaze, blinking fast to preemptively block any tears from forming. She'd been furious when she'd found out what happened the night of the event. Then, she hadn't left my side since except to shower and use the restroom. "But you belong up in New York, I can see that. Maybe I'll come visit you sometime."

"How about next month?" Noelle grinned. "I was going to tell you earlier, but with this whole debacle happening I hadn't found a good time."

"What?" I smiled back. My best friend's infectious grin was brightening my expression. "Don't leave me hanging, Noelle!"

"I got hired on as a stylist for New York fashion week!" Noelle's cheeks turned pink with excitement.

"Noelle, that is amazing!" I clasped my friend in a gut-busting hug. My glee was coming out so strong I couldn't let her go. "You deserve that and so much more. Honestly, congratulations. You are... I always knew you'd be a star."

She waved a hand. "I'm hardly a star. It's for a small show off the main stages, but I like to let people think otherwise." She winked. "But it's a start, ain't it?"

"A start? This is a huge step!" I held her at arm's length, speechless as I looked into her face. "I'm gonna come up and support you. I've got that money from the bartending event. I'll save that up and get a job at the cafe to cover rent for now. This is gonna be a vacation, Noelle. Me and you in the big city. Can you imagine?"

"I've been dreamin' of this day since I moved away!"

"I'm sorry I couldn't come up there earlier." I hesitated slightly. "I... I'd been meaning to, but things always cropped up."

"Stop it, Scarlett Powers. I was comin' back here anyway. I'd never expect you to fly up there. But if you wanna come we can tour the city..."

"Sip wine? Sightsee? Maybe we can look at the Statue of

Liberty." I felt the excitement bubble up in my own chest. "Maybe I'll drive to the city beforehand and buy a real dress to wear to your show. Wouldn't that be something?"

Noelle's eyes gleamed. Then she let out a huge sigh of relief. "Man, it sure does make saying goodbye easier when I know I'm gonna see you again soon."

I nodded. "I'm hardly even sad anymore. I'm just tickled pink for you."

We joined for one last hug before it was really time for her to leave. Promising to get in touch with me about dates, times, and possible flights, Noelle waved goodbye as she loaded her trendy suitcases into her parents' vehicle. Then, all three of the Summerses blew kisses to me, which I caught and blew right back, as they pulled away, headed to the airport to send their daughter back to the Big Apple.

Meanwhile, I turned around and made my way to the dusty rental car I'd been given from the inventory of Joe's shop until I got my car back from the police. I climbed in, and I headed in the opposite direction, back to my tiny little house, alone in the country.

CHAPTER 57

Dear Diary,

I ALWAYS KNEW NOELLE SUMMERS WAS gonna be a star. And she's doing it. She really is. That girl deserves her dreams more than anyone I know. I'm just as lucky as can be that she still calls me a friend.

Now, if I could just be sure that Gray got a new nanny and hear a word from Mack that he's okay, then I'd be all set. I'd be able to focus on getting my life back on track. Heck, maybe I'd even look for a real career, take a few classes, get my GED. I've been meaning to for a while but just never took the necessary steps. Maybe this is the kick in the pants I need to start the next phase of my life.

As for Mack, I tried not to think about him, but as I opened the door to my house, the quiet seemed to suck me right in, making me feel more alone than I'd ever felt in my life. The thoughts of him just crowd my mind until my heart aches and I can't bear it any longer. In the lonely hours after the storm, there's nobody around to listen.

Except you. I think I'm in love with you, Diary.

Love, your secret admirer,
Scarlett

CHAPTER 58

Dear Diary,

IT'S BEEN THREE GODDAMN WEEKS. Excuse my French. I don't mean to write those nasty words in here, Diary. I don't wanna be the one to ruin your virgin ears. But you understand me, right? I'm not asking Mack for a goddamn marriage proposal. Just a note. One word to tell me he's all right.

Instead, I'm still sittin' here.

Thinkin'.

Wonderin'.

Waitin'.

At least, I *was* waiting, but not anymore. See, I'm sick of waitin', Diary. I've got a job at the cafe, and I'm getting ready to finish the requirements for my GED. I might not be the most independent woman around yet, but I'm working on it. I've even been looking into taking classes online. After I get my GED, maybe I'll go to college. I could get a business degree or even study creative writing. I could be a preschool teacher! The options are endless, Diary, and I can't wait any longer. Maybe I'll look out of state and really spread my wings. I hear Southern California is nice this time of year. Maybe a change of scenery would be good for me.

Don't you worry, Diary. If I leave, we're going together. I'd never leave you.

Love,
Scarlett

CHAPTER 59

Diary,

NOELLE HAS BEEN TALKING ABOUT me visiting her up in the city, but we haven't set a date yet. She's been pretty vague about her schedule, and I don't wanna press. Plus, I'm keeping plenty busy between school and work, so maybe we'll hold off until it's time to finally celebrate me getting that GED.

Anyway, I'm not sure what's happening around here today, but there is *something* going on in town. A big rigmarole. A big commotion with cars comin' and goin' all day. I stopped by the cafe to see if Mary Anne needed help with the extra folks, but she shooed me away and told me to go study on my day off.

I've been working a few shifts a week there to make ends meet financially. I thought it'd be a short-term job, but she's expanding onto the plot of land next door and mentioned she might have a permanent job as a waitress opening up, what with the additional space she'll need covered. Construction has been going for weeks now, though I've yet to see what it looks like. It's not supposed to be done for another three weeks, and then I'm hoping I'll get a full-time job offer from her. In the meantime, I'm focusing on my schoolwork.

It's time I took action, Diary. I've gotta do *somethin'*.

Love,
Scarlett

Chapter 60

I was just getting ready to go for a nice long walk into town—enjoy the beautiful day, soak up some sun, and see what the commotion was all about. Just as I pulled on a light jacket over my tank top and jean shorts, a knock on the door distracted me.

I glanced in the mirror, happy enough I'd decided to put on a tad of mascara, as well as a swipe of lip gloss that Noelle had left behind. I wasn't going to win any beauty awards, but I could pass for presentable.

I forgot all about looking presentable when I opened the door.

There, on my front steps, with a smile so shy, it softened my heart, stood Mack.

My Mack.

And in his hands was a bouquet of big, beautiful sunflowers.

"Mack?" I was too shocked to state anything but the obvious. "What are you doin' here?"

"I came here to see you." Mack extended the sunflowers.

Grasping them, I took a sniff of the floral scent, more out of habit than anything else, and continued to stare at him as if he were a ghost. Or a unicorn. Or any other creature I would never expect to see in real life, let alone on my doorstep.

"What are you doin' here?" I asked again.

"I came to apologize," Mack said. "I promised you I wouldn't disappear, and then I went and did it anyway. I don't expect you to forgive me, and I don't expect you to have a drink with me, but I didn't want to stay away for ten years again."

I swallowed hard, unable to respond.

"That's a lie. I did want to stay away." Mack's eyes darkened with sadness. "Runnin' away is easy for me, sweetheart. I'm good at it. But this time, something was different. I couldn't get over missing you. I missed that smile on your lips, the way you crumble into my arms when life gets too hard and makes you cry. I want to be that shoulder you cry on when you're overwhelmed. I want to teach Gray how to ride a tricycle with you. I want to eat SpaghettiOs for dinner, and I want to sneak into the drive-in theater and watch movies, even if we can afford to pay for the tickets nowadays."

I set the sunflowers on the counter because my hands were shaking too hard to hold onto them.

Mack took a tentative step forward. "I'm sick of runnin' away from stuff that doesn't go my way, and I want to stop it. I miss you, Scarlett. I don't blame you if you don't want to give me another chance. I just hope you can understand why I disappeared this time. My father… if he had laid a finger on you…" Mack shook his head, a cringe scrunching his face up in anger. "I wouldn't have been able to live with myself."

"I understand." I reached for Mack and rested my fingers on his wrist. "I'm just glad you came back. I only wanted to know you were okay."

"I don't want you to understand why I left," Mack said, his voice coarse and hard. "I want you to understand why I came back."

"Mack, you don't need to explain." I stepped forward once more, and his blue eyes looked down to mine.

He stood less than a foot away, and his hands slowly made their way around my back. "I'm not sure if I can say it in words, but I'd like to kiss you if you'll let me."

His soft gaze, the way his strong arms held me tight, and the safety I felt from his presence was all too much. My throat constricted. I rose to my tiptoes and planted a feather-light kiss on his lips.

Mack responded almost instantly. His fingers curled into the skin above my hips, pulling my body so close that we melded into one figure. His arms encircled me in a sphere of warmth, and the knot that had been plaguing my stomach for a month slowly dissolved. He kissed me for so long that my world disappeared. When he gently broke the kiss, cradling my head in between his hands, I wobbled as if I'd just guzzled an entire bottle of champagne.

"Wow," I murmured. "I think I'm woozy."

"Let's continue this later," Mack said, releasing my face to clasp my hand. He nodded toward the same black Audi he'd had a few weeks ago. "I have something to show you."

CHAPTER 61

"**Y**OU'RE BRINGING ME TO THE cafe?" I asked, wrinkling my nose. "I was just here this morning. Mary Anne sent me home."

"Not exactly." Mack climbed out of the car, came around to my side, and opened the door before I could do it myself. He guided me like he might a fragile little birdie. Wrapping one arm around my waist, the other hand lightly touching my stomach, he hardly watched where he was going. Instead, he kept his head cocked in my direction and his gaze on mine.

My lips were still swollen and raw from that miraculous kiss, and I floated on cloud nine all the way to the front of The Cozy Cafe. I knew in my head I should've asked for more of an explanation about his sudden disappearance, but for the moment, I was going with my heart. And my heart told me that Mack meant what he said. I couldn't imagine what he'd been through, knowing his father had been behind everything. If Mack needed time, I'd give it to him.

I'd had three weeks to think about how much I missed Mack. Now that he was back, I wasn't going to let him go so easily.

"Well if you're not bringing me to the cafe, then why are we here?" I looked up at The Cozy Cafe. It had been familiar before, but now that I worked there more days than not, it was a second home.

"I may have been gone for a few weeks, but that didn't mean I wasn't thinkin' about you the entire time." As Mack smiled at me, I already couldn't believe the moment was real.

"I don't need any surprises, Mack. I'm just glad you're home." I regretted my choice of words instantly. "Back, I meant back in Luck. I know it's not your 'home' anymore, per se."

"It'll always be my home. Now, can we finish our chatting later? I have a lot to say, but I wanna do it with the drink in hand that I've promised you."

I couldn't help it. I gave him one more peck on the cheek. "I still can't believe you're real. That you're here. Holding onto me."

"Well, you're gonna have to suspend your disbelief for one last second, all right, Miss Scarlett? Because we worked on this surprise for a full month for you."

"We?"

"I couldn't have done it alone."

I furrowed my brow, wondering who would be sitting inside The Cozy Cafe, waiting for me. Instead of pulling the door open to the cafe, Mack kept on walking right past it. He walked right up to the construction happening in the empty plot next door.

The construction crew had built a sort of wall out front so none of the townsfolk could stick their long noses over the fence and peek at the design. There had been talk of a big unveiling party down the line, where everyone would get the opportunity to see the new building all at once, but that wouldn't be for a few months. For the time being, we had to make do with the plastic sheets roping the area off, obstructing our views.

"Do we get a sneak peek at the construction?" I gave Mack a light smack on the arm. "Did you ask Mary Anne for permission? She is gonna slap you hard upside the head if you didn't ask first. She's been real hush-hush about the project."

"As a matter of fact, we are doing an unveiling." Mack stopped in front of the construction project. He secured one arm around my waist, with the other balancing on my hip as if holding me steady. "And yes, we have Mary Anne's permission. In fact, she helped me with the idea of it, along with Noelle Summers, and your friends from that band, GURLZ, or whatever."

"Tiny, Tallulah, and Tootsie were in on it? Oh, this is gonna be fun."

Mack grinned. "I sure hope so. Are you ready?"

I clapped my hands and gave a little jump up and down. "Let's see the new cafe!"

"That's the thing," Mack said. "It ain't a cafe. In fact, it's barely even connected to Mary Anne's place."

I frowned again, but I didn't have time to ask more questions because Mack winked at me, that mischievous expression back on his face. His excitement at the surprise had already won me over, and it was enough for me just to see his lips smiling again. I didn't need anything else that day, or ever, not really.

While I was distracted by the joyful expression on his face, he took advantage of my hesitation. Tilting his head back, Mack shouted loudly and clearly, "She's ready, ladies! Let 'er drop!"

All at once, a series of hoots, hollers, and whistles erupted from behind the white sheet blowing in the breeze. Someone rushed forward and handed a package to Mack, but I didn't get a good look at who since I was distracted by what was happening in front of me. There was a *snap*, a *rip*, and the loud *crinkle* of the wind catching the plastic and whipping it back and forth as the sheet fell to the ground, exposing the structure behind it.

The fully finished structure.

Once my brain caught up to my eyesight, I realized why Mack had both of his arms around my waist. When I read the sign above the door, I just about collapsed. My legs went weak. They wobbled so much it was like I had two limp noodles sticking out of my jean shorts. Mack's arms circled around my waist, and his laugh gave me a jolt of life, thank God, as he propped me back up on my feet.

My jaw worked hard, trying to get the words out of my mouth, but it wasn't doing a great job. I looked first at the construction site, then at Mack, then at the ladies scattered all around the land, staring back at me with beaming smiles as big as bananas.

"What do you think?" Mack asked.

"Is it… did you…" I paused, doing the rounds with my gaze once more. When it landed on Mack, I picked right up where I left off. "Is this what I think it is?"

"I felt bad, Scarlett." Mack pulled the package from behind his back. It was a rectangular box about the size of a Bible, except instead of paper pages lining the edges like a normal book, the outside was made from wood. My body was too confused to do much of anything, seeing how I was torn between swooning and fainting. "I felt so bad when I disappeared a second time. I knew I'd have to make it up to you somehow. Well, I thought of one way that might do it."

I swallowed, the saliva sticking in the back of my throat. I scanned those blue eyes staring up at me.

Mack moved a hand to my waist and held me steady. "I want to make your wish come true, Scarlett."

"Mack, no… you don't gotta do that." I lowered my voice. "I already believe you. I was gonna get a drink with you. I want to hear what you've got to say. You don't gotta do this."

"It's not what you think." Mack gave me a kind smile. "Listen, Scarlett. I don't know if I'm the man to give you the happily ever after that you deserve. Some days, I find myself hoping and praying that someday I might be that person. But the thing about marriage is that it's a two-person decision. I owe you a lot of answers before we even *start* to worry about that. So for now, I hope this can come close enough. You deserve your happily ever after, Scarlett, and if this can help you get there, then it's yours."

I blinked, tears stinging my eyes. Then, I pulled Mack in toward me, wrapped my arms tightly around his neck, and let those stubborn tears leak out. But not before I looked up at the brilliant new construction, attached by a small hallway to Mary Anne's cafe.

The petite little building was so cute. It could have doubled as a gingerbread house in Hansel and Gretel. The red bricks stacked up to hold a roof sturdy enough for the members of the GURLZ band to stand on top of it. The three ladies must have cut the white plastic sheet and unveiled the building. With glinting scissors dangling from their wrinkled hands, they waved down from the roof, faces beaming.

The front lawn of the cottage had already been landscaped, complete with flowering bushes, bright trees, and a winding stone path that crossed over a bubbling fountain. To the left of the fountain sat a bench where Noelle Summers and Mary Anne leaned against one another, watching me with smiles so bright they could light up a dark room.

I turned my gaze back to the store... *my* store, apparently, and I read that name one more time. The beautifully carved sign hung above the weathered, wooden door that looked as if it might lead to Narnia. On that sign were three little words.

Happily Ever After.

Below it was a smaller inscription: Luck's First Bookstore.

"Mack, I can't accept this." I turned to him, hauling myself to my feet. My head was as foggy as if I were in a dream. "This is too much."

"It's nothing." Mack crossed his arms. "This is all yours, completely paid off. The first year of property taxes, fees, anything you might be worrying about. All of it's taken care of."

"Mack, no."

"This is *nothing*," Mack said, shifting a bit. "I'll let you see the price of my condo in the Hollywood Hills, then you can tell me this is too much. Plus, it wasn't all from me. The ladies did some fundraising too."

"We played a concert!" Tootsie shouted from the roof. "Made five bucks in tips. We paid for the 'H' in the sign."

"And Mary Anne's been donating all her tips to the fund for the last couple of weeks, and Noelle held a fashion show up in New York for the cause," Mack said, gesturing in a circle. "We love you,

Scarlett. You're the only person in town who'll do this store justice. Now, will you please take these?"

I'd almost forgotten about that wooden box until Mack pulled it out from behind his back again. On the outside, in fancy letters decorating the front, the words Happily Ever After danced across the top. When Mack lifted the lid of the gorgeous box, a set of keys lay inside. But not just any keys. These keys were large enough to get into Dumbledore's private office, I'd bet.

I made eye contact with everyone surrounding the bookstore. Each of them nodded encouragingly, and as much as I wanted to argue about how I couldn't accept this as a gift, I caved. I wanted to see the inside.

My hand reached out of its own accord and gently pulled the key ring from the box. My heart raced as my feet carried me up the front path, over the bricks, and past the hiccupping fountain to the front door. Before I slid the key into the lock, I turned back once more, and that time, my gaze locked on Noelle.

She was grinning just as big as could be, swinging her legs on the bench. I gave a quick wave, gesturing for her to join me up front. She leapt up, followed closely by Mary Anne. Mack hopped in line behind them.

From the roof, Tootsie called down, "Go on in! We're gonna figure out a way down, and then we'll be there."

"Should we call the fire department?" I shielded my eyes from the sun and looked up at the trio of old ladies.

"The way you're talkin', it's like you think we're old or something," Tiny said. "We ain't old. We're young and nimble."

"I'll go up there since I couldn't convince them to stay off the damn roof," Mack whispered, disappearing around back and leaving Noelle, Mary Anne, and me to open the door.

"I can't believe you're back." I clasped Noelle in a hug close to me. "I could get used to this, seeing you once a month."

Noelle laughed. "Well, you just might have to. Now, open up

already. I wanna see the expression on your face when you open that door."

Fumbling with the keys, my body trembled with just about more excitement than it could handle. I rested one hand on that heavy wooden door and twisted the lock with the other. Then, holding my breath, I gave it a push.

Inside Happily Ever After was a greater nirvana than I'd ever imagined. The first room could've been taken right out of *Beauty and the Beast*. Shelves lined every wall, books lined every shelf, and sliding ladders completed the ambiance. The reading room boasted plump couches, and their new fabric was spotless and bright. Oversized armchairs circled a crackling fire. Tables and chairs lined the middle of the room for those needing more of a research-type environment. The register had been placed near the front and was covered by a canopy of books.

It was magic.

I turned to Noelle. "This is gorgeous."

"That's not it." She let out a high-pitched giggle then grabbed one of my arms while Mary Anne grabbed the other. Together, they marched me through a hidden doorway, which was covered by shelves of books, and into a room out back. Although, it looked more like two rooms joined into one.

Along the right side sat a beautifully finished wooden bar with eight stools in front of it. It looked completely stocked, judging by the bottles on display behind the counter. A large chalkboard menu topped it off. The drinks scrawled on a chalkboard fit the theme of the place—beverages like Tequila Mockingbird and Bridget Jones's Daiquiri. An appetizer by the name of Deviled Eggs Wear Prada was listed under the specials for today's date.

A set of hands landed on my shoulders and turned my body to face the opposite direction. A partition separated the bar area, which was nothing more than a few lounge chairs and fluffy couches, from the other half of the room.

"This is the stuff I picked out," Noelle said, leading me into the back-*back* room by the hand. "What do you think?"

I stepped around the partition and burst into a fit of uncontrollable laughter. "Noelle! Nobody in town will go for this!"

All sorts of lingerie lined one wall, while books with sexy titles lined another. A small section was titled Bachelorette Parties. Underneath the sign, an array of risqué toys, suggestive candies, and rude congrats cards were stacked in a beautifully organized display.

"Isn't it perfect?" Tiny asked, elbowing her way through the crowd. She'd made it down from the roof in one piece, much to my relief. "Just what this town needs. A little sugar and spice."

I turned, strolling back into the bar where Tootsie and Tallulah flanked Mack on both sides, looking a bit ruffled from their trek down from the roof. Noelle and Mary Anne filed in as well, followed by some more elbow-throwing from Tiny.

"I don't know what to say," I said. "This is incredible. Thank you so, so much. I'm overwhelmed."

"Happy Grand Opening," Tallulah said, her soft, soulful voice gliding across the room. "And *Happily Ever After*."

"We have one more thing to show you." Mack nodded toward the front room.

The rest of us followed him, though I couldn't possibly imagine what else he could show me. It was already too much.

"I brought a special visitor to add one last touch to the shop." Mack pulled open the front door. "Come on in here, buddy."

Gray's little body shot through the door so fast I barely had time to bend over and throw my arms out. In a whirlwind, he launched himself at my chest, and I wrapped my arms around him and squeezed tightly.

"Miss Scarlett, I have something for you. From Mack," Gray said after a moment of hugging me tightly. His little fingers played with my hair. "My mom's holding it for me."

I never thought it would be possible, but the look on Mrs.

Annie Harper's face was almost sheepish. She glanced hesitantly around the shop then took one step inside. Clutching a shopping bag in her hands, she focused her eyes on the floor.

"Hello, Miss Annie," I said. I couldn't hide my excitement over seeing Gray, but I still couldn't forget how his mother had treated me. "Can I help you?"

"I owe you an apology. I acted stupid, without thinking, and I'm sorry." She shook her head. "I don't expect you to forgive me, or come back to nanny for Gray, but if you can accept my apology for Gray's sake, I'd appreciate it. He just hasn't been the same since you left." She bit her lip, finally looking me in the eye. "He doesn't wanna sleep. I have to force him to eat. He needs you, Scarlett. I'm sorry I didn't recognize it sooner."

I hugged Gray close. "I need you too, buddy."

"Congratulations on your bookstore." Miss Annie glanced around. "It's beautiful in here."

"Yes, it is. And thank you for your apology. I accept it, of course, and I wanna be part of Gray's life." I hesitated. "We might have to discuss schedules changing now that I'll be spending a lot of time down here, but I think Gray might like spending a few days at the store with me, if that's all right with you."

Mrs. Harper smiled. "I think he'd like that very much. Oh, I nearly forgot. Here. This is for you. We scrounged up as many as we could find."

Mack reached out and accepted the bag before I could, which was just fine with me because I didn't want to let Gray go, not just yet.

"These belong right here." Mack carried the bag over to a wall behind the counter, a shelf I hadn't noticed, probably because it was empty. But there was a plaque attached at the top that read Local Authors.

Mack reached into the bag and pulled out one of the stories I'd written for Gray. The pages were worn and torn, the color fading from the cover, but he stuck it on that shelf anyway. Then, he stuck the next and the next and the next ones there, until the whole shelf was filled with stories Gray and I had created together.

Once that was finished, Gray's mother took a step forward. "I had this made special for you and Gray," she said, taking something out of her purse. "He said it's his favorite."

When she handed the surprise over, I gasped. "This is magnificent."

I looked up at her, my fingers running along the edges of a real, leather-bound book that had the title of a story Gray and I wrote together on the cover. It was printed on gorgeous, thick paper with illustrations as brilliant as a rainbow. She walked right up to the shelf and tucked it on the end. When she turned to me, it was with a smile. "A real book. You should be proud."

The sight nearly made me melt into a puddle right then and there.

"I am a lucky girl," I murmured. "I don't know what I did to deserve any of this."

"That's where you're wrong." Mack threw his arms around my waist, smiling around the room at the gathering of friends. "Luck is fortunate to have you." Mack pulled me close, and he gave me the softest kiss on the forehead. "Welcome to your very own Happily Ever After, Scarlett."

Chapter The End

Dear Diary,

A ND SHE LIVED HAPPILY EVER after. Just kidding. I've got a lot more adventures before I write the words: THE END.

Love,
Scarlett

NOTES FROM THE AUTHOR

If you've enjoyed getting to know Mack in this story, then check out his appearance in Lacey Luzzi: Seasoned! This book is available on Amazon and is free in Kindle Unlimited at the time of publication. Stay tuned for the release of *The Little Things* Book 2 coming early summer with more Scarlett and Mack!

** **

Don't worry, I haven't forgotten about Lacey. Her next adventures are due Spring 2016. Release date TBD, but will be announced soon via my newsletter at www.ginalamanna.com.

Now for a thank you

To all my readers, especially those of you who have stuck with me from the beginning of Lacey's story, and now Scarlett's adventures.

By now, I'm sure you all know how important reviews are for Indie authors, so if you have a moment and enjoyed the story, please consider leaving an honest review on Amazon or Goodreads. I know you are all very busy people and writing a review takes time out of your day – but just know that I appreciate every single one I receive. Reviews help make promotions possible, help with visibility on large retailers and most importantly, help other potential readers decide if they would like to try the book.

I wouldn't be here without all of you, so once again – *thank you.*

ALSO AVAILABLE FROM GINA

If you're interested in receiving new-release updates, please sign up for my newsletter at www.ginalamanna.com.

ABOUT THE AUTHOR

Originally from St. Paul, Minnesota, Gina LaManna began writing with the intention of making others smile. At the moment, she lives in Los Angeles and spends her days writing short stories, long stories, and all sizes in-between stories. She publishes under a variety of pen names, including a children's mystery series titled Mini Pie the Spy!

In her spare time, Gina has been known to run the occasional marathon, accidentally set fire to her own bathroom, and survive days on end eating only sprinkles, cappuccino foam and ice cream. She enjoys spending time with her family and friends most of all.

Websites and Social Media

Find out more about the author and upcoming books online at www.ginalamanna.com or:

Email: gina.m.lamanna@gmail.com
Twitter: @Gina_LaManna
Facebook: facebook.com/GinaLaMannaAuthor
Website: www.ginalamanna.com

Thanks again for reading, and I hope you enjoyed the story!

Made in the USA
San Bernardino, CA
03 December 2019